GUILTY AS SIN

GUILTY AS SIN

Judith Cutler

severn
House

This first world edition published 2015
in Great Britain and 2015 in the USA by
SEVERN HOUSE PUBLISHERS LTD of
19 Cedar Road, Sutton, Surrey, England, SM2 5DA.
Trade paperback edition first published
in Great Britain and the USA 2016 by
SEVERN HOUSE PUBLISHERS LTD.

British Library Cataloguing in Publication Data

Cutler, Judith author.
  Guilty as sin. – (The Lina Townend series)
  1. Townend, Lina (Fictitious character)–Fiction.
  2. Antique dealers–Fiction. 3. Aristocracy (Social
  class)–Fiction. 4. Detective and mystery stories.
  I. Title II. Series
  823.9'2-dc23

ISBN-13: 978-0-7278-8536-4 (cased)
ISBN-13: 978-1-84751-639-8 (trade paper)
ISBN-13: 978-1-78010-705-9 (e-book)

All Severn House titles are printed on acid-free paper.

Severn House Publishers support the Forest Stewardship Council™ [FSC™],
the leading international forest certification organisation. All our titles that
are printed on FSC certified paper carry the FSC logo.

MIX
Paper from
responsible sources
FSC   FSC® C013056
www.fsc.org

Typeset by Palimpsest Book Production Ltd.,
Falkirk, Stirlingshire, Scotland.
Printed and bound in Great Britain by
TJ International, Padstow, Cornwall.

For the clergy, churchwardens and congregation of All Saints' Church, Kemble
With great affection and gratitude

ONE

'Torquay isn't so very far from Exeter, Lina,' Griff said, his tone halfway between persuasion and wheedling. On the table between us he put a brochure, its cover featuring his and hers feet in dance shoes. 'It would be nice to combine business with pleasure. Or the other way round. It's a good time of year for the seaside, now the kids are safely penned in school. It would help Dee out, too. A couple have dropped out – at this late stage, for goodness' sake.'

Griff was my mentor and dearest friend, who'd rescued me almost literally from the gutter and made me his business partner. How could I deny him anything? In any case, now he'd recovered from his bypass operation there was no need to mollycoddle him. Not really. For a man of his age, bang in the middle of his seventies – for all he claimed to be ten years younger – he'd recovered well. But this current plan was crazy: combining a Saturday antique fair in the very uninspiring premises of Matford market, a location I'd vowed never to visit again, with a ballroom dance weekend twenty miles down the A380 at the famous seaside resort.

'After all,' he continued enthusiastically, 'it's scarcely worth going all the way to Devon from Kent for a one-day event. We'll set up the Tripp and Townend stall on the Friday after noon, nip off to the Mondiale for supper and dancing in the evening, and then return to Exeter on Saturday morning. Do a few deals. Pack up. Back to Torquay for the fancy-dress dance in the evening. Home on Sunday. Easy. And indeed peasy.'

'Absolutely.' Absolute idiocy, more like. Do both? More sensible, given the distance – a 500-mile round trip, give or take – to do neither. But he looked as hopeful as a dog expecting walkies. Picking up the brochure to suggest I was enthusiastic, I felt truly, miserably guilty. Of course I should feel enthusiastic. I must try harder for Griff's sake.

As part of his post-operative therapy, Griff had returned to one of his early loves, ballroom dancing, taking me along with him to the weekly classes held in the village hall. We were learning ballroom and Latin, really useful if ever I went clubbing. OK, enough irony. Clubs weren't my favourite places anyway. But I wasn't at all sure about the dance classes, to be honest; it's one thing not enjoying activities a lot of people my age do, but quite another to find myself with a bunch of pensioners who might just have been younger in years than Griff but were almost all older in attitude. Many couples had been together forty years or more, a niggling reminder of my single state.

I did have one nice mate my own age, Carwyn Morgan, a police officer recently promoted to detective sergeant. We were fond of each other and had occasional low-key dates. He worked long shifts; I worked long hours. And now Griff was better and wanted to go to antique fairs again, I had to chauffeur us to a lot of locations involving an overnight stay. Neither Carwyn nor I, then, had what the experts called a good work-life balance, and the relationship wasn't going anywhere fast. I suspect Griff hoped that a stray thirty-year-old Prince Charming might be learning the rumba – the dance of love – and that, without missing a step, we might fall head over heels with each other. Griff, of course, had long ago found his own Prince Charming, in the form of a rich dilettante called Aidan, who was far too old to be a prince, and, to me at least, was rarely charming. To be honest, I wouldn't have trusted either of the old ducks if a handsome young man had smiled winsomely at them.

But there were no young men in the class, handsome or otherwise, to make my heart beat faster. And though Griff was a most wonderful dancer, better by far than any of the others, the idea of two evening dances bookending a stint in the least attractive premises I've ever sold china in didn't appeal in the least.

Our shop receptionist and general angel, Mary, now officially and blissfully Mrs Paul Banner, encouraged me to see the brighter side of Torquay: 'There's a lovely department store down by the harbour. Expensive, but a lovely range of clothes

– and despite what they say about Torquay being full of older people, this place definitely caters for the young.'

And, assuming I got a chance to shop there, when would I ever wear the lovely new clothes? Not while I was restoring exquisite china in my workroom in Kent, or visiting my father, Lord Elham. Despite his title, Pa certainly wasn't noble, not in his behaviour, in the past at least. He'd never made any attempt to provide for me, even though I'd had to spend most of my life in care after my mother died. Despite this, I was the only one of my siblings who'd ever bothered to come back into his life. I suppose that I'd taken him on as a restoration project, much like the work I did on china for Griff. Now I'd repaired some of the cracks, as it were.

Pa lived in Bossingham Hall, a stately home just south of Canterbury. It was there I had to head now, so I put on some of my older jeans and a washed-out t-shirt. You see, Pa didn't live in the posh part of the hall that the public paid the trustees to see. He lived behind the green baize door that had separated the family from the servants, the haves from the have-nots. He wasn't quite a have-not, because he shared his accommodation with a filthy load of assorted china and bric-a-brac, some you couldn't give away, some priceless, which he looked to me to sell whenever he needed a new supply of champagne. This was his favourite, indeed at one time his only tipple. When I came on the scene, in addition to confiscating all his beloved Pot Noodles, I'd sternly introduced green tea into his diet, along with such outré items as green vegetables and fresh fruit.

You were supposed to approach his below-stairs area via a track so pot-holed he'd been blacklisted by every single delivery driver. To protect the Tripp and Townend van's suspension, I'd taken to sailing up the impressive public drive, using the staff parking area – I'd only been told off twice so far – and walking through the gate marked STRICTLY PRIVATE. Pa didn't like this; he preferred to have advance notice of visitors so that he could stow the tools of his forgery trade well away from suspicious eyes. That was another problem in my relationship with Carwyn: having a career criminal as a father. Carwyn had met and liked Pa, without knowing, of course, the full details of his erratic income – though I can't imagine he hadn't heard rumours: at least one of my police acquaintances was gunning for him. Pa approved of Carwyn, profession apart, and, like Griff, would have been delighted to see me respectably married to a decent man, tending children rather than priceless china.

Today Pa greeted me – his fingers so clean I suspected he'd spent a long time scrubbing the ink from them – with a triumphant flourish of a piece of paper. 'Got those trustee buggers! They're going to pay for that track to be repaired!' He stared at me. 'Come on, that's good news! You're supposed to dance a little jig – quite a fancy jig, with all those dance classes under your belt,' he added waspishly, jealous as always of what he thought might be fun time spent with Griff.

'With a chassé reverse turn?' I demonstrated. 'Anyway, it's really good news about that track. I don't suppose they want you to pay anything towards the repairs, do they?' I had to add.

'Only ten per cent.'

That might be quite a lot of cash, and to the best of my knowledge Pa simply didn't have it to hand – unless he'd completed a really big forgery recently and conned someone spectacularly gullible. 'I'd better find something exciting to sell for you, hadn't I? The Chinese market's flourishing at the moment. Let's see what's in your hoard . . .'

When Griff had first taken me under his wing, I'd had to rely on a strange instinct I've never understood, let alone been able to explain. With no knowledge to base my judgements on, I'd simply know if something was worth having. It was as if I was a water diviner, with a twig twitching when I got near a spring. It wasn't water I was after, of course. It was precious items. These days, thanks to Griff, I knew my stuff all right – but still this divvy's nose of mine came in useful, sometimes disconcertingly so.

It was the knowledge part of my brain that I'd used to organize Pa's jumbled accumulation of tatty china and treen, mid-price collectibles and absolute works of art into some sort of order, so I could easily lay my hands on a pair of Guangxu enamelled fish bowls. When I'd first found them I'd literally had to unearth them – or is it dis-earth? Someone had filled them with potting compost and though the geraniums they'd grown were long since dead, the dried-up soil remained. Nearby was a *sang de boeuf* vase less than a foot high, its paleish neck running down to a tubby little body. It always made me smile to look at it. Now the cheque might make Pa smile even more.

'Devon?' he repeated, as we sat in his kitchen drinking green tea. Once it had been as filthy as a set for a Dickens movie; these days, afraid that if it was ever that gross again I'd stomp off in a huff, he kept it – almost – pristine. 'Why Devon?'

'Because that's where our dance teacher has decided to organise a weekend get-together,' I said. 'She could have chosen Harrogate or Malvern, but she chose Torquay.'

'Hmph. You're sure, Lina, that you're not having it off again with that lounge-lizard of a dealer, Harvey Whatsisname? I really do not approve.'

'Neither would I. So no, I'm not.' I'd almost had an affair with Harvey Sanditon, a specialist in top-end china and porcelain, who was one of the sexiest and most gorgeous men I'd ever come across. I didn't mind him being twenty years older than me, but then I discovered he had a wife and ended the relationship. As for Pa himself, when he'd had affairs, he'd never worried about age differences or indeed begetting so many children out of wedlock I sometimes thought he'd lost count (I hadn't – it was over thirty). But where my sex life was concerned, he was an arch-Puritan.

'And there's that nasty little man who fancies you must be his granddaughter. Arthur Somethingorother. The toad lives down there, doesn't he?'

Arthur Habgood, owner of Devon Cottage Antiques. He'd been so annoyed by my refusal to take a DNA test to prove it that he'd actually made very serious – and untrue – allegations about me to the police. Charming.

'Why go to Devon at all? Far too dangerous. You'd do much better to stay at home.' He sounded as plaintive as Mr Woodhouse in the Jane Austen novel Griff had once read aloud to me.

I couldn't tell Pa that I agreed with him one hundred per cent: that would be disloyal to Griff. So, pointing out that Devon was quite a large county, with a correspondingly low risk of running into people you'd much rather not, I enthused about staying in a newly refurbished hotel and meeting people from our dance teacher's other groups. Dee taught in a different village hall every night of the week, and apparently used these autumn dances as a chance to bring all her students together. There were so many of us she needed a hotel geared up for conferences – and one, of course, with a ballroom.

Pa brightened considerably when I confided Griff's hopes that Dee would find a young and hetero partner for me. 'But what about young Carwyn?' he asked doubtfully.

'Wouldn't you be happier if I wasn't dating a cop? You know he wouldn't – couldn't – protect you if he found you and Titus Oates were up to your old tricks. Again. And don't tell me how cunningly you hide the tools of your trade – you know that when the police are determined to track something down, they rarely fail.'

'That was in the days when there were enough of them. You know we have to share our best detectives with Essex now? What use is that if there's a crime?' Pa sounded as self-righteous as if he was genuinely law-abiding.

'I don't think they all hang out in Essex – there are enough left over here to carry out a dawn raid if they wanted to. Couldn't you and Titus turn your hands to something legal for a change?'

'We might just be. Highly legal. Highly respectable.' With an enigmatic smile he touched the side of his nose.

For some reason I wasn't reassured about his career choices any more than he was by my travel plans. But that was all I could get out of him.

In fact, he changed the subject sharply. 'Are you sure Griff's up to all this wandering about the countryside with you?'

Of course, I didn't want to drop Griff in it by pointing out the whole Devon trip was his idea, so I said blithely – and truthfully – 'He wanders a great deal without me. He works out every week in a post-op cardio keep fit class and he's joined the church choir. He's even joined the church team that visits sick parishioners and offers them Communion.'

'Church this, church that – I suppose all this God-bothering means the old bugger's cramming for finals.'

TWO

Griff and I had a late supper that night, because in addition to dancing I'd started to go to a Pilates class that had just started in the village. I didn't go for pleasure so much as necessity: all the restoration work was doing vicious things to my spine and I was afraid I'd end up looking like a question mark, so it made sense to take action now. I'd expected to find everyone lying on mats, but it seemed that mat classes only ran in the daytime, when of course I was working or, occasionally, keeping an eye on Pa. The evening session was in a studio with all sorts of equipment that looked as if it might have come from a dungeon run by the Spanish Inquisition. Three or four of us women shared the space, an incredibly muscled guy running the show (gay and in a partnership, before you ask).

It made a nice change to have the company of people nearer my own age, and there was talk of us going out for a drink at some point. One woman had a baby to hustle back to, but Laura, Honey and I would linger in the changing area talking of this and that. They tended to talk more than I did; I'd had a far from conventional childhood and youth, and still found it hard to pick up the nuances and subtleties of my contemporaries' chit chat, especially as we three really didn't have much in common. On the other hand, parachute me into a gathering of fellow dealers and I could have talked till the cows came home – assuming they still did: our local ones seemed to live indoors these days.

Honey worked in Fenwick's in Canterbury; she was always immaculately made-up, with nails to die for, and each class was scented with her latest perfume. Laura, a council administrator in Maidstone, had wild blonde hair and an interesting line in printed t-shirts; for some reason she was wearing a Tommy Cooper Comic Relief one today. Honey and Laura had known each other since their schooldays, which in my case had been decidedly limited, since social workers had transferred me to a seemingly endless series of foster carers and the schools nearest them. Not a lot of continuity there – or indeed learning, as far as I was concerned.

It was Griff who, taking me in as a sort of feral apprentice, had taught me to read and to listen to music, to shop intelligently and cook the ingredients I'd bought, and who'd put me through the more formal training with restorer friends of his which meant I could earn my own living – and now his too. In fact, the restoration side of the business was doing so well in comparison with the shop next to our cottage that our accountant had insisted we made it into a separate firm. But none of that made for good conversation with casual acquaintances, especially as part of the psychotherapy Griff had also paid for had been to learn to forget the worst parts of my life. Consequently there were some very big gaps.

And if my job didn't sound very interesting – mending old china – I could certainly not talk to Honey and Laura about my father and his work.

Griff was now well enough to be back in charge of the kitchen again, so I was welcomed home by gorgeous smells. I grabbed a glass of water to take up to the shower. By the time I'd finished, there was a glass of something else ready – and his favourite Thai green chicken curry on the table.

Griff was no keener on hearing about Pa than Pa was on learning about Griff's latest exploits, so I asked about his day – church work, some of it. That afternoon he'd been part of the church's home Communion team, visiting an elderly parishioner. They'd taken a wafer and some wine that had been blessed the previous Sunday.

'Dodie's house reminds me in many ways of your father's quarters before you got him organized,' Griff said, gently swirling his glass of sauvignon blanc – he was supposed to drink red, for his heart's sake, of course, but occasionally he'd allow himself a holiday.

It had taken a long time for Griff and Pa to meet, so he'd never seen Pa's rooms at their worst. I snorted with laughter. 'Nothing could be as bad as Pa's place as it used to be! If social services or the medics had got anywhere near him they'd have had him sectioned. Remember, the only thing you'd want to touch was his TV.'

He squeezed my hand. 'By *normal* standards, then, Dodie's is pretty dirty. She does have carers, of course, but it's not their job to clean the whole place.' Griff paused ominously.

He wasn't about to suggest that since I had both rubber gloves and expertise in handling china I should offer my services, was he? 'Why don't you ask the women from the church cleaning rota?' I suggested hastily.

'What a good idea.' He sounded genuinely impressed. 'After all, anyone doing home visits is supposed to have a Criminal Record Bureau check – you remember the palaver that irked me when I joined the team?'

I did. He'd been so infuriated by what he saw as quite spurious enquiries about his bank balance and past addresses, he'd thrown both pen and application form across the room; I'd been afraid that despite his clean bill of health he was about to have a heart attack.

'Oh, it's not called that any more, is it?' he said. 'It's DBS – something about disclosing and debarring. All these changes for their own sake,' he chuntered.

'But will the women have been checked? Just for cleaning?'

'No, no. Most are involved with other things too – the youth club or the playgroup. And if they work with children or vulnerable adults they have to be checked; it's Church of England as well as government policy,' Griff declared. He added, 'All the same, if you weren't as honest as the day, it'd be easy to steal the odd item, because there are simply so many, and poor Dodie's eyes aren't what they should be. Nor her memory, of course.'

I gathered the plates as Griff topped up his glass. It was good to see him enjoying his food and drink again, particularly as he exercised it off one way or another every day.

There was something in his voice, however, that made me pause. 'Your eyes and memory are spot-on. What's worrying you?' I sat down again and poured myself another drop.

'I just have a feeling . . . Most of what she's got is rubbish – maybe worth a few bob at a car boot sale, if you like tatty souvenirs of Weymouth or wherever. But in the midst of the miniature vases, lighthouses and cottages I find a netsuke. About which I know absolutely nothing, so it might be my brain playing tricks.'

'What sort of tricks?'

He touched my hair. 'Sometimes I think some of your dowsing instinct must have rubbed off on me. Mind you, I'm a bit old to discover my inner divvy. But you know how sometimes, without knowing anything about an object, you know it's special—'

'Or conversely that it's rubbish.'

'Quite. I know this is special. A tiny rat clutching a candle. Perfect. What on earth is it doing there?'

I spread my hands. 'A present? Have you tried asking her?'

'It's nothing to do with me. Certainly nothing to do with why I'm in her house. I'd be embarrassed. All I'm supposed to be doing is praying and watching Tony Carr give her the wine and the wafer.'

'So what's the problem?'

'Just the mismatch . . . At least it was until Tony and I went to see her today.'

I knew every intonation of his voice better than I knew my own. 'It's gone walkabout, has it?'

'It may have done. May. Or someone might have picked it up and put it down somewhere else – maybe even Dodie herself. She'd rearranged all the photos on her piano the other day, and Tony found one down the back of the sofa.'

'I suppose it wasn't possible to ask her about it?'

'It might have been last week – might be again next week. But today all she could do was chunter about never seeing her family. The sad thing is that they visit regularly.' Griff shook his head as much in anger as in sorrow.

'Who says? I mean, one person's regular is another's once in a blue moon.'

He sounded defensive rather than certain. 'They know someone at church.' As if that was any answer at all.

'Even so . . . OK, so they turn up from time to time with food and drink and flowers. Could it be that they've realized the little rat's valuable and have removed it for safekeeping?'

'Or removed it full-stop? Or maybe one of the carers has taken a fancy to it?'

I said bracingly, 'Surely they're all DBS checked, too?'

'Of course. But have you any idea how dreadfully little these women are paid for doing the most intimate work?'

'If they wanted to steal anything, they'd have to know it was valuable. Griff, there's no problem, is there, and if there is, it's not yours. Speak to Tony if you're really worried.'

'I may just do that. And I'll float your suggestion of getting the cleaning team to help with Dodie's housework, too.' He got to his feet. 'There is someone else we could mention it to: Carwyn.'

A suspicion as vague as that? I wasn't at all sure he'd be interested. In any case, he wasn't even in the country at the moment. 'He's on secondment to Europol at the moment, remember.'

'Of course, that training initiative, whatever that means. Tony it must be. Ah, well. Peppermint tea, sweet one?'

Sometimes Griff could still surprise me. Like the evening a few days later when he announced, with some trepidation, I thought, that he'd got something to show me. I knew he'd been pottering round in his shed, something he'd not done for months before his operation, but he'd been notably quiet about what he'd been up to.

'You know that the Saturday night dance in Torquay is a fancy-dress affair? And that this year's theme is London Life?'

I nodded, though it had hardly registered. And then stopped short. All this work in the shed – he'd not been building a miniature Big Ben or Buckingham Palace, had he? Or even the Shard? He was a man for plaudits, was Griff, and if there was a prize going, even in the most obscure raffle, he wanted to win it. He'd want to go as something no one else – no one in their right mind, at least – would ever think of. And there was no doubt he was embarrassed as he flung open the shed door.

The first thing I saw was a Pearly King outfit. Perhaps he'd simply been sewing on endless buttons. Then I registered that there was no Pearly Queen outfit beside it, just a large wire structure painted gold. Inside was a frivolous dress, very short, with a bustle – more a short train, really – of feathers. A feathery headdress sat beside it. The whole outfit was pure Kylie Minogue.

'If we don't win first prize I'll eat my hat, pearls and all,' he declared. 'The whole cage is very light, so all you have to do is hold these little perches and walk normally.' He demonstrated. 'And then you step out and we sing, "Only a bird in a gilded cage". And you'll look lovely in that little dress,' he said – probably truthfully.

At first I was revolted – there were all sorts of Freudian undertones I might not understand but which I really did not like. However, Griff was trying so hard that I couldn't reject all that forethought and planning out of hand. 'How do we get it in the van? With all the things we need for the fair?'

'All these wires push back together.' He demonstrated. 'And the bottom ring that holds them in shape just unclips.'

We were left with a structure like the flimsy ribs of a very tiny canoe.

'That's how you get in and out. You just push the verticals back and – bingo!' He looked at me like a dog hoping for a chew for performing a clever trick but fearing a kick.

'You were wasted as an actor – you should have been an engineer.'

'If you could see some of the props I designed – and made!' He sighed, but not necessarily at the thought of glories past.

'OK. I'll go and try on the costume. It'll need stage-quality tights, of course, or I shall be the far side of indecent.'

'They're tucked inside the headdress. Actually, there are some little knee breeches there too, if you'd prefer them.'

The old bugger had thought of everything, hadn't he? I trooped off to my room with all the gear. I had a sudden weird frisson: at one time I must have dressed up in something pretty for my mother, whom I barely remembered, to be honest – just these tiny fragments of something too vague to be called a memory.

I'd never have worn an outfit like this, however. Belatedly entering into the spirit of things, I applied some slap: over-the-top glittering eyeshadow and shiny lipstick. And popped on my dancing shoes. Wow. It wasn't me anymore. I was ready to razzle and to dazzle. Though I did think the matching knee breeches, if a bit tight, were more appropriate for Dee's pupils.

I shimmied my way down to Griff. 'I wasn't convinced by the cage, to be honest,' I admitted, 'but this more than sets me free.'

'I hope all the old gents have their heart pills with them,' Griff mused. He put his head on one side. 'I think we may need to change your hair a little, but otherwise I think we have fancy-dress perfection. How would you feel about blue nail varnish to tone with the feathers?'

I inspected my working paws, scarred by glue, paint, lacquer and goodness knows what else: even with varnish there was no hope for them. 'It'll have to be false nails, or even glitzy gloves, but let's go for it. Yes!'

The other preparations were considerably less exciting. Trade wasn't good these days, not surprising given the length and depth of the recession. Victorian was going out, and Art Deco coming in. Russian was good, Chinese was better. On the other hand, the good citizens of Exeter might not be up to trend yet, so we packed a selection of our old reliables. Those that didn't make the cut went into plastic storage boxes which I took to the self-store unit down the road. I made space for them by removing three other carefully labelled old-fashioned cardboard boxes of stuff Griff had collected before my time.

He was eagerly rubbing his hands together as I carried the cases into the kitchen. 'I've forgotten what I've got. Dear one, this is like Christmas, isn't it? Which shall we look at first? Russian?'

Icons – quite a number. We both scratched our heads as we looked helplessly at each other. One of us would have to do a lot of homework. What was this? Fabergé? A whole lot of Fabergé? I gaped.

Gently Griff reached across and put my jaw back into position. 'Beautiful as the items are, convincing as the marks are, they're all fakes, dear one. I bought them as fakes and will have to sell them as fakes.'

I nodded: honesty was Griff's middle name, and now mine

too, of course. But my enthusiasm bubbled over. 'Look at this pill box. All this lovely enamel. And surely that's a genuine diamond in the middle of the lid? Taking your daily dose wouldn't be nearly so bad if all you had to do was flick this open.'

'It does rather put NHS bubble packs into the shade, doesn't it? But even though it's a fake, my love, it doesn't mean it's worthless.' He fished in the box and removed a scrap of paper. 'Here you are. Twelve years ago I paid six hundred pounds for it – so allowing for inflation and the huge surge of interest from Russia . . . Let's say I'd expect it to fetch at least double, possibly triple or quadruple, my original investment. And this little cigarette case – for all people don't smoke these days, it's lovely in its own right, and some denizen of St Petersburg may well take a shine to it.' He touched the view of the city on the lid. 'I'd hope to earn a nice lot of roubles for this too.' Then he frowned and put them hurriedly back in the box, not even opening the other tempting packets.

'Griff? Are you all right?' I was already hunting for the emergency spray he'd not used once since his operation.

'Perfectly,' he assured me. 'It's just something our lovely Paul was saying the other day. An accountancy issue. Accountancy and tax. Like when we separated the restoration from the retail sides,' he added hurriedly.

But judging from the serious expression that always smudged Griff's face when they'd been closeted together, I suspected they were plotting something more serious. I was very puzzled. Without positively throwing money at the Inland Revenue, Griff always declared that if you were fortunate enough to earn enough money to pay tax, you should pay it without grumbling. The tax avoidance and evasion schemes – I could never remember which were the worst – that some of our acquaintances dabbled in were anathema to Griff and, let's be honest, incomprehensible to me.

Squaring his shoulders, he patted another box. 'This might be more what we need. Far less profit.'

I couldn't understand why he should want to turn his back on a large increase in income, but lifted the one he indicated on to the table.

'Lacquer boxes,' he said. 'I only paid a couple of hundred each for most of these: we'll get a nice manageable return, I'd say.' He removed about a dozen. 'Meanwhile, let's pop the rest back into store, shall we?'

I felt my face fall. 'Can't we look at the china?' I excavated a pretty tea set. 'Oh, that's really pretty. Cup, saucer, pot, creamer and sugar bowl. All that loveliness for just one person,' I added sadly. 'I wonder what the servant carrying it to her mistress thought.' I shook my head. Enough of this preoccupation with upstairs-downstairs differences. 'Why not sell this at least? After all, we're supposed to be porcelain specialists.'

'We'd make more if we did it online and tickled international interest.'

'You make it sound like fishing.'

He sighed. 'How much do we make from the shop these days?'

'Just about enough to cover Mary's wages. If she ever left I'd wonder whether we should close it. As for the big exhibitions – when did we do more than break even at the National Exhibition Centre events?' Or at potty little local one-day fairs like the one at Matford.

'But I love the social side of it, my love. Meeting punters, greeting old friends – though sadly there are fewer of those by the month.'

The implication was that they were dropping like flies; in fact many were simply retiring or had the same view of fairs as I did. But I didn't want to argue, so I changed the subject. 'Have you mentioned that netsuke to Tony yet?'

'As a matter of fact I have. He took it quite seriously, in fact. His wife has oversight of the vulnerable adults in the congregation and she's going to visit Dodie and talk about it.'

For some reason I changed my mind. Sometimes kindness and goodwill aren't enough. 'And she's a trained police officer? No, I thought not. Tell you what, I will text Carwyn and see what he has to say.'

'Very well. In the meantime, let's see how Moira gets on, shall we? At least she's used to talking to old ladies.'

THREE

The first evening in Devon passed pleasantly enough. Waltz; quickstep; cha-cha-cha; rumba – I did them all. Mostly I danced with Griff, but I did stand up with other partners, although not the handsome thirty-year-old Dee had hinted at. Why did I doubt if he'd ever existed? The old guys danced well, but handsome princes they were not – nor was I tempted to kiss any of them to see if I could transform them.

For me, the high point of the first evening was when Griff and I finally took the floor for the Charleston. The hour or so he'd made me practise in the kitchen paid off, especially when I decided to finish the number with a couple of cartwheels. And then the jive, with more cartwheels . . . Yes! I could have jived and Charlestoned all night. But Griff couldn't – not, he assured me, because of his heart, but because his muscles simply weren't used to all this exercise. And we had to get up early in the morning, didn't we?

To go to Matford.

As you'd expect from a livestock market, there was a lingering smell not caused by roses, though it had to be said that the industrial-strength air-freshener had done a better job than usual. Customers weren't directed to types of antique – 'Nineteenth Century China', for instance, or 'Retro Clothing' – but to 'Sheep Pennage' or the 'Dairy Cattle Sale Ring', and might be further confused if they were looking for our stall: of course Tripp and Townend were present, but so, over there, was Townsend, Chartered Surveyor. And we had our usual location, over which less scrupulous dealers might have felt the Sword of Damocles hanging: Devon County Council Trading Standards Service's sign competed with ours.

Although I'd tried to sound relaxed when Pa had mentioned the name of the man who might well, on reflection, have been my mother's father, I really did not want to meet him again. Pa had been pretty accurate in his description of him. So when I saw the Devon Cottage Antiques sign I was far from happy. At least someone had a sense of humour: he was based under an advert telling you how to keep your livestock free from pests. Of course, he might have sold the business or have an employee on duty that day, and I'd have loved to wander over to check out his stock with my weird divvy's sixth sense to see what was genuine and what was fake. However, even though you're sure all the explosives have been cleared you don't necessarily want to go for a stroll in a minefield. And there was another little bomb waiting to go off too – he'd always wanted to check my DNA, and here was I spreading samples of it all over every plate or vase I touched on our stall. All he needed to do was buy one. For a nano-second I froze, ready to bolt. Years ago, that's what I'd have done. But though inside there was all too often a terrified little girl desperate to hide under a bed, outside I was a poised-looking woman capable of holding my own as an antiques consultant in exalted homes in Paris, not to mention earning an appropriate fee.

A bit of mature composure was called for now. I ran a mental check. Rather than muffle up in thick layers and a shapeless fleece, I'd resorted to sleek thermals under cashmere, topped with a leather jacket. Boots, of course, over skinny but not embarrassing jeans. As usual, Griff had cast an eye over my make-up, and my hair, although it was overdue a cut, was newly washed and at its glossy best. I know, I know – the look would have been far more appropriate if the venue had been a stately home or even a posh school. Only my hands – their usual tatty selves – wouldn't have been out of place on a *Tess of the d'Urbervilles* location like this.

Predictably, Griff was wandering around the stalls, greeting old friends and making new ones. To look at him no one would know he'd been a few heartbeats from death only months ago. Even I found it hard to imagine that he'd danced for a cool two hours last night without showing any fatigue less than ten hours later. Eventually he returned and it was my turn to scan the room, not so much for friends, but for items to buy cheap and sell dear. That was what dealers did. We tended to focus on one area – a man dealing in Jacobean art might come across a Clarice Cliff teapot on his travels, but it would never sell alongside a portrait of one of James I's cronies; it needed a china specialist. A jewellery expert might fall for Victorian brass weights – hard to imagine, but people do – but they wouldn't be at home with gems; they needed a kitchenalia expert. Equally people kept their eyes open for what regular customers collected: Griff had become friends with a woman who rarely bought our china but who always stopped by to see if we'd found spectacle cases to add to her collection. As luck would have it I found a beaded Victorian case that was pretty if not perfect. I took a quick photo for her, getting a text back within the minute: *Buy!* Anything else? My antennae simply refused to twitch: perhaps today was a day for working, not waiting to be inspired.

Over by a sheep-dip advert, a middle-aged woman I'd not seen before was selling nothing but teapots, many best described as novelty. But amidst the country cottages and the teddy bears (my bedtime friend Tim Bear would have turned up his furry nose) were a couple of oldish Worcester ones, both with blue underglaze crescent marks. The smaller was as perfect as anyone could expect of something 250 years old; the larger had a rivet holding the knob to the lid. Not a good repair. Then I unearthed a really funny pot in the form of a cauliflower of about the same date. I was about to point out to the woman that they were all seriously underpriced when she started to extol the virtues of a Humpty Dumpty pot. Feigning naivety, I asked about the cauliflower. It was worth the other two pots I liked put together, possibly all the other items on her stall put together, but she looked at it disparagingly and said I could have it for twenty. So I didn't haggle down the others too much. She felt she'd done well to sell three items before the punters got in; my conscience itched a bit but I silenced it by reminding myself how long it would take to clean up the cauliflower, which would probably end up with a higher end dealer like Harvey Sanditon, to make it presentable. The others would go on our stall and if necessary on to our website.

I parked them all with Griff, to his coos of approval, and then forced myself to stroll past the Devon Cottage stall. Unlike most others, this had a bit of everything, even a tray of tatty jewellery, mostly fit for scrap, to be honest. Did I hear anything calling? Yes, I was afraid I did. A pretty Victorian brooch in the shape of a heart. What looked like glass beads outlined the heart, but I wasn't at all sure they were beads. If they were, why had someone bothered to solder a safety chain on the back? You wouldn't do that unless it was an item of value. What if that blue bead was a sapphire, the green one a little emerald? Maybe that was a ruby? And what if that yellow setting was in fact gold? Any hallmark there might be was hidden under layers of grime. Not that I'd have been prepared to use my jeweller's glass, which would have alerted the jaded-looking woman on duty straightaway. I haggled the price down to seventeen pounds and strolled back to base, proud of myself.

But something stopped me. I'd missed something, hadn't I? Something important. Where was it?

Of course, I didn't even know what 'it' was. Just that I had to stand very still and wait for it to call me more loudly – not bad for a completely silent object.

An answer of sorts slid into my brain: I had to go back to Habgood's stall. Which, having in one sense diddled him out of a hundred pounds or so, I wasn't keen to do. So I walked slowly in the direction of a picture-dealer acquaintance of mine, merely scanning Devon Cottage Antiques with sideways glances. Yes, there was something there. Something small. I'd wait till the assistant was dealing with someone else before I went foraging. Where next?

'Are you actually looking for something or are you on one of your hunting trips? Pardon the pun!' Will Furzeland, the paintings and miniatures stallholder, greeted me. He was big and broad and looked as if he'd stepped straight out of a Hardy novel. His smile was not especially friendly. And why would it be? My gift didn't make me universally popular in a trade that depended not just on luck but also on hard-earned know-ledge. My colleagues might take their hats off to me as a restorer, but they put them on again when I was in divvy mode.

'Griff's partner Aidan has a birthday coming up, and we

were wondering about another miniature for his collection.' I took a big risk. Looking him in the eye I added, 'And I know you're an honest man, Will – not one to have nicked the pictures you're trying to sell.'

To my surprise, he gave me an awkward hug. 'Yes, it was a bad business, that boyfriend of yours doing what he did. You're not still seeing him, I hope?'

This wasn't the moment to insist I never had been *seeing* the young man in question, so I merely shook my head. Thinking about Aidan, whom I loathed almost as much as he loathed me, was enough to make me look glum. But I smiled as I saw one of Will's miniatures. 'Now, that young woman there, she'd grace any collection, wouldn't she? Shall I send Griff over so you can fix a price between you? Assuming he likes her as much as I do.'

Will took her off his display unit and held her beside my head. He looked from one face to the other. 'She's the very spit of you, isn't she? So he'll probably like her too much to give to anyone else—'

And Aidan wouldn't like her at all!

'Something about the eyes – and definitely your nose,' he continued.

'In other words, my father's nose. She must be some ancestor or other,' I said ruefully. 'I don't suppose she's got a name, has she?'

Ostentatiously he covered the label. 'She hasn't but the artist has. Go on, tell me! And I'll give you an extra five per cent off.'

I shook my head. 'Despite the now absent bloke, miniatures aren't my area, you know. And he's not going to be giving me many lessons, is he? Not from prison.'

'Go on,' he insisted.

'OK. Brushwork: excellent. Colour: radiant. The detail in the hair: amazing. It's top class, isn't it?'

'You're right there. So who's the artist?'

'Not even for an extra twenty per cent . . .' But something was coming through the quagmire of my memory – the image of a wonderfully flattering self-portrait of a handsome man. The words came out of their own accord: 'John Smart. It's a John Smart.'

'Good girl. So you'll tell old Griff it's kosher?'

'Old Griff's forgotten more about things like this than I shall ever know,' I said, looking over to our stall. Griff was deep in conversation with a man about his own age, dressed in that weird country gents' uniform of bilious mustard cords and a tweed hacking-jacket with elbow patches. Actually bilious wasn't a tactful word, come to think of it: the man looked prey to persistent indigestion or worse. He was a bad colour and very thin. 'I'll send him over when he's free, I promise. Can you tuck it away for him? Thanks.'

As he slipped it behind his counter, he asked, 'When are you and Arthur Habgood going to end this grudge match of yours?'

I'd have liked a bit of Griff's stagey hauteur: what could he possibly be talking about? But it was easier to be straight. 'He tells the police I handle stolen goods and has me arrested.'

'He never did!'

'Oh, yes. Not very friendly at all.' I hit my stride. 'Now, if I look at your stock, do I find anything halfway dodgy? Of course not. You've got provenance for everything. Look at anything on our stall. Could you tell if it had been restored? No. But I make clear from the outset on the label stuck firmly underneath whatever it is. Always have, always will. The first piece Habgood bought from me, pretty well the first I'd ever repaired, just an apprentice piece, he sold as perfect. And he pursues me for years with a gobswab on the grounds I'm his granddaughter. So, between you, me and the gatepost, I don't care that much about the man.' I clicked my fingers with a flourish.

'I don't blame you. I can see I shall have to put a few people right about him.'

We exchanged a genuine hug. If only Will was twenty years younger . . . Oh, and single.

Meanwhile, I still had to not think about the item that was calling me. That's right – *not* think. I had to let it come to me in its own time.

To keep my brain empty I retired to the ladies', applying a bit of gloss to my lips to kill more time. But any moment now the punters could come in and I'd have to be on duty. Shoulders straight? Smile ready? Back into the arena, then.

And on Devon Cottage's table, there it was waiting for me. A netsuke. And guess what – it was a rat eating a candle.

I could have been sick on the spot. Which wouldn't have done any good at all, would it? Instead I strolled on to our stall, where Griff was still nattering to his friend, and grabbed my phone. Instead of texting, however, I put it in camera mode, zooming in on Devon Cottage's offerings. I even risked a couple at slightly closer range. There – time and date recorded. I even sent them to Carwyn for safe-keeping, as it were. And then, calm as you like, I sauntered over. The woman was a bit surprised to see me again, but I explained I was buying on behalf of a client whom I'd had to phone. We haggled over the price a bit, to the extent that I said I'd have to check if my client was prepared to go so high. OK, a further ten pounds off. And my client wanted a written receipt – sorry to be such a pain.

I'd have sung and danced my way back to our stall except one just didn't do that sort of thing. In any case, Griff was looking decidedly apprehensive.

It seemed his friend, whom he introduced as Noel Pargetter, another resting thespian, was desperate for Griff to lunch with him the following day. Personally I'd rather have been on the road by then – the A303, full of families returning from their weekend cottages, was never pleasant on Sunday afternoons. Never pleasant full-stop, actually. But the later you left it, the more clogged it was. Until I judged how keen Griff was, however, I'd say nothing. I caught his eye and waited.

Whenever Griff was asked to do something he wasn't keen on, he would give me a little signal with his signet ring finger. It didn't so much as twitch when Noel repeated his invitation. But it was clear that Noel didn't expect me to be part of the deal, though Griff didn't seem to realize that, and blithely accepted for both of us. Normally I'd have said I already had plans, and begged to be excused, but something was happening that made me fall in with Griff's plans with alacrity. It was the sight of Harvey Sanditon in the doorway, looking around before he stepped inside. I knew from the smile on his face that it was us – more likely me – he was looking for. He'd never yet let slip the chance to spend time with me, even under

Griff's close chaperonage, and though we were clearly unavailable today, he might spring an offer for Sunday lunch too. In this case it was rather the devil you don't know than the devil you do, and more to the point the one I'd rather keep at the far end of a long spoon.

Surprise, surprise, Harvey had the best of excuses for wanting to talk to me. He'd bought a pair of eighteenth-century Worcester lidded vases, one of which needed minor restoration. He showed me a couple of photos: mouth-watering Chinese-style hexagonal ones, with wonderful birds in panels against a blue ground. I knew he'd never try to sell them as a perfect, because from time to time I checked his website to see how he advertised other items I'd worked on. Recently he'd added '*by Lina Townend*' to the original words, '*Minor restoration*'. As a way of wooing someone, it was pretty original, I had to concede.

'If I might bring the vase to where you're staying it'd save me an enormous amount in courier's fees,' he said.

He sent so much to me that the courier and I were practically friends, but I couldn't argue with his logic.

'What about tomorrow morning – before Griff and I go out to lunch?' I suggested. It might be harder to be passionate over coffee.

He bit his lip. 'I can't do that, I'm afraid. I've got a family lunch party myself in Manchester of all places, so I shall be on the road very early. What about this evening?' He didn't leer; Harvey never leered or ogled, but he looked at me with a quite embarrassing hunger, so obvious that other people must have noticed. Why did he expose himself – and me – to behind-the-hand mockery?

'I'm sorry. Griff and I are absolutely tied into an event this evening. But we'll have a word with the hotel reception team and make sure they put your vase straight into their safe. The Mondiale in Torquay – up on the hill.'

'Oh, yes,' Griff put in helpfully, 'it's the highlight of our dance classes – a fancy-dress ball. Can't miss that.'

I couldn't reach to kick him.

You could almost see Harvey working out how to capitalize on the information, but the point he made was valid enough.

'If the ball's at the Mondiale, would one of you be able to leave the dance floor long enough to sign for it? At about seven? Tricky people, insurers.'

Griff smiled, but clocked the first customers making their way over. 'Of course, of course. But right now it's all hands to the pumps, Harvey. We'll see you this evening.'

I never bollocked Griff in public or in private, but I could have had a stand-up row with him just then. However, I confined myself to shoving him off quickly in the direction of Will and his miniature.

What should I say about the netsuke? Nothing yet, at least – some of our regular customers were already handling items we'd brought with them in mind, and there was work to be done.

FOUR

'It does look just like Dodie's,' Griff said, moving his glasses up then down his nose, as if to help himself focus not just physically but mentally. We were having a mid-morning lull and risking the coffee. 'But I only saw hers for a few moments, remember, and it was only a glance, not a close inspection. And I know so little about Oriental art, I've no way of knowing if each netsuke is unique or if they were produced in their hundreds. How much did you give?'

'Not enough, I suspect. I came up with this cock and bull story about a client ready to do a deal, and she blinked before I did. But I also got a receipt and a photo on my phone showing where it was on the stall. With the time and date, of course.'

'So your thinking is that we should keep this dear little chap as putative evidence in a case that may not exist.'

'Put like that it sounds crazy. But yes, that's what I want to do. If it's not Dodie's rat, than we can sell it at a profit, probably. If it is hers, we've no right to sell it anyway.' I knew I sounded stern, but all I really wanted to do was yell at him for exposing me anew to Harvey's loving eyes. 'Anyway, I saw the look on Noel's face when you told him I'd be joining him for lunch, poor thing. So what we'll do is this: I'll drop you off wherever he lives and go and hit the shops. And then I'll pick you up, either at a time we arrange beforehand or when you send an SOS. Sound good?'

He patted my hand. 'It sounds excellent, but for one thing. Noel lives out in the sticks. In a hamlet just beyond Moretonhampstead. So it wouldn't be shops you'd hit. At best a view, at worst a pony.'

'No problem. You can invent someone I'm meeting – Harvey, if you insist – and I'll get the Mondiale to organize a packed lunch for me and I'll enjoy a bit of nature. I'll Google the area before we set off – I might even nip into town here if it continues as quiet as this and get an Ordnance Survey map, just to annoy Sally the Satnav.'

Griff looked around, spreading his hands. 'I see no ravening hordes. Off you go, my darling. And, dear one, I'm sorry about Harvey descending on us this evening. I'll fend him off, don't you worry.'

What Griff and I had forgotten was that the Great Fancy-Dress Parade would take place at seven, at the exact time Harvey had invited himself along. And what neither of us had imagined was that, rather than page one of us, the hotel staff would send him, clutching his priceless parcel, direct to the ballroom. He must have entered just as I exited my cage. I'd decided against the rather tight breeches in case I wanted to do a few more cartwheels. Of course the little skirt was decent enough, the sort tennis players wear, with built-in knickers, and I wore long gloves to cover my working hands.

Because I was being a demure – indeed, dying – little bird, I didn't look up . . . until I heard a sickening thud. Cardboard, bubble wrap, something else I didn't even want to think about . . . Then I looked. *Restored by Lina Townend? Reconstructed by Lina Townend,* more like. The demure little bird became an avenging angel, flying the length of the ballroom to the stairs down which Harvey had fallen and yelling abuse at a man stupid enough to drop something 250 years old, even if it was his to drop.

I'd read somewhere that, in the event of a motorcycle accident, no one at the scene should attempt to remove the crash helmet until the patient was in the operating theatre, because the helmet was holding the possibly fractured skull in the right place. The tissue and bubble wrap were performing roughly the same job for the vase. So I wouldn't open the box, and wouldn't let anyone else open it, not even the owner, until I got it home. I cradled it briefly before returning it to the owner's hands.

As for him, he could lick his own wounds.

How coherently I was explaining all this I've no idea. Not very, I suspect. But at last I gathered enough breath to ask Harvey how he wanted to play the insurance. 'How about

damaged in transit?' I asked, stifling a hysterical giggle. 'OK?
So you might as well drop the box off at reception this time
round. And I'll collect it when I go back to my room.'

'You termagant,' he breathed. He added a lot of other things,
much more loudly, rounding off with, 'You bitch!' There were
even a few additions to that short sentence, too.

'That's me,' I agreed, trying to sound cheerful, but suddenly
realizing how much I'd miss his constant admiration. 'And
now you must excuse me. Griff and I were about to sing.' I
made a fluttering walk back down the ballroom. We'd arranged
to do our duet with me outside the cage. But on impulse I
stepped back in and gestured Griff to begin. He did, in his
still clear tenor.

I warbled the first chorus solo. And then the whole room
joined in. As the last note rolled round the room, Griff made
another unrehearsed move. He unlocked the cage to let me
take flight. Tentatively at first, I stepped out. Then I spread
my wings. No, I wasn't about to flap about in an ungainly
manner: I cartwheeled the length of the room. Bloody Harvey
was still there. So I seized the box from his unresisting hands
and, as if it was part of the act, ran up the stairs and away.

It would have been far more effective, I suppose, if I hadn't
had to go back down again to beg the reception staff for a
spare keycard. And it would have been better, with my puffy
eyes and snivelling nose, if I could have stayed with Tim the
Bear and not had to join the others for supper – as an afterthought I put the breeches on; tough if I looked less like a
bird and more like Gainsborough's 'Blue Boy'.

The trouble with being a show-off is that while some people
want a repeat, others are genuinely offended by your antics.
So I got a mixed response when I slunk into the dining room,
hoping my recent tears weren't too obvious. While a lot of
folk gave me a round of applause, several very ostentatiously
didn't, and I did hear, as Griff and I got up to accept the bottle
of fizz for our prize, which now seemed far too hard-earned,
some sharp intakes of breath and some disapproving tuts
amongst the generous cheers. It was also noticeable that when
we withdrew to the ballroom, fewer men asked to partner me;

perhaps the tirade I'd directed at Harvey – though I couldn't recall using a single swear word from my extensive vocabulary – had shocked them. Certainly his stream of abuse would have been offensive to most people of that generation, and I'd been the one to provoke it.

But I wasn't without help. Just as I wished the floor would open, Dee came up to me. She was as short as I was, so she could look me straight in the eye. 'Is it true that that man broke twelve thousand pounds' worth of china?'

Griff had exaggerated a bit, but I wouldn't dob him in. 'Give or take a few hundred. Actually, take quite a lot now. I'll probably be able to do something with it, but I can't magic it whole again.' Drat: another sob was worming its way up. 'I don't know why he took it into his head to come here tonight. He was supposed to have had Griff summoned to reception. That was the deal. Not to gatecrash your event. I'm so sorry.'

She didn't seem to want an apology. 'Has he been stalking you?'

I gave that some thought. 'Not quite. But he's always wanted to change what I think should be a purely professional relationship.'

'He's old enough to be your father!' She sounded outraged.

'Quite. He's also very powerful. He could ruin my business if he puts the word around. And I wasn't very polite to him.'

She pursed her lips firmly, perhaps thinking that there'd been enough bad language for one evening without her adding even a mild expletive. 'If I were him,' she said very deliberately, 'I wouldn't say anything. He didn't come out of it very well, and not just because he broke something precious. If he hadn't been – well, I've heard the expression *devouring someone with one's eyes*, and that's what he was doing to you, he wouldn't have fallen, would he? What did he expect you to do with the parcel anyway, once it was in your hands?'

'Take it straight up to my room. Why?'

'And do you suppose he'd have stayed tamely down here talking to me or the DJ?'

I stared.

'Quite. Sex, that's what he had in mind. You're a victim here, Lina.'

I shook my head firmly. 'I don't do victimhood,' I said firmly. 'I do survival.'

She laughed, reaching to squeeze my hands. 'Well you'd better survive the next dance, then − I know it's the foxtrot and you find it hard, but you know all the steps you'll need and the tune we'll use has a good, clear beat . . .' After a very public hug, she headed off to talk to other guests. I'm not sure what she said to them, but the looks were much kinder after that, and one very old lady went so far as to pat my cheek when we met in the loos.

One thing in favour of the foxtrot was that I had to concentrate so hard on my feet I didn't have spare brain space to think about anything − or anyone − else. For once, however, when Griff tried to apologize for his part in the fiasco, I let him get on with it instead of shutting him up. And I did hit him with one low blow: 'Even Pa would have tried to protect me from Harvey,' I said with unkind truth, 'not encourage him as you did. But that's an end of it, Griff. I just don't want to talk about it now or tomorrow or ever again.'

'But your therapist—'

'Maybe to my therapist. But that'll be at a time of my own choosing. And I won't be trying to do a heel turn at the time.'

FIVE

Shepdip Farm huddled in the lee of a rather grand hill, defeating Sally the Satnav's attempts to find it. The dear old-fashioned OS map, however, led us straight to it. It was a broad, low-browed building, probably Elizabethan, the slate roofline sagging with age. I'd have liked a drooping thatch, of course. The lower windows were mullioned, the upper ones prettily emerging from the roof like surprised eyes under pointed eyebrows. There were too many chimneys to count in the time I had available.

'You rather expect to see Jan Ridd striding out to greet us, don't you, my dear one?' Griff observed, waving at the frail old man who was opening his front door a crack. 'Now, you'll be back here at two-thirty sharp?'

'And earlier if you text me. Assuming there's any signal round here,' I added gloomily, waving to Noel, whose signet ring gave the sort of flash in the sun for which only a socking great diamond could be responsible, and reversing back up the steep track to what passed for a main road but was in fact a single-track lane with passing places for random sheep.

My efforts to take my mind off the Harvey business had involved spending a lot of the previous night Googling things to do on Dartmoor – things that didn't involve walking gear and sensible boots, of course. Deciding against obvious family attractions, I opted for a look at a couple of churches, both managed by the Historic Churches Preservation Trust. According to Google, the best ones were to the west of Dartmoor, but I was on the east, so choice was a bit more limited. By chance, there was one St Sidwell's in the Moor – famous, according to Google, for its medieval rood screen that somehow escaped the depredations of both Henry VIII's men and Cromwell's vandals – that was only about five miles west of Noel's, so I headed for that, picking my way down a not-very-well-made road like a toddler testing the sea for the first time. After all, in addition to what remained of Harvey's vase, I had our own stock to think about.

I was certainly glad I hadn't met the vehicle parked by the tiny church on its way up. This was a white van, the size favoured by decorators and so on. To say it was parked, actually, was to flatter the driver – abandoned might be a more accurate term, since it occupied the entire layby. Should I park across its bows, to make a point? Instead I crept on past the church to find a gateway to reverse into. Since the chain holding the gate had rusted solid, I took a chance that no one would be opening it in the next fifteen minutes. Meanwhile, I took a photo of the offending van, for no other reason than it so annoyed me. Then I padded into the church – no longer used for worship since its only congregation would be sheep or ponies. But someone was working in it. White van man, no doubt.

Not working. Hacking at the famous rood screen. Two men had already removed one panel, now they were starting on a second. No signal for me to dial 999, of course. They were making so much noise that they didn't register my presence, or the quiet snap of my phone as I took as many photos as I could. Then I did two more things – one sensible, one downright foolhardy, considering the size of the vandals, both six-foot bruisers: I hid the phone under a pile of leaflets and, seizing a handy pole – a churchwarden's staff, as it turned out, unaccountably left there even though the church wasn't used – I ran at the men, screaming.

Stupid or what, when they had chisels in their hands? But they were so surprised they actually dropped them and ran. OK, they gathered up one priceless panel, but they abandoned the second. I ran after them – God knows why – still yelling. By now they were angry – as you would be if attacked by a persistent wasp, I suppose – and drove the van at me. All I could do was dodge and impotently jab the pole into the side as they drove away. If they stopped for a second attack on me I was lost. But thank goodness they simply scarpered.

Catching my breath, and wondering how I'd been so damned stupid, I withdrew to our van. But I had to go back for my phone – all that evidence – so I took another risk. Leaving

the engine running, I hurtled into the church, retrieving the
phone and the badly damaged panel, which I shoved on to
the passenger seat. I really needed a signal to call the cops,
not to mention putting space between me and White Van Men.
Time to dash. Which I did, straight into the path of an oncoming
police car.

At least we both stopped in time. I almost fell out of the
van, racing towards the car and gesturing frantically back up
the road. My story wasn't helped, however, when they found
the smashed medieval panel on my passenger seat. For a
moment I was sure I was about to be arrested. Fortunately the
photos I'd taken went a long way to convincing the young
sergeant, whose blonde curly ponytail made her look about
seventeen, and her even younger male constable, his homely
face dotted with acne, of my innocence. They volunteered
their names: Sergeant Pat Henchard and PC Toby Drake. In
return I handed over one of my business cards and suggested
they could get someone to look me up online; they couldn't
themselves because there was no dratted signal, of course.
Eventually, prompted by the photo of the awful bit of parking,
they put out a call for the white van, though they were swift
to warn me that without the CCTV that covers towns and even
villages like ours, it'd be hard to catch someone in the vast
deserted acres of the moor.

They let me reverse the van the thirty or so yards to my
gateway, then parked alongside, rather blocking the lane, but
clearly making sure I could not make a run for it. With an
ironic bow, I handed over the panel for their safe-keeping;
both officers blushed at their lack of forethought.

Their gasps of horror matched mine as we surveyed the
damage. 'Of course someone must secure the place, not just
as a crime scene but as a repository of priceless works of art,'
I declared. Whenever I wanted to impress people I tried to
speak as Harvey would have spoken. Authoritative, not quite
arrogant. I wished I hadn't thought of Harvey, but they took
the sudden surge of tears as a sign I was truly sincere.

'You really care about this stuff, don't you?' PC Drake
turned to look at me.

'Yes,' I said simply. 'It's my life and my livelihood. I can't bear to see works of art spoiled, especially deliberately. And when it's a couple of low-lifes presumably stealing to order for some rich bastard, I'd get out the guillotine, I can tell you. And sit there knitting.'

He laughed. 'You wouldn't operate it yourself?'

'It depends what they'd damaged. This rood screen was unique,' I said, walking up to it but shoving my hands deep in my pockets lest I reach out to touch it. 'Nine centuries or more it's been standing there, quietly helping people to worship. It's totally irreplaceable. Of course, if you ever find the missing panel it can be mended, but it'll take a genius to do it invisibly,' I said, thinking about Harvey's vase again.

Sergeant Henchard crowed with pleasure at the sight of the vandals' chisels, which she stowed in evidence bags. They banged against her thigh as she walked.

A glance at my watch told me that I'd soon need to start back to Noel's place if I wasn't to get Griff into a tizzy. But Henchard and Drake were talking urgently about something, and I was loath to interrupt. So I took the opportunity to look round the ancient place. The rood screen must have been added to an already old building – the font looked Norman or even earlier, and some of the monuments were definitely pre-Crusades. The arches were Saxon. How dare those animals violate so lovely a space! Would it be wrong to hope they rotted in the hell that the screen depicted? The remaining panels showed a vast evil mouth, opening to receive a variety of terrified-looking figures. Some were greeted by monsters, others by flames. As if aware of my stillness, the two officers stopped talking and moved beside me, also caught in silent wonder.

I pointed to the walls, where, despite damage caused by damp, vivid paintings showed how colourful the whole place must once have been: St Michael was weighing the souls of the dead, to judge where they'd end up.

The spell was broken by Henchard's radio. She snapped an expletive I'd have thought twice about uttering in church, even an unused one. 'We need to have this one made secure first,' she told the person crackling at her. 'The bastards may loop back. Excellent. We'll go the minute they turn up.' She turned to Drake and, curiously, me. 'Scene of crime team's on its way, as is a team from the Historic Churches Trust. And some uniform back-up. Meanwhile, there's been another theft from another historic church, St Rumon's. Back towards Moretonhampstead.'

'May I tag along?' I asked mildly. 'I've got to go that way to pick up my business partner, and it'd be nice to have an escort. I know our van's pretty inconspicuous compared with some, but it's still got our name on it.'

'Like the hardware superstore people,' Toby said, in a decent impression of the horrible mockney accent of the guy doing the voice-overs for the Wickes TV ads. 'What do you think, boss?'

'I'd stick to the day job if I were you, Toby. OK. You can come. But you're not to interfere or take any risks. Understood?'

St Rumon was new to me, but according to the leaflet in the church he was associated with an abbey in Tavistock; why anyone had chosen to dedicate such a tiny and on the face of it unimpressive building to him, goodness knows. This time the thieves had taken not wood but stone. The leaflet drew our attention to two unique pieces of sculpture in the north wall, possibly dating to the reign of Cnut; it was these that had been sledge-hammered out.

'Not a theft done on spec, surely,' I muttered. 'How dare they, Pat, how dare they? If only the fabulous beasts could turn round and bite them.' I touched the illustration – fearsome heads indeed.

'I've never known anyone so passionate about art.'

I nodded. 'I'm not alone: my boyfriend's with Kent Police's heritage department. He's on secondment to Europol at the moment.'

'I suppose you work together a lot?'

Not after my first police-officer boyfriend. No way. 'I'm more antiques than heritage,' I said mildly. 'I don't even know if there's anything else worth stealing here.'

'Whether or not, we'll secure the scene,' she said. 'Seems a funny policy to leave precious stuff like this where anyone could just waltz in and nick it. That's the Church for you.

Now, I shall be busy here for a while. Do you want Toby to escort you back to your partner? Then – and I know it'll hold you up – but we really need you to come back to Newton Abbott to give a formal statement, see if you can pick out our friends. I know we'll do wonders with your pics, but that's procedure. Do you want to pick up your partner first or just give him a bell and say you'll be late?'

I checked my watch. Noel didn't seem to be the sort of man Griff would want to be dumped on for a couple of hours more than he'd bargained for. 'I'd like to go and collect him first, please. And I'd really love Toby to keep an eye on me.'

SIX

Griff deserved some explanation of my late arrival, though he got a slightly edited version of my adventures. His eyes widened when he registered the presence of Toby, who'd been tactful enough to park some distance from the gate. After all, not everyone liked a visit from the police.

We processed to Newton Abbott without any more excitement. I persuaded Griff to come into the police station with me; he was already sleeping off his lunch in the waiting area when Toby escorted me through security to look at photos of well-known antique thieves and to download the images from my camera, none of which showed their faces in full. The people trained to run the facial recognition software were off-duty till the following day, so we had to rely on my eyes and memory. From time to time my stomach rumbled alarmingly, and soon Toby and I were working our way through the Mondiale picnic, washed down by machine coffee, as we scanned ugly mug after ugly mug. Desperate as I was to point an accusing finger, however, I couldn't see today's miscreants – though I did see other faces I knew from here and there, not least my father's bosom pal, Titus Oates. It didn't seem necessary to claim acquaintance with him. On to a formal statement, then.

Pat Henchard arrived back in time to read it through, just as I hoped I could leave.

'You really were very stupid, you know,' she told me helpfully. 'A couple of blows from those chisels . . .' She drew her hand across her throat.

'Adrenaline,' I said, by way of apology or explanation. 'I might have been able to outrun them, leap into my van – and run into you two, of course.' We grinned at the absurdity of the scenario. 'But I ought to head home soon. I don't suppose you've found that white van yet?'

'We know it was stolen from a yard in Tavistock, but that's all.' She pulled a face. 'I might just get some of our mates to keep an eye on you if you give me some idea of your route . . . Kent? Bloody hell! Still, there are lots of cameras watching over motorways, and we'll alert Traffic. You should be all right. We'll lead you as far as the A38.'

It seemed rather lukewarm reassurance, but it was all she could give me.

'If only I'd not succumbed to the temptation of Noel's Chablis,' Griff lamented. 'But I really don't think I'm fit to drive, my dear one. In fact I'm finding it terribly hard to keep my eyes open.' Tell me something I didn't know! 'Unless it would help you to concentrate if we talked?'

'Find something jolly on the radio,' I suggested, 'and I'll sing along to that.' And as he fell into his inevitable doze, I could keep an eye open for white vans – the afternoon sun seemed to have brought them out in swarms – and the less frequent patrol vehicles. On the plus side, none of the vans seemed to have scars inflicted by a churchwarden's staff, and the possibility that they might have receded by the mile.

By now Griff was awake enough to tell me all about his prolonged lunch with Noel, and I was happy to let him chat away, taking, to be honest, very little interest in a man Griff described as an old bore even when he was young.

'Why did he give up acting?' I asked idly, just to show Griff I was still listening.

'Why do we all? Lack of roles, dear one, lack of roles. But I've an idea he came into money. Quite a lot, I presume.'

'A lot? And he lives in a dump like that?'

'It's by no means a dump inside: rather gloomy, of course, but a sort of Victorian Scots baronial décor. And it's not his main home. He has a place in London, one gathers. Is all well, dear one?'

'Absolutely fine.'

It was amazing just how many white vans did have scars, of course. And my driving was accordingly – and illogically – twitchy. Perhaps I was simply tired. I pulled over at Solstice Park Services, parking where the security cameras could see us. Surely no one would have followed me this far; they'd have been more interested in dumping their very heavy loot.

Which set me on another train of thought. I texted Carwyn: what would be the best time to phone him this evening? And did he or his Europol mates recognize these chisel-wielding thugs? A text from him in response told me he'd get in touch late on Monday – meanwhile, I should watch my back.

So on Monday I simply got on with the day job. Actually, not quite simply. I had a bit of a moral dilemma: usually I deal with my repair jobs in strict rotation, unless really urgent action is required by a gallery, for instance. Because he paid me so much, I also eased jobs for Harvey up the queue. Should I this time? Would he even pay me, thinking that somehow the damage was my fault? Not for anything would I contact him, however. So his box went on to the pending shelf, and I reached for the one at the top of the day's list, a really tricky bit of Crown Derby, with all its extravagant gilding. Absolute concentration and a steady hand were required. If I allowed my thoughts to wander for one moment in Harvey's direction, I – and the wonderful plate – would be sunk. Griff had to take responsibility for checking the firm's emails, and I stuffed my mobile under the sofa cushions well away from my workroom so I couldn't hear the cheery warble of an incoming text even if I wanted to. Carwyn never contacted me in the daytime, even when he was in England, so he wouldn't update me till later this evening.

After Pilates, in other words.

And, as it turned out, after a quick drink with the other women. My social life being close to zero, I was happy to adjourn to the newly refurbished and renamed Pig and Whistle – though part of me was already rechristening it the Rat and Candle, after the netsuke Griff was taking to show Tony. Once there I had a doubt or two. Laura and Honey managed to look sleek and elegant in their tops and leggings; I merely looked as if I'd been working very hard indeed, which of course I had. I had hopes that a piece of equipment called the barrel would restore my shoulder blades to their rightful position.

Over water, then wine, we exchanged blow-by-blow accounts

of their weekends, Honey's sounding rather less than inspiring since she'd worked both days on the cosmetics counter, which explained her wonderful make-up. Laura had been to the seaside with her boyfriend. I'd combined the work and the seaside, of course, not to mention winning the fancy-dress prize. They were dead keen on seeing my outfit, so I fished out my phone: I'd accumulated eleven calls and nineteen texts. The wine, a jolly Prosecco, suddenly tasted sour. I thumbed quickly to the photos, skipping the ones of me in the cage, incidentally.

After all the giggles, Laura said quietly, 'Something's upset you, though, hasn't it?'

For answer, I showed her unread text envelopes. 'Bloke trouble,' I said. 'The sort of bloke that won't take *no* for an answer. Not even, *no – piss off!*' I added truthfully, if inelegantly.

They were duly outraged on my behalf, and wanted the details, topping up my glass.

'I really fancied him till I found out he's married,' I admitted. 'And to be honest, it feels as if I've been fending him off for years.'

Honey giggled. 'What made you fancy him in the first place?'

I scrolled through my photos to show them.

'Wow! George Clooney, eat your heart out!'

'Quite. But as I say, he's married and he's old enough to be my father,' I said, with a sudden frisson of horror at all the implications. *To be my father.*

Griff, Pa, Aidan, Harvey . . . I suddenly saw stretching before me a lifetime of worrying about old men. 'What I need is a toy boy!' I declared, more to myself than to Honey or Laura, adding less dramatically and more accurately, 'Or at least someone my age.'

'So are you going to delete all those messages without opening them?' Honey asked. 'That's the best thing.'

'It's tempting. But some of them may be to do with work.'

'Go through them now, then we'll get in some more drinks. Come on.'

I dealt with the texts first – at least two-thirds were from

Harvey, increasing in frantic contrition. Worryingly, the last one told me he was so desperate he was on his way to see me.

My reply was succinct: *No. Absolutely not. Go home now.*

The calls were all from him. The last two or three sounded as if he was on the road. Honey and Laura looked from me to each other. 'You're going to have to call him back – let's hope he doesn't answer so you can leave a really firm message. Not a teary one,' Laura added.

'I'll need a few deep breaths,' I said. I dialled. And got to him direct. I would not panic. 'Harvey, this has got to stop. If you're on your way to Kent, then just turn round and go back home. And don't try phoning or texting,' I said, over-riding him, 'because I shan't respond.' I cut the call. The girls applauded. They didn't know I still had thousands of pounds' worth of shards to put back together. Or did I? Was his vase not now his problem? I could return it to him in the state in which he'd left it. Easy. But would a surgeon refuse to treat a patient on the grounds that its parent had annoyed her?

Even if I'd considered talking over the situation with Griff – hard, since it was he who'd accidentally dropped me in it in the first place – I got home to find him in a worse temper than mine after a meeting of the Parochial Church Council. Why he'd ever consented to join the PCC was beyond me – if there was such a thing as a committee man, Griff was the antithesis. To stop him grumbling about the slowness of arcane procedures, I asked about the netsuke. To be honest, I didn't care much: the extra Prosecco was catching up with me. If I wasn't careful I'd take out my rather tipsy anger with Harvey on Griff himself. When I was younger, I would have smashed anything or anyone within reach; supposedly my counsellor had suggested ways of dealing with anger, but all I dared do tonight was keep a lid on it.

'Tony thought he might have seen our little rat on Dodie's table,' he said, taking it from his pocket and stroking it absentmindedly, 'but he couldn't be sure. And like me he doesn't want to cause trouble where there isn't any. So it's all been left hanging in the air – unlike our bat-droppings problem,' he added. 'You'll never guess where they've started fouling now . . .'

At this point I decided l really should get in touch with Carwyn.

'My Europol colleagues were quite interested in the pics you sent,' he said.

'Even though they don't show their faces properly?'

He laughed. 'Would you believe, there are people working on ear recognition these days?'

That was something I knew about. 'Like fingerprints? They get them from windows and other places they may have touched . . .'

'That's old hat. They've known about that for years. But actual ear shape . . . I've been on to DCI Webb, by the way.'

'Freya! Why on earth . . .?'

'Because when I emailed her, Henchard said she was afraid Chummie might just have seen your van. Might not, of course. But I thought – and I'm not trying to put the wind up you, Lina – that the Kent Police in the form of DCI Webb ought to know you could conceivably be a target.'

I snorted. 'And they or she could do something about it? Whenever I see her all she can talk about is cuts and budgets and police commissioners and the sheer impossibility of doing anything except run to catch up. Actually, she's right, isn't she? I was looking up some stuff online the other day.'

'Yes. It's bad.'

'You sound as if you need a hug. Hell's bells, Carwyn – you're not being made redundant, are you?' Actually, my heart sank: what if he was offered a permanent job abroad? I'd really miss him. Really, really miss him.

'No. Not until I've worked off the amount it's cost them to second me, at least. Any news about Griff and the netsuke?'

I updated him. It would have been nice to have some advice; instead he cut in with a question.

'Have you two had a falling out?' he asked.

'It'll pass.' I kept my explanation as low-key and rational as possible, but then admitted I'd had to fend Harvey off this evening.

'He'd come all the way up from Devon to apologize for swearing?'

'Not quite. In fact, I don't really think it's anything to do with his awful behaviour,' I said, the possibility dawning on me at last. 'I think he just wants to get back into my good books so that I'll repair the vase he broke.'

'And will you? After all that shit?' He wasn't usually a man to swear, and there was a distinct edge to his voice.

'I said I'd do it before he broke it again, so I suppose that's some sort of verbal contract. But he can whistle for it till it reaches the head of the queue – which is three or four months' long. Sometimes in the past he's paid for preferential treatment, when he's got a buyer waiting, for instance. And check out what he says on his website about restored items I've handled – a really good advert for me.'

'I have – and it's weird he refers to you by name. Why doesn't he say "*Repaired by Townend Restoration*"? That's the name of your company, isn't it? He's just trying to get into your knickers by flattery. Your pa's right – the man's a posh toe-rag.'

'A married toe-rag too – and given my pa's history, remember, I don't do married men.' I'd learned by painful experience that it just didn't work. And I suspected the same applied to men married to their work. What I needed was a nice boy next door. Perhaps life would be better when Carwyn moved back this side of the Channel.

SEVEN

W hat I got was a police car passing the front door a couple of times during the next week; this was presumably Freya's best effort at keeping me safe. Reassured – possibly – I got in a couple of days' uninterrupted work. As usual when I was under pressure, Griff took over the running of the house, and Mary Banner dealt with any sales. When she'd been the widowed Mrs Walker, we'd always addressed her formally; now she'd remarried, she'd inexplicably regained her first name. Mary was equally at home in the shop or on the internet. Despite our worries, the shop was doing well this week, with internet sales down slightly: perhaps the pleasant weather and absence of schoolchildren was bringing out the punters. The weather was pretty irrelevant as far as I was concerned, apart from the early evening walks that had been Griff's road to recovery and now proved my back's salvation.

'Are there any emails or texts I should know about? Harvey apart, of course,' I asked as we headed up the hill to the church, the highest point of the village and once quite a testing walk for him. Now he kept up with me pace for pace, and had enough breath to talk.

'There was what looked like a standard email from Devon and Cornwall Police saying that they were doing everything in their power but hadn't yet solved the crime that you witnessed. Let me just pop this card into the postbox over there, my love – a little thank you billet for poor Noel, so much more personal than an email. There. I do wonder if I shouldn't have sent him a little something. It felt very poor form to turn up without so much as a bottle of wine or a bunch of flowers.'

'I don't think petrol station versions would have filled the bill either, do you?' I gave him a sideways look. 'OK, what did you find out when you Googled him?'

'As if I'd do such a thing! As it happens,' he said, dropping his voice as if the yew hedge we were passing might sprout ears, 'he's turned up in the *Sunday Times* Rich List a couple of times. How about that? No, you're never impressed by money *per se*, are you? My dear one, I can't undo what I did on Saturday morning, can't unsay it, but I wish with all my heart I could. You must know that.'

There and then, halfway up Church Hill, we stopped and had a hug. 'Let's not talk about it anymore. Pa will be pleased, anyway: he refers to him as a lounge-lizard, which always sounds pretty disgusting. OK, this here netsuke and Dodie's other goodies – what are you going to do, you and Tony?'

'Take her Communion again tomorrow, as it happens. I don't suppose you would have time to come along too?'

'Imagine me being DBS checked! OK, I know I don't actually have a criminal record, not so much as a parking ticket, but I'd hate the process even more than you.'

'You'd be chaperoned so you wouldn't need one.'

'And how would you explain my presence? There! Gotcha!' It was lovely to share a laugh together. 'However,' I said, 'I do have a serious suggestion. Our security people could install a hidden camera as easy as winking. We've even got one, haven't we, in our caravan, disguised as a radio?' We never took the caravan to gigs these days so it was pretty much going begging. In fact, we might as well sell it.

Griff froze, hands in the air. 'And you're thinking we could take the fake radio and leave it there?'

Was I? Perhaps I was.

'Oh, dear,' he continued without a break, 'we'd have all sorts of regulations to deal with, my love. Violations of privacy, that sort of thing. Even if Dodie herself said she'd like it, who's to say she's *compos mentis* enough to make that sort of decision? I couldn't.'

'Would you really have to tell anyone? If you saw anything that did arouse your suspicions, then—'

'Get thee behind me, Satan!'

'OK, how about you simply see if she thinks she might have lost the rat? Come on, Griff, you're wonderful with old ladies. If anyone can extract a sensible answer you can.'

'I'll try.'

We walked a bit further in silence. Then I had an idea. 'If you've got regulations for dealing with people, there must be someone around who's drawn them up – and whose job it is to reinforce them. That's the person to consult. Oh, look – there's Honey, the woman from the Pilates class.' I waved.

Rather to my surprise, she crossed the road to join us. As always, I introduced Griff as my grandfather. His honorary status was something we kept between us.

Her smile dismissed him as an elderly irrelevance. 'Hey, fancy a drink? I was going to text you.'

Griff gave me a little push. 'Off you go, my dear one. Let me know if you want me to hold back supper.'

I did wish he'd stop arranging my social life for me; as it happened, I didn't mind this one, but he wasn't to know how I felt about the arrangement. But I smiled and said that since it was a work day tomorrow it would have to be a very quick drink.

Laura was already in the Pig and Whistle with a slick young man she introduced as her boyfriend, Jay. A jug of Pimm's was on the table in front of them. I soon had a full glass in my hand, rather weaker than Griff made it but fine for all that. And then two other guys drifted in, Luke and Spencer, the latter of which turned out to be Honey's brother. Luke was an estate agent – always, Honey told me, a good person to know if you wanted to get a toe in the property market; Spencer never made his occupation clear, but since I wasn't interviewing him for a job, perhaps that didn't matter. In any case, I was used to people having to 'rest' – most of Griff's actor friends were what one might loosely call 'between jobs' at any particular time, and I knew I was more than lucky to have more work than I could handle, with a home thrown in. How many graduates and post-graduates were reduced to filling supermarket shelves, assuming they even got that lucky?

It soon became clear, however, that Honey and Luke were an item, and I guessed that the girls were trying to take my mind off Harvey by setting me up with Spencer. In his mid- to late twenties, he was nice enough, but with a face that would disappear in a crowd. Personality ditto. He certainly didn't set my pulse racing. On the other hand, he seemed quite taken with me, particularly my dancing. Did I sense a touch of betrayal here? Had Honey lured him with promises of my extravagant costume and presumably exotic sexual tastes? I was ready to bristle. But it seemed he'd always liked *Strictly Come Dancing* and would love to have a go himself. Laughing darkly, I gave him details of Dee's classes; let him make of the other students what he would.

To my surprise, the next day Griff summoned me from my workroom, where I was trying to help a china amputee, for coffee with Tony, the man who gave Dodie home Communion. Tony, who looked like a retired bank manager and turned out to be exactly that, hesitated over the indulgence of a biscuit, but when I told him that Griff had cooked a batch to take up to Dodie and had a few left over, he sensibly succumbed with gusto.

'I gather you marked that model rat before Griff took it up,' Tony prompted me. 'Some sort of invisible ink?'

I nodded. 'Just in case . . . What did she say when you showed it to her?' I asked Griff.

'Oh,' he replied, in an old lady's voice, 'I wondered where that had gone. I thought I must have put it with the others for safe-keeping. I never got round to looking, of course, and the poor girls who come to care for me wouldn't have time. But,' fake Dodie continued, rubbing anxious hands over her face, 'where did you find it, Mr Tripp?'

Tony watched fascinated as Griff returned to himself. 'It's a long story, Dodie,' he said. 'You're sure it's yours?' Then he was Dodie again: 'Yes. Look, there's the tiniest of chips just here, which reduces its value, of course. That's why I kept it down here with all that tatty rubbish. It wouldn't matter if one of the girls damaged it while she was dusting.' Griff, as himself once more, shot me an impish glance.

Tony reached for another biscuit. Then she repeated her question – where had Griff found it? I thought Griff might wriggle out of that one, but he told her the truth. And she . . . she seemed to understand.'

'So who would have taken it?' Dodie-Griff demanded. 'And how did they know which to pick out? Because I didn't take it to a sale, Tony – and I certainly didn't find it there and bring ⋅ it back, poor thing.' Griff's hands were old, of course, but rarely unsteady; now, as they stroked the invisible rat, they were those of someone who needed help to get dressed. He shot bright eyes up at Tony. 'Would you and Mr – Mr . . . the other kind gentleman see if the others are safe? I can't imagine why they shouldn't be, but I'd be happier knowing.'

'So up we had to go into her roof space – it's not big enough to call a loft. And what should we find there but a locked box. Japanned metal – not a safe but heavy. The sort you store important documents in. Big strong padlock. No key.'

'You wouldn't,' I observed, 'keep the key with whatever it is you need to protect. But how on earth would you recall where you'd put it? Assuming your memory was going, that is?'

'Going, but not quite gone. And now it's in our – the church's – safekeeping.'

'Hang on – the key or the box?'

'The key. The box was too heavy for us to lift. Three receipts we wrote out—'

'Hang on, Tony – where did you find the key?'

'You know those things you get by mail order – things you can't even think of a use for, let alone use? Well, she got herself a little safe that looks like an electric wall-socket. She pointed straight to the right one. And there, amongst a few trinkets—'

'Some a bit better than that, Tony. She had some really good pieces – Georg Jensen rings and brooches, and other modern designer jewellery. And don't forget that diamond crucifix. Anyway, the key was there. And when we opened the box, still in situ, by the way, since neither of us had backs that could reach it down, we found thirty or so netsuke, all as lovely as the rat. It seems her husband spent time in the British embassy in Tokyo. And that little old Dodie was in British Intelligence.' The two men, much of an age, shook their heads in silent horror at what she had become.

'Remind me, my dear one,' Griff said, 'when I finally drift into a hospice or a care home – a very luxurious one, mind – to have a large notice printed that I can carry with me everywhere—'

'So long as you remember to pick it up,' Tony interjected.

'To go round my neck, then. Or be tattooed on my forehead.

This man played opposite Vanessa Redgrave. This man starred with the young Colin Firth. Any road up, as my Midlands friends say, clearly this morning at least Dodie's marbles had made a welcome, if temporary return. And she wants to know how the little rat went on its unauthorized journey.'

I could think of another, larger rat who had made an unauthorized journey, but asked quietly, 'Did you mention my hidden camera idea?'

Tony nodded. 'With reluctance, I might add. Because though she was with us today, she might not be tomorrow.'

'All the more reason to protect her, then, surely. Is she likely to have told anyone else about her little safe?'

'Who knows? What a tragedy, to have those lovely things and not to wear them or have them on show. Not even to be able to see them without help.' He shook his head sadly. 'We all have to leave behind things we've treasured, and I believe we won't miss them one scrap in the Afterlife, but at least I've got the pleasure of knowing that my family will inherit and treasure them. As you do, Griff.' He smiled at us in turn as we clasped hands briefly. 'But Dodie doesn't like her relatives particularly. We at the church understood they visited her regularly, but she assures us that they don't. Assuming she doesn't forget them the moment they drive away.'

'So why not leave her netsuke collection, say, to a museum?' I asked. 'And her jewellery to be auctioned for her favourite charity? It's only convention that stuff should stay in families. Actually, in her place I'd go one better: I'd give it now, so I could go and see it in place.'

'Like those medieval rings you found,' Griff said with a smile.

'Almost. They never really belonged to me in the first place. Meanwhile, now she trusts you, couldn't you fetch out her goodies each time you see her so she has the pleasure of them for a short time at least? You've got the keys, after all.'

'And who would the finger of suspicion point at if anything else disappeared?' Tony asked, setting down his coffee cup rather hard.

'But if she had the camera in place . . .?'

'She did seem quite happy with the idea. Couldn't you discuss the problem with Moira – she's the person with responsibility for our vulnerable adults policy, my love,' he added in an aside.

Tony nodded agreement. 'Of course. I'll report back after church on Sunday. And I'd better mention it to Lydia, too – as senior churchwarden she likes to keep her finger on the pulse, Lina. But she might want to pull the whole problem to the entire PCC.'

Decision by committee, in other words. Griff stifled a groan.

'With all due respect,' I said, 'I don't think you should wait that long. Each time a carer or relative visits, there's an opportunity for him or her to steal something. I know that little rat is dye-marked, but it's like the police having DNA samples – they don't count as evidence until someone with the matching DNA turns up. Why not phone Moira now? I'll leave you to it,' I said, returning to the little shepherdess with a missing hand.

But I'd only just worked out the proportions I'd need to build a new one when Griff asked me to join them again.

'My dear one, Moira says we should act today, while she's *compos mentis*. She'll tell Lydia at an opportune time. And since you're the only one of us who knows how to set up the camera . . .'

Punctiliously but painfully easing herself from her chair, Dodie shook my hand. But she retained it, staring at my face, first from one angle, then another. 'I've never met you, Griff tells me, but I certainly know that face of yours. Dear me, I really am gaga, aren't I? What a thing to say!'

I squeezed her fingers reassuringly. 'Why don't you sit down and I'll explain about the face. There. Comfortable? You're not mad. We've never met. But maybe you once met my father, Lord Elham. People say we're incredibly alike, though I can't say either of us can see it – and neither of us feels terribly flattered.'

Still holding my hand, she closed her eyes. 'Bossy Elham. You're never his daughter.' She looked at me searchingly again. 'You are, though, aren't you? Dear me, I hope you don't take after him. What a dear scoundrel he was. What my father called a loose screw. But Griff tells me you live here in the village with him. You're his partner. Dear child, isn't that a bit of an age-gap, if you'll forgive me asking?'

Behind me, Tony gasped. I'd have expected Griff to roar with laughter but he was curiously silent. 'Not that sort of partner,' I said. 'He's my business partner – and my adoptive grandfather. He took me on as his apprentice when no one else would have touched me with a bargepole.'

'And now she's got an international reputation for art restoration,' Griff said proudly.

'Goodness me. And what does Bossy make of that?'

'You could ask him if you like. If you're old friends, would you like me to bring him over to see you?'

Blow me if she didn't blush. 'No . . . Seeing me like this . . .' Perhaps the word *friend* had been the wrong one. Pa wasn't known for long-term platonic relationships, after all. Forty, even thirty years ago, those faded but delicate features must have been stunning, and Pa wouldn't have worried one jot about being a toy boy, would he?

'Would you like me to send your regards?' I asked, hoping the word was appropriate.

She looked as if the notion exhausted her.

It didn't take me very long to find a good place for the radio, which had the bonus of actually working quite independently of its clever little gizmo, which I focussed on the table with all the gee-gaws on. Its range also meant it would ensnare anyone tampering with the photos on the piano – all in good solid silver frames, after all – and the fake electric socket safe.

I explained that one of us would need to return regularly to check the footage, but by now she seemed too weary to take in very much. Surprising myself, I kissed her goodbye.

'Bossy's daughter,' she murmured, almost asleep. But then her eyes shot open. 'That crap on the table.' From such old lips the word jarred. 'The wife of one of my children thought it made the place look more homely. A year or so ago I'd have had the strength to argue. But I don't want to make matters worse between her and my son, stupid boy. Crap.' She made a wafting gesture with her left hand, and, still murmuring, did indeed sink into a doze.

EIGHT

Spencer's arrival in the village hall dancing class was like a fine young rooster turning up in a run of moulting hens, his modest good looks and decent enough figure turning heads a lot more grown-up than mine – but not, of course, mine. So when Griff announced that his back was hurting and he might need to sit out the rumba, I warned him in no uncertain, though very quiet, terms, that if he did he might have a couple of bruised shins to worry about, too. Genuinely bruised shins – where I'd kicked them. It was either that, I pointed out, or me lose my nicely painted toenails: Spencer was trampling all over his own feet, and threatened Dee's too when she tried to help him. All the old dears insisted that the rumba was a very tricky dance, with its awkward timing, and he'd soon pick it up, but none of them offered to partner him to demonstrate the steps. Perhaps they were put off by his cologne, which was what Griff might describe as shouty.

Spencer was wondering aloud if we all adjourned to the Pig and Whistle after our exertions. I put a firm hand on Griff's chest: 'Don't even think about it,' I hissed. 'I've got that saucer to unglue tonight.'

'The work of moments, surely, my love. He seems a nice young man – it's a shame to be unsociable.'

'You go, then, with Arthur and Jenny. And see how long he stays.'

He stared at me for a minute. 'Very well. I will.'

Oh, dear. Griff and his penchant for young men. 'I'll have supper ready for eight forty-five,' I said. 'And not a minute later. Or you won't sleep, will you?' I added unkindly.

I wondered, as I headed home, if I might be cutting my nose off to spite my face. I might object to being so crudely set up, but I did enjoy the girls' company and snubbing Spencer

like that might offend them. Too late to worry now – I needed
to start cooking the brown rice.

It dawned on me rather belatedly that if anyone was going to
check on the hidden camera footage, that person was going
to have to be me. Griff never had got the knack of it, usually
managing to simply wipe everything. But I wouldn't, indeed
couldn't, go anywhere near Dodie's Aladdin's cave without a
chaperone, which meant either Griff or Tony. We also had to
work round the carers' visits, which seemed to be rather
randomly timed. Sometimes she was up and dressed by seven-
thirty in the morning; once or twice we found her still in bed
at eleven, weeping with hunger and embarrassment. If there
was ever a way to make a sometimes flaky old person thoroughly bewildered, that was surely it.

The first piece of footage showed that the radio had drawn
the attention of one of the carers at least. It seemed there was
some brief discussion about whether Dodie wanted it switched
on; apparently she didn't. We reminded her that the camera
worked even when its host was belting out Classic FM, but
that was one piece of information she didn't seem able to
grasp or remember. Or perhaps she simply didn't like the radio.

Griff and I debated endlessly as to whether we should tell
Pa about her. Griff was more concerned with Dodie's welfare
than with Pa's need to know, and he pretty much vetoed a
visit, a point I was disinclined to argue. However, I did remind
him that Pa was lucid these days, apart from when he decided
he might as well finish off a bottle of bubbly he'd opened only
that afternoon. But he only did that when he thought I wouldn't
be going round to check up on him; the occasional un-
announced visit worked wonders. Meanwhile, he was long
overdue a visit, probably because I really didn't want to talk
about the Harvey business and had needed another topic of
conversation to divert him.

I'd no idea how he'd take the news I'd come across one of
his old flames, so I took a bottle of what he always called
'shampoo', just in case he was upset. He listened intently,
sipping slowly and nodding with great sadness when I told
him her situation.

'She was so lovely,' he breathed at last. 'So very beautiful. And so very reluctant.'

Probably because she was so very married, I thought – but then I'd never experienced the louche society that had been Pa's milieu. Thoroughly lower middle class, that was me.

'And you say she remembered me? Even if just for a minute? Look, Lina, you know these things. What if I sent her some flowers? For old times' sake?'

'I can't think of anything better,' I said truthfully. 'Do you want an Interflora job or do you want yours truly to do the honours?'

'Interflora wouldn't work if she's unable to answer the door, would it?' he retorted sharply. 'Find a nice pot to sell and use the proceeds.'

'There's still about two hundred and fifty pounds left over from the Guangxu fish bowls. Maybe more.'

'Very well. Spend some of it on flowers and some on getting her tarted up a bit: hair, nails, that sort of thing. They let themselves go, these old people,' he declared, without irony. 'I can't visit her if the place smells, mind.'

'Let's not cross that bridge yet, Pa. She's not well and she may not want visitors – even you. But I promise,' I added as his face fell, 'that I'll talk to her about the possibility. Now, I'd like you to do something for me. You and Titus. And it's so legit it might even get you a reward.'

'What are you waiting for?'

The account I gave of our Devon trip was brief, concentrating on the notion that I hadn't wanted to play gooseberry when Griff lunched with Noel Pargetter.

Pa scratched his head, inspecting his fingernails to see what he'd harvested. 'I know that name from somewhere.'

'You're not confusing him with Nigel Pargetter on *The Archers*?'

He gave me a sour look.

'Actually he used to be an actor, so you may have seen him on stage.'

Pa shook his head. 'I never was much of a one for the West End. No, no . . . I'll ask Titus. He'll know.'

Which didn't augur well at all. 'Anyway, he's retired now. He came into some money,' I added idly.

'Lucky bugger,' he said, again with no apparent irony. 'Anyway, this reward. How do we get our hands on it? Nothing dodgy, I hope . . .' he added, at his most sanctimonious. 'Stealing from *churches*?' he exploded as I finished my little story. 'That's outrageous. How low can you get?'

Forging church and other documents for a start, I could have said. But I encouraged his outrage and embroidered, just a little, their anger at being pursued by a girl with a pole. 'If anyone's got his ear to the ground it's Titus,' I declared, adding very quickly and hoping he wouldn't notice the hiatus, 'and you.'

'I don't like the idea of your being in danger,' he said. 'You'd best come and camp out here.'

'Don't worry – Kent Police are keeping an eye on me,' I lied blithely. I'd not seen a patrol car for days now. 'But the important thing is this: you're not to put yourselves at risk either.'

'I don't hurtle round the country in a van with my name and address on it. Very well, I'll ask around. It sounds like a steal-to-order job, doesn't it?' Ever the professional, my pa. 'I'll bet it's heading overseas – did you hear about a brass lectern nicked from a place in Gloucestershire that turned up in a market place in Romania? Did you say you'd got some photos of them?' He squinted at my phone, shaking his head at the lack of facial features. 'You interrupted them? Men with chisels like that? My God, what sort of idiot did I breed?'

'The sort that's been protecting you and Titus for umpteen years. This here project, Pa, that's supposed to be making your fortune: what is it?'

He touched the side of his nose. 'Wait and see.'

Griff was never at his sunniest when I'd been to visit Pa, but he looked quite hang-dog when I returned, fussing unnecessarily with the morning's post.

'I – we've – had an email,' he said, keen to get it off his chest at once.

'Harvey and his dratted vase?'

'Precisely. He's reminding me we've had it in our possession for a week and that he has had no written estimate, which
he needs for his insurance company. He'd be grateful for an
immediate response. All very formal,' he added anxiously.

'We could always send him an equally formal reply stating
that pressure of existing commitments is such that we can't
deal with his request until next Friday at the earliest? No?
OK, I'll get on to it. Is Paul around? I wouldn't mind an
independent witness. And you can't get much more worthy
than an accountant.'

'You mean he did that himself?' Paul stared at the pieces of
the vase as I removed the packing, which, to do Harvey justice,
had done its best.

The good news was that it wasn't shattered, but had broken
along existing fault lines – they were slightly brown, whereas
new fractures would have been pristine white.

'Not deliberately. He dropped it as he fell down some steps.
Come on, Paul – Griff must have told you and Mary all about
his gatecrashing the fancy-dress dance.'

'He was very subdued – none of his usual revelling in detail.
So how do you go about preparing an estimate?' He sounded
genuinely interested.

'A subtle equation of the hours I shall need to work on it
and how much I want the job. In this case I'd be more than
delighted if he got a quote from someone else and they undercut
me. So I'd say . . .' I named a figure that sent his eyebrows
skywards. 'Well,' I asked, 'what do accountants charge per
hour . . .? Quite. And there are a lot more of you around than
people like me.'

He looked at me steadily. 'I want you to buy Griff out of
this company. Soon. And if possible buy him out of the retail
antiques company, too. Actually, perhaps the other way round.
I'll give it some thought. Do you have any cash reserves of
your own that I don't know about?'

'You're my accountant! You know every penny I've got.' I
didn't need to mention the contents of our secret hidden safe,
the whereabouts of which were known only to Griff and me.

'You could try for a bank loan – with your turnover you

shouldn't have too much of a problem. All the same . . . Would your father help out?'

'He doesn't have a bean, and when he dies the trust will claim back his living quarters.'

'And you won't even get his title?'

'I wouldn't even if I was legitimate. I'm by no means his first-born. Or his last.'

'I can't believe you still visit him.' Paul shook his head.

'He's a bit like this vase – a difficult project. You can't imagine what a mess he was when I first came across him. He functions as a normal human being, these days. Almost,' I conceded, in the name of honesty.

Paul patted my shoulder. 'I know what you did for Mary, when she needed help so much. Which is why I want to stop you ending up in the most awful financial mess where no one will benefit except HM Revenue and Customs, some lawyers and – yes, some accountants like me. I'm working on it, Lina – you and Griff will just have to trust me, even when I give you unpalatable advice.' He added sternly, 'Do you realize how vulnerable you are, Lina? When Griff dies, you lose your home and your work. Half at least. To be honest, though, I can't see a solution either of you would like.' And with that he was gone.

I checked the poor vase one more time and jotted down some figures. In the end I couldn't inflate them – not much, anyway. If ever there was an artefact that needed my skills, this was it. Some might have thought my estimate high, but I knew of very few other freelance restorers who would have considered doing it for any less.

NINE

Well, well, well . . . Who should drift into the Pig and Whistle as we recovered from our Pilates class with quantities of mineral water, but Spencer! With Honey sitting right beside me, I couldn't tell him straight out that I didn't want his company. I tried to make it clear half an hour later that I didn't need him to walk me home, but Honey and Laura decided they'd all had enough too so we set out as a foursome, awkward on the narrow and uneven pavements. Was I surprised when we split into two and Spencer fell into step beside me?

'I didn't know you were famous,' he said.

'Neither did I!'

'Well, I Googled you and you're all over the place.'

'It's just because of my work,' I said modestly, hoping I was right; I'd never bothered to check. 'I bet you are too, aren't you?' It took me a moment to realize my mistake. But I couldn't unsay it. Anyway, we were almost home and the girls were giving me girlie hugs – in which Spencer had to join, of course. At least it was no more than a hug, but I really wasn't comfortable. I just hoped I wouldn't have to dance with him at the next class. Come to think of it, hoping wasn't enough: I was going to have to speak very firmly to Griff.

Dodie clapped her hands in delight at the sight of Pa's flowers – I'd chosen roses and lilies, since I always found the seasonal chrysanthemums on offer so depressing. Because I really did not want to root round in her possessions, even with Tony and Griff to keep an eye on me, I'd taken a glass vase from stock we'd set aside to dispose of – sometimes at auction you have to buy a job lot of tat just to lay your hands on one decent item.

But the mention of a possible visit was a step too far: her eyes filled and she picked at her hair and clothes. There was no need for words. Shapeless tracksuit bottoms and a heavily pilled sweater wouldn't fill anyone's heart with optimism. Why did she have to wear garments guaranteed to make her miserable? I'd have asked point-blank but this wasn't my father, who rather liked to be bullied; it was a woman I hardly knew.

As it happened, one of her team of carers arrived just as I was leaving – the one who'd been interested in the radio. Her smile was perfunctory, mine the one I use when I want to inveigle someone into doing something they don't want to do. In this woman's case, she probably didn't have time for conversation, or to answer my question: 'Doesn't Dodie have anything better to wear? And what about her poor hair?'

'I talk to you, I don't have time to talk to her. OK?' And she disappeared inside.

She was right, of course, a point Moira Carr made when I ran into her in the village deli.

'There's no reason for her to be in such a state, surely,' I expostulated over the cheese counter. 'There must be someone who could drop in and do her hair and sort out some better clothes. I know they must be machine washable and mustn't need ironing, but even so . . .'

'Why not talk to her social worker . . .?' Moira suggested reasonably. 'Lina? What have I said?'

'It's no good, I can't deal with social workers,' I said. 'I know they all mean well and they're underpaid and overworked, but they messed up my life good and proper and if I had my way I'd—'

Her face was very tight, but she managed to say, 'Perhaps you didn't know that I'm a social worker. Retired now, of course.'

Retired. Of course she was retired. Practically everyone who did voluntary work for the church was retired.

I took several gulps of air. After all, I needed this woman on my side, and she hadn't personally ruined my education. 'In that case,' I began, grasping desperately for the sort of lingo that would impress her, 'you'd have all the skills and know-how to approach them. They wouldn't be able to blind you with words and phrases that simply don't mean anything to me. And you wouldn't annoy them, would you?' I added, pleading despite myself.

Her face softened a little. 'It depends which words and phrases I used in return.'

'And you're not in an – an . . .' It was ages since my vocabulary had upped sticks and run, which it always used to do when I was stressed, which was most of the time. I tried again. 'I'm in a strange position. I'm not a friend of hers, though my father was. I deal in antiques, and some people might construe my presence in her house as – well, as casing the joint. Mightn't they?' I looked her straight in the eye, suspecting there'd already been gossip to that effect.

'Yes. Have you finished your shopping? In that case, let's pay and have a coffee.' She gestured at the tiny café they'd managed to squeeze into the side of the shop.

'If you had a wish list with regard to Dodie,' Moira asked, scooping the froth from her cappuccino, 'what might it include?' She looked at me from under her remarkably straight eyebrows, which owed more than a little to poorly applied pencil. The rest of her make-up was equally amateurish, with every seam between colours showing, as if she'd painted by numbers. Her sea-green eyeshadow, with no modulations at all, was quite startling. Perhaps it was all of a piece with her suddenly clichéd language: I'd seen 'with regard to' in print but never heard it spoken.

'I'd like someone to care for her properly – not just dash in to see to her immediate needs. Look at today – wouldn't it be lovely if someone could pop her into a wheelchair and let her enjoy the sunshine? One of those emergency buzzers to hang round her neck – surely that's essential for any old person living on her own? Someone to do her hair and nails – probably her feet, too. And someone to ensure that she has clothes that don't make her cringe – there must be some in her wardrobe.'

'And you've looked?' she rapped back.

'Certainly not! I've not been DBS checked, I'm not family; my only role is to see if any incriminating footage crops up on the hidden camera I've installed. Oh, and to take her some flowers from my father, who knew her years ago.' I smiled sadly. 'He'd love to visit her, for old times' sake, but Dodie doesn't want him to see her in her present state.'

'You're not thinking of some sentimental Darby and Joan reunion, are you? Because that might be prejudicial to her mental stability.'

Should I tell her she'd got froth on the end of her nose? 'Aren't company and stimulation supposed to be good for the elderly?' Whoops – Moira was no spring chicken herself. 'Lunch clubs and seated aerobics? That sort of thing?'

She eyed me with as much enthusiasm as if she herself was Dodie's overburdened social worker. 'Who are you expecting to do all this? Not you, obviously.' It was a decided accusation.

'I work full-time. I look after my father. Even so, I'd love to do more, and would, but as I said, I've no legal right even to step into her house.' I added something I'd heard on the radio, 'Fear of litigation has made cowards of us all.' It sounded quite impressive, come to think of it.

It did the trick. 'I'll endeavour to talk to social services for you, though I must tell you their budgets have been slashed and with outsourced carers they have very little direct contact with their clients.'

Humbly I asked, 'Is there a retired hairdresser in the congregation who might volunteer her services? Maybe even give her a manicure? And, oh, Moira, find her some better clothes?' Catching her eye, I dabbed my nose.

She took it for what it was, a woman-to-woman gesture, and smiled as she wiped away the froth. Getting to her feet, she said, 'I'll make due enquiries and get back to you.'

And she left me to pay the bill.

Surprise, surprise, Harvey accepted my quote for the repair, provided I could give it immediate priority. I'd never known an insurance company insert that sort of clause before, so I got Griff to email back our standard reply, to the effect that it was impossible to guarantee the repair of any object by a specific date. Griff eyed me anxiously, however, and I agreed to move it a little further up the queue than I really liked. The only reason I could see for what I saw as toadying to Harvey was a desire I actually shared, to get rid of all traces of the wretched man.

I also had a rare communication, if you could call it that, from Titus Oates, who used the phone as if he was being charged by the nano-second.

'This church crap, doll – I'm on to it. But keep your pretty little nose out of it – right?'

'Hang on, Titus – this stuff my dad's doing for you? What is it?'

'Absolutely kosher.' End of call.

I made that twenty words.

Actually, from Titus, they were pretty significant words, because he never actually lied. They implied the church thefts were the work of serious villains, and that for once my father wasn't breaking the law.

There was no option but to dance with Spencer at the next village hall class. Gerry, the man who regularly helped Dee demonstrate the men's moves, was *hors de combat* with a snapped Achilles tendon, a disaster for a man who loved his tennis, his dancing and his gardening to the exclusion of all else – even, it was rumoured, his wife. She never came to classes, though she did deign to turn up at some of the dances Dee organized for her combined groups. The only other obvious choice of partner for Dee was Griff, of course, a far better dancer when he wasn't hampered by me.

I suspect some of the sentimental old dears' hearts beat faster to see us young people in each other's arms. Or maybe it was with relief that none of the womenfolk had to expose their feet to the onslaught mine suffered, largely because Spencer thought it was cute and charming to chatter. My response was to count audibly and, sinfully, to lead him. We had to end up somewhere, after all, and he knew no better.

Annoyingly, his attempts to talk didn't end there, and he dug himself so deeply into conversation with Griff that he ended up walking home with us, although he was thwarted in his apparent desire to spend the rest of the evening in our cottage. Griff had the nous to say we had a complicated order to put up, and bade him a firm goodnight.

However, as I set the table for supper, he said, 'I wish you didn't make your dislike of him quite so obvious, my dear one. He's a pleasant enough lad.'

'Sorry – he's not pleasant enough to encourage. Not enough to ditch Carwyn for, certainly.'

'But you say yourself there's no future in that relationship. And you're playing more than hard to get when it comes to Harvey.'

I put the cutlery down with a sharp little clatter. 'I am not playing hard to get. Harvey is married. I've told him repeatedly that I don't want a relationship with him.'

'Married or not, he'd keep you in very good style—'

'Heavens, Griff, I don't believe it! It almost sounds as if you're pimping me!'

'I want to secure your future, my dear one. I'm not immortal, you know. And Paul's been saying frightful things about death duties and capital gains.' He met my eye at last. 'Has he said anything to you?'

There was no point in lying. 'He wants me to buy you out of the restoration business at least. And the shop.' I shrugged. 'I don't see how. We're not making much profit, but think of the stock we're holding – that Russian stuff, for instance. All that would have to be valued. Not to mention the stuff in the secret safe.'

He raised a finger. 'But that *is* secret. That's the whole point. Only two of us know about that. I could give it to you and no one would be any the wiser.'

'Until a hundred thousand pounds' worth of stuff finds its way on to the market.'

He looked defeated for a moment, but suddenly snapped his fingers. 'I may just have an idea. Involving your father . . . No, I won't say anything more, not until I've spoken to him. But if anything happens to me before then, you say nothing, do you hear me, nothing of that to the tax people. Nothing to Paul. You'd have to find a way to dispose of it yourself. Promise me you'll keep it as your nest egg?' He took my hands and gripped them.

I had no option, did I? Even if what he wanted me to do was tax evasion at best? Or was it avoidance? I'd forgotten again. 'I promise.' Oh, dear. It was one more reason not to get any closer to Carwyn. Then I asked the question I should have asked two minutes ago. 'Why should anything happen to you? What's been going on, Griff? No, don't pretend you've got to see to something on the hob. Sit down and tell me.'

Griff looked guilty, anxious and scared, all rolled into one. 'It's not a thing a gentleman of my generation finds easy to talk about, my love. The euphemism is waterworks trouble.' He coughed, blushing.

'Don't think I haven't noticed how many times you use the bathroom during the night.' Or during the daytime either. Hmm. This had been happening for less than a week though, surely. Did that sort of thing inevitably spell a death by prostate cancer? 'And our current GP is a woman and you'd rather sit around worrying about death than have her finger up your bum,' I said, deliberately crude. 'OK, I'll fix you an emergency appointment for tomorrow.'

The surgery had a computerized booking system which generally let you book appointments for a couple of weeks after the symptoms subsided of their own accord. But there was an emergency button, which popped you up the queue, provided you were prepared to tell them the symptoms that were troubling you.

Facing an eight-thirty appointment the following morning, Griff dealt with the problem over supper by chatting briskly about absolute rubbish. At least I thought it was until I heard the name Noel Pargetter again.

'I've had such a peculiar email from him,' Griff was saying. 'Such a strange tone from one old friend to another.'

'What does he say?'

'He tells me that sometimes it's best not to renew acquaintanceship but to remember good days in the past. Something about my having divided loyalties. And then he says he'd rather I didn't take up his suggestion that we meet in London for lunch next week.'

'What a strange way of putting it. Why not say he's going to be busy and will have to postpone it? That's what people do when they change their minds. And eventually the other person loses interest.'

'Quite. How many times have I done that?' he chuckled.

'What does he mean about divided loyalties? Is he jealous of Aidan?'

'Aidan and I were an item of sorts when Noel and I first met. Nothing's changed. All we'd agreed to do was have a civilized lunch at his club, not embark on a torrid love affair. I'm not sure how to respond, to be honest.'

'Normally I'd suggest just a dignified silence. That's what you'd advise me to do. Delete it and move on. But the funny thing is that Pa's heard of him, apparently in a different context. And worryingly, he was going to talk to Titus about him.'

'Oh, dear. In that case I shall certainly not pursue the acquaintance.' He shifted with embarrassment. 'Dear me, is that the time? Bed for me, my love.'

Me too. But first I'd give myself the pleasure of hearing Carwyn's voice: we nattered happily about precisely nothing of importance for about ten minutes. He sounded pleased that my contact with Harvey was now limited to formal emails written by Griff, and wanted to talk about my current repair job as a rest from thinking about people-trafficking.

It was only when I caught him in a giant yawn that I remembered that France was an hour ahead of the UK, and I was ready to end the call. Before I did, however, I told him about the Noel Pargetter email, which puzzled him as much as it did me. He was also interested in the sudden burst of money and then his disappearance from the Rich List. However, he told me his immediate theory for the cessation of pleasant relations between the men: that Griff must have farted at the wrong moment. That seemed a good note on which to say goodnight.

TEN

'Cystitis? But everyone gets that!' I told Griff as he returned home, a silly grin all over his face.

'I know, I know.' He returned my hug. 'But she still wants to run some tests. And she frowned all the time she was tapping into her computer. Not like old Doctor Allinson – he'd sit you down and have a proper natter.'

'The poor things are all target-driven – haven't got time to blow their noses,' I said, pouring coffee. 'But it's so far, so good – right? So I can go and finish retouching that revolting piece of Majolica.'

'Absolutely. Don't forget we need to check Dodie's camera, will you?'

'Drat. So we do. It's very odd it's picked up nothing so far.'

But this time it had. It had picked up a hand – well, a hand picking it up. And moving it to where we found it, right by Dodie, so the only thing it could photograph was the probable victim herself.

'My son,' she said dryly, patting the radio. 'Being kind. I told him it was good exercise for me to get up and switch it on but he insisted. By the way, tuning it to Classic FM was an act of genius. For some reason I'd stopped listening to music. My silly old ears, I suppose. But, do you know, I'm beginning to enjoy it again. Now, I have some news – and I suspect, dear Griff, that your Lina may have had something to do with it. Tony says some ladies from the church are going to come and . . . I believe the expression is *tart me up*. Not that a church lady would use it, of course. One is going to wash and blow-dry my hair, another give me a pedicure, would you believe. A chiropodist – through I think she's got another name, which I always forget – comes in because of my diabetes, but imagine the joy of having the nails painted! And a manicure, too!' She stopped fiddling with the alarm on a cord round her neck – well done, Moira – and gestured rather grandly.

I squeezed the hand lying on her lap with pleasure. 'Now, Dodie, forgive me if I'm speaking out of order, but you might feel better in some nice clothes. I could reach some for whichever of your carers gets you dressed.'

'Would you really? Oh, I do hate these drab things. They so encourage dwindling – and one thing I dread is slipping into senility. I want to be me when I die.'

'Those slippers *are* pretty dwindly,' I said.

'You darling girl! When I think I used to wear heels like this . . .' She gestured – three-inch stilettos, by the look of it. Not the footwear she could dream of wearing now, of course. Nonetheless, she twisted her foot to show a once well-turned ankle. 'And clothes, darling. Dior. Balmain. All the great couturists . . .'

I didn't find any Dior in her wardrobe because I didn't find any clothes in her wardrobe – apart from two pairs of baggy tracksuit bottoms and three shapeless tops, all stained. My hope was that some of the church ladies had taken the rest to wash them, and that Dodie had forgotten. My fear was that someone had spirited away a load of expensive clothes, something that would never catch the eye of the radio-camera, of course. Good shoes, too, though perhaps she'd got rid of them when she became unsteady. On the off-chance, I looked in the spare room wardrobe, too – absolutely bare.

I walked slowly back down, wondering how on earth to break the news. This was something I very much wanted recording, so I sat close to her, taking her hand again. 'I was wondering if you'd asked someone to have your clothes cleaned or washed,' I began.

'Why should I?' She added, to my astonishment, 'Are you telling me that my clothes have gone the way of my netsuke? Perhaps they'll come back in the same miraculous way, but as you youngsters say, I'm not holding my breath.'

Griff moved closer. 'Dodie, do you remember when your radio-camera was moved? Because it's not the only thing that isn't where it should be. The netsuke's gone again.'

'It has, but only a little way.' She dug in one of her pockets.

'Here he is. He keeps me company. Oh, dear, oh, dear – I was hoping to get out of these weeds.'

'You will. I'll find you something myself. But what do we do, meanwhile, about the missing clothes? Your social worker needs to know, as does your family.' Not to mention the police, though that might not be what she wanted. 'Moira, the lady from church who organized your hairdo and pedicure, will know what to do. Shall we phone her and ask her to come over?'

Remembering that Moira had considered that even tea with my father might harm Dodie's emotional balance, I thought that having her entire wardrobe purloined might harm her even more. When Moira arrived, I slipped out to cast an eye over the rails in one of the two charity shops in the village. Replacing couture wasn't even in my mind: just finding something to fit. Elasticated waists were probably a necessity in both skirts and trousers. Having found three skirts and two pairs of trousers in what I guessed were Dodie's size, I turned my attention to tops, of which there were plenty. I could only choose what appealed to me – bright, a bit off-beat. The kind volunteers insisted that if she didn't like them I could bring them back and replace them with something more subdued. Jewellery was going for a song: several stylish costume pieces joined the clothes. Shoes? No, too specialized. But I'd love her to have something better than those Velcro-fastening monstrosities. Then I made one last, off-the-wall, purchase.

Moira had summoned a gloriously confusing meeting in Dodie's living room: on one side, by the television, were a harried and equally polysyllabic social worker under a pile of paperwork, and a resentful son dragged from what he kept telling everyone was a vital meeting, and on the other, by the door, a police community support officer being told that she was no use and that someone with investigative powers was required.

Dodie sat looking from one to the other, increasingly bemused, as if a loud Wimbledon game had just descended into her space. She'd been entirely what I should imagine was her old self before; any moment now she'd regress into a weepy old lady. I shooed the lot of them into her kitchen, small and cramped enough to encourage a quick decision. Meanwhile, I stayed behind to show her my booty, over which she nodded approval. No one could have raved over the skirts, but she held the tops up and made me find a mirror. She was happy for me to take all the clothes away to wash them, but nothing would separate her from some gorgeous beads, which might have been but probably weren't amber. There was a super chunky ring too, not Georg Jensen, of course, and not silver, but with real pizzazz.

'True anti-dwindling devices,' she declared, slipping them on.

Finally, with the sort of smile I remember giving when I had a mother to buy me non-useful presents (after she died I'd had so many practical gifts from temporary foster parents I came to hate Christmas), she reached into the bottom of the bag.

'A teddy! Bossy, he's just like my old Mop.' And not unlike my own Tim. 'Thank you so much, my darling.' She smiled sweetly and promptly fell asleep holding him. So much for washing him, which Health and Safety would probably have decreed.

Bossy, eh? Surely that must be short for Bossingham? It would certainly be appropriate for my pa's selfish demeanour. And everyone said how alike we looked. It was a good job the social worker hadn't overheard. It would have shot my insistence that she was lucid and furious right out of the water.

There was no point, I told myself, in interrupting the still rancorous committee, and I had work to do before I did a supermarket run for Pa.

'Robbed! What bloody mongrels! Stealing from a helpless pensioner! What is the world coming to?' Pa raged. Just in case, I removed the eggs from his clutches and transferred them to the little rack in his fridge. 'Old ladies and churches. Whatever next?'

Unable to think of a satisfactory response that didn't involve kettles and pots, I did the next best thing: I made mugs of green tea for us.

'When can I go and visit her?'

'Not until she's had her make-over,' I said firmly. 'And until

I've got her some more clothes, of course.' I told him about my emergency dive into the hospice shop.

His blood pressure must have been soaring. 'Buying someone else's leavings! What were you thinking of, Lina? The widow of the former ambassador to Tokyo reduced to rummaging in a charity bag?'

Stung, I responded, 'It was me doing the rummaging, actually, not her, largely because I don't know where else to shop for old ladies' skirts at a moment's notice. But I take your point, because it raises another. She's not exactly living in style, and ambassadors aren't known for their poverty. If her husband's dead, he must have left her a pension, probably quite good, which she ought to be drawing. How come she's eking out such a miserable existence?'

'You'll have to find out. By the way, I could do with your selling a few more pots for me – more of that Chinese stuff. I've been watching that TV chappie – he's always talking it up, just as you are. Internet sales, that's what you need.'

How did he think I'd sold the last batch?

'I'll see what I can find. Any news for me on the church thefts, by the way?' I added caustically, hoping to catch him out.

He might have been tricked like that when I first met him but not now; maybe it was the green tea. 'If I did have, I'd tell young Carwyn, not you. They're dangerous, these people. Very dangerous. And no more asking Titus how we're making our money – I'll tell you when we're good and ready. Now, have you managed to get rid of that Devon creep of yours yet?'

Which one? There were two in my life, come to think of it. One I'd given absolutely no thought to, of course, was Arthur Habgood, owner of Devon Cottage Antiques. To my absolute horror I'd completely overlooked his part in the reappearance of Dodie's netsuke. The only excuse was my wretched erratic memory, not to mention all the goings on involving Harvey and then the church robbers. It'd be much easier to stay schtum – but I'd already told Carwyn about it, and it would look much better if, now the police were actively involved, I reminded them of my part at least. Wouldn't it? Even if Habgood did claim to be my grandfather.

Griff nodded soberly when I asked for the name of the
police officer Moira had demanded and finally got: DS Hunt.
'Are you dobbing Habgood in because you think you should
or because you still harbour resentment against him?'

'It's not tit for tat, if that's what you're worried about. If I
had the chance, I'd go down and tackle him myself. But with
that huge backlog of repairs, I don't have time, Griff. Especially
as Pa now wants me to add buying clothes for Dodie to my
list of pastimes.'

'I thought you already had – and put them through the
machine. They look excellent to me. And you can always buy
her clothes online, so they can be returned if they don't suit.'

'Of course. I've not been thinking very clearly, have I? But
Pa made a very good point: why is she reduced to garments
from the hospice shop, given her background? Did whoever
nicked her clothes nick other things, too? And there's one question I really don't like to ask – who will pay for her new gear?
Not the stuff I've bought – that can be a present. But anything
from Marks and Spencer or wherever will cost a lot more.'

'You're already several hundred pounds out of pocket for
the little netsuke, aren't you? I noticed you didn't put it through
the firm's account but your own. It'll have to be a conversation
with Moira, won't it? A serious one.'

'Moira. And the police.'

I strongly suspect that DS Hunt was just going off duty when I
rolled up in Maidstone, but she was too polite to do more than
sigh and check her watch every two minutes. She wore a wedding band and was the right age to have a child at home,
waiting for its supper. Perhaps she herself had eaten too many
junk food suppers on the hoof: though not fat, she was pudgy
rather than chunky. How would she meet the fitness and endur-
ance levels Carwyn worked so hard to maintain?

'If this is inconvenient,' I said pointedly, 'I could come back
first thing tomorrow. No? Well, these are the pictures I took
of the Devon Cottage stall at the antiques fair in Exeter, with
the netsuke in situ. And here's the receipt for it. I'd say it was
underpriced by at least a hundred pounds, probably more,' I
added, thinking of my haggling.

Hunt's eyebrows shot up. 'You think they were trying to get rid of it fast?'

'I'm not sure. They sold me a gold brooch set with precious stones for under twenty pounds, so maybe they're just not very switched on. But I was worried enough to send DS Carwyn Morgan the photos. He said he'd referred them back—'

'Oh. *Those* photos. I didn't have a clue what he wanted doing with them, since there was no evidence of a crime being committed.'

'There is now, isn't there? And just for the record, Dodie recognized it as hers in front of a witness. Here are the pics from the hidden camera.' I handed over the memory stick onto which I'd downloaded everything – a duplicate of which, incidentally, I'd kept at home.

'I can't think what possessed you to set up your Boys' Own surveillance equipment,' she said pettishly.

'Would you people have had the resources to?' I countered. 'It's a shame her son moved it, isn't it?'

'Are you making an allegation there, Ms Townend?'

I held up my hands in mock surrender. 'I've never met the man. I don't know anything about him. I'm just doing what Carwyn says people should do – giving you all the information and letting you sort out what's relevant and what isn't.'

For a moment she showed why she might have been attracted to the police in the first place. 'It is weird, isn't it? All those clothes going missing . . . Why steal clothes? Assuming the old dear didn't just give them away.'

'There's a lot of interest in designer clothes   retro chic.'

'Would they be that good?'

'If there was evening wear, it would be good enough to go to embassy balls—'

'Come off it! A poverty-stricken old bat in a one-horse village in Kent owning Chanel or whatever?'

I asked quietly, 'You do know her background? That she was married to a career diplomat?'

I must have pressed the right buttons. 'What? My God, what if the media get hold of this? Tell me everything you know.'

And suddenly I was useful. As was my father.

'Lord Elham, you say?' She practically curtsied to me.

'Yes. But I'm not his heir or anything like that.'

'Not a *lady*? Nor even an *honourable*?'

I shook my head sadly. 'Just honest.' Most of the time, at least.

ELEVEN

The unexpectedly lengthy interview over – I hoped Hunt could claim overtime – I was drifting back to the town centre, wondering whether to take advantage of a late opening evening to do a little shopping, when I ran into Spencer. It took him a few minutes to switch his face to the *How nice to see you* position – perhaps my snubs were beginning to get through his thick skin at last. However, his smile soon reached his eyes and he was offering me a drink. Better still, a pizza or a curry or something.

I settled for a diet Coke at a handy pub. I wasn't sure what we'd talk about, since I really didn't want to encourage his Google-inspired explorations of my life. For once Pa seemed a good bet: I let it be known that he lived alone south of Canterbury and I did my best to keep an eye on him.

'I thought you looked after your grandfather – at least, that's what he says.'

'Did he tell you that he also looks after me? Because he does.'

He frowned as if he'd forgotten an important part of his homework. 'I thought you only went to the dance class so he could exercise gently after his heart operation?'

'That was what got us going. I suspect if I stopped going he'd give up too, which would be a total shame, because he's so light on his feet. And it's good to keep learning things.' Good for both of us. 'What about you? Still thinking it's like *Strictly*?'

He pulled a glum face.

I provided an answer myself: 'Not a lot of fake tan and sequins around. Nor many men lifting their partners.'

'More's the shame – the local osteopaths would have a brisk trade.'

I was so surprised he could quip, I almost forgot to laugh. But he'd been talking families, so perhaps it was time for me to find out something of his. 'If I'm following Griff into the business,' I said, somewhat underplaying my role, of course, 'what about you? Have you got a family firm to go into? Didn't I recall Honey saying something . . .?' I couldn't, of course, because Honey was as non-committal about her life as Spencer was.

'What's she been saying?' he snapped, before I could finish the fake question, not to mention think of a satisfactory lie.

'Oh, something about going nowhere at Fenwick's, that's all, and wishing she – No, I can't recall her exact words. What about you?' I repeated. 'Or are you – as Griff puts it – resting? Between jobs,' I explained.

'Why all this cross-questioning?'

By now I did have some sort of response. 'Because for me my job's so much a part of my identity – as you've seen on Google,' I said, with what I hoped was a disarming smile. 'And knowing how someone spends their days – or nights – helps place you. But not everyone wants to be placed. Especially as accurately as Google places you.' My grimace was genuine. But why had I gone into appease mode for a guy I wasn't even remotely drawn to? An irritating imp, however, quite inexplicably popping up from the depths of my brain, told me to continue. 'Or, to be accurate, places *me*. Another drink?' It was my round, after all, and a few moments at the bar would give me time to consider which way the conversation ought to go. Sport? It was time to go fishing.

At least Spencer's leisure time didn't involve a rod and line. But it wasn't much better, from my point of view. It would have to be rugby, wouldn't it – a sport about which, thanks to Griff's aversion to blood injuries, I knew next to nothing. But in my time I'd learnt a lot about nodding intelligently while others held forth, and to be fair I'd gained a great deal of information about the world in general and my small antiques part of it in particular. This was a chance to pick up on what Spencer might accidentally let slip, not for me to be entertained.

Apparently he'd played rugby since prep school, which presumably meant private education and therefore money. Then a public school I'd never heard of. He didn't mention playing

at university, but he did mention Maidstone second fifteen –
again, that meant little to me, bar the fact he wasn't up to first
team standard. I floated questions about injuries and training
when he paused for breath. It transpired he had cover for
private medicine. So there must still be money around somewhere. But I didn't quite dare to ask about it, not yet. Instead
I came up with a sensible question: 'What would your team-
mates think about your ballroom dancing?'

For answer he told a long story about two male ballet dancers
dealing with bullies by doing one of those Carlos Acosta ballet
leaps and kicking them in the teeth. I wasn't sure where that
got us, but I spoke earnestly about core muscles, a term I'd
picked up from Pilates. For response he pulled his t-shirt tight
and made his stomach ripple up and down. Weird. Actually,
post-Pilates, I could do it too, but not in public.

Dare I ask how his rugby training (presumably) and playing
fitted in with his job? On the whole, since he was now checking
his mobile and texting, I thought not. It was better to end the
session amicably.

Would I have been better off spending my evening shopping? Probably.

But you never knew.

In the past, I'd wanted action and I'd wanted it immediately,
sometimes going out of my way to provoke it. Now, perhaps
since not so long ago someone had threatened to break all my
fingers, I was more circumspect, realizing that just as I had a
queue of repair jobs, other people, like DS Hunt, had other
cases to investigate, possibly more urgent and almost certainly
at the same time. According to Carwyn, though she was probably carrying the caseload of an inspector, she wouldn't have
enough colleagues to delegate to and an appeal to her superiors
for more would lead to hysterical screams of laughter. With
that in mind, I completed a couple of urgent museum jobs
over the next couple of days, content, if not actually happy,
in the knowledge that social services and the police would be
dealing with Dodie's theft with all the information I'd been
able to give them.

I also popped round to see Dodie myself, not just because

Pa texted me to ask how she was, but to review the CCTV
pictures and take the newly laundered clothes. I was pleased
to see her wearing a softly pleated navy skirt with a toning
sailor-striped top, the ensemble completed by a red scarf I
didn't recognize, but which one of her carers had given her.
I felt humbled: these women earned, as Griff had pointed out,
a pittance, but one had found the cash from somewhere for
an act of kindness. Moira, whom I ran into as I was coming
out, assumed a cool managerial smile when I told her: it
seemed that carers were forbidden to receive gifts from their
clients and in all probability strongly advised not to give them.

Blithely ignoring her Eeyore face, I launched into an attack
on the awful shapeless slippers. But I did so with an eye on
what I hoped was the appropriate jargon. 'What Health and
Safety rules they violate,' I said, 'I can't imagine. But if she
should ever fall and damage her hip, I would hold whoever
lets her wear them entirely responsible. Wouldn't you?' I fixed
her with my beady eye, knowing that social workers were at
least as target-driven as the police, with lower pay and even
fewer resources. And their tiniest slip provoked the most
vicious media attacks imaginable.

'I will certainly bring the issue to the case-worker's attention, coming as it does so soon after the incident of the clothes.'

'I was so grateful you were there,' I said, speaking, as it
happens, from the heart. 'You handled everything so well.'

'The process is one thing, the outcome is another,' she
declared with a nod. 'Ah, here's Frances, our retired podiatrist.
Perhaps she'll be able to advise as to the most suitable
footwear.'

Cleaning the cut edges of the Worcester vase was the first
stage, not to be hurried. Any dirt would weaken the join when
I eventually got round to applying adhesive, a job I had to do,
needless to say, in total calm and with complete concentration.
I even went so far as to give up booze and coffee for forty-
eight hours, as if I was training for a sporting event. The
retouching would require a similar regime, but I could give
myself a couple of days off once the groundwork was done
to my satisfaction and a vase stood proudly in my workroom

where once a pile of shards had lain. Who wanted to go to the pub with the Pilates girls and stick entirely to water?

Come to think of it, who wanted to go to the pub with the Pilates girls at all? Not me, to be honest.

'The trouble is,' I confided in Griff over a mid-afternoon cup of tea, 'that after that drink with Spencer, I have this niggling feeling that they want to find out about me, while giving nothing away about themselves.'

'You have a very unusual career, sweet one. No wonder they're interested.'

'But they block any questions about themselves. Not as crudely as Spencer, but they simply don't want to talk. Yes, I know it could be my problem – I've never had anyone to have girlie chats with so I've still got L-plates on – but I'm wondering if I should take a little risk. What if I suggested we pick up a take-away after the pub and brought it back here? Would the other girls do the same next week and the week after?'

'Quite a long-term experiment. With luck it might end in genuine friendship, of course. But not if you undertake it simply hoping to catch them out. That's not how you make friends.'

'I know. Speaking of friends, did you ever ask Noel Pargetter what you'd done to offend him? I know Devon's a big county, but what if he's a mate of Arthur Habgood? Or – oh, dear, oh, very dear – a friend of Harvey's?'

He looked at me under his eyebrows. 'I thought we agreed I should take him at his word? But you may be right. Perhaps I should contact him and assure him of my undying devotion and beg for another reunion? Or not!' he added, with an ironic grin. Then his face became serious again. 'There's no reason why I shouldn't simply ask what he meant by such a peculiar email, of course. Let me think about it. Meanwhile, for your little venture, may I suggest plenty of white wine in the fridge? Aidan's invited me to supper, as it happens, so I may stay in Tenterden overnight to sleep off my excesses. But I'll be back for a late breakfast – it's Dodie's day for home Communion . . . What have I said?'

'This sounds as if I know more than the experts, but . . .

Griff, what if we could take her to church? She'd need a wheelchair and some support, and there's no way she could kneel at the altar rail or anything. But wouldn't it be good for her just to get out? She must be going stir-crazy!'

'You may be in danger of judging her feelings by your own, my love.'

'I'm judging them by what she told me about her fear of dwindling. And by the changes to Pa that came once I'd torn him kicking and screaming from Bossingham Hall. And he'd got a more varied environment in his quarters than Dodie has in hers. He still likes me to wait on him hand and foot, but that's because he's so jealous of you. I know he goes out with Titus—'

'Albeit not, if possible, to such public places as supermarkets bristling with CCTV cameras,' Griff said tartly. Pa wasn't the only jealous one.

'But he's cleaner, sprucer and pretty much a signed up member of the human race. I'm not saying we should expect any miracles for Dodie—'

'Though we would be taking her to the right place for them!'

'But she might just like to see unfiltered daylight for a change. Could you get Tony to discuss it with Moira? She'd know how to get hold of a wheelchair, provided Dodie was interested.'

'And are you going to get your father to turn up for morning service as well?'

I couldn't quite work out his tone. 'Not without Moira's permission.'

Which seemed to be the right answer.

TWELVE

Sadly for my old friends at the Indian place, Honey and Laura were massive Chinese fans, insisting we try the new take-away, which had once been the baker's shop. We ate at the kitchen table. The food, which we kept warm on one of our rarely used heated trays, was just about acceptable, provide it was washed down with copious quantities of the white wine Griff had put in the fridge.

Honey, fresh from a row at work with someone who had always, apparently, had a down on her, gave a blow by blow account of a conversation I suspect she wished she'd had as opposed to the one that actually took place; at least I hope so, because I'd have bet Harvey's vase that at least two of her sallies would have got her instant dismissal.

'I'd love to be like you,' she declared, 'your own boss.'

'I had a long apprenticeship first,' I said, 'and Griff and I are a legal partnership, so I'm still answerable to him.'

'But you wouldn't say he was your boss. He must be pretty well retired.'

'I owe Griff everything,' I said, truthfully. 'And until he's ready, I wouldn't dream of suggesting he retires. In fact he does so much I honestly couldn't function without him.'

'So what does he actually do?'

'He holds the whole enterprise together.' I peered at the bottle. 'There's so little wine it's not worth saving. Honey? Laura? There you go.'

Laura told us about her brother becoming an intern with a London advertising agency that paid him zilch, not even travel or food expenses. 'I should think work experience in a place as pretty as this—' she looked back into the living room '—would be lovely. Would you let us handle the china?'

'You could handle the pieces in there because most of them are damaged – that teapot over there, for instance.' I fetched it. *'I'm a little teapot . . .'* I recited. 'But when it comes to pouring out, you wouldn't get much, would you?' I turned it round to show it had lost most of the reverse side.

'Surely you couldn't repair damage as bad as that,' Laura exclaimed.

If it had been world-class porcelain, instead of just a pretty domestic piece worth virtually nothing, I actually could these days by rebuilding it layer by patient layer, but they didn't need to know that. 'I repaired that jug over there as an apprentice piece.' Drat, I shouldn't have used the technical term. 'It's OK, but no one would want to buy it.'

They peered at it. 'But it's fine.'

'To the naked eye. But it wouldn't fool an expert.'

'What if someone tried to sell it to someone else as perfect?' Honey asked, sounding really interested.

'When I do a repair, I log all the details of the original damage and what I've done to put it right.' I knew I sounded pompous but I could have added a lot more – how I sent the owner a copy and kept one for myself, signed by both me and the client. For insurance jobs, there was another copy which went to the company.

'And people actually credit your work on their websites. Wow.'

I didn't recall mentioning that, but her brother might have told her when he Googled me. 'Just the name of the firm. Not me.'

'I thought that George Clooney lookalike mentioned you by name. Or was that just because he fancied you? Has he changed it, now you've told him to piss off?'

'I've not looked.' And didn't want to.

Although Laura was having difficulty smothering her half-a-bottle-of-wine yawns, Honey said, 'Where do you work? Let's go and see!' She'd downed nearly a bottle.

Two tipsy women amidst all that precious stuff!

'I wish you could. But my insurance insists everything has to be kept locked away, I'm afraid. Two reasons: risk of further damage and confidentiality. People don't want folk to know their priceless heirloom's got a great fresh crack down the back.' To prevent argument, I pointed to the coffee maker. 'Now, do you want to try Griff's new toy?'

Since I also fished out liqueur glasses they were more than happy to.

'What about other stuff?' Honey asked. 'Can you repair that?'

'It depends what. And how good a job it has to be. I could do something with glass, but no one would give me any prizes.'

Laura looked wildly around. 'What else do people need repairing?'

'Wood,' Honey said swiftly. 'Stone.'

'There's plenty of wood to practise on in a building this old,' I said, 'if I ever did. But there are specialists for that. And for stone.' Why had I added that? Come to think of it, why had she asked?

'So if I fell over a table and broke it and the pot on top of it,' Honey said, 'then you could fix the one but not the other?'

'If you'd insured it because it was valuable, I'd certainly do the pot but suggest an expert for the table. But if it was just a favourite vase and any old table, I'd tackle both if you really needed me to.'

'But you'd want me to pay?'

Damned right I would. 'Mates' rates,' I said with a grin. 'But I'd move the table and vase if I were you.'

'But you could do it?' Honey insisted.

I wished she'd let it go. Maybe she was too drunk to. I hoped she wasn't on an early shift the next day.

Perhaps Laura picked up my irritation, though I tried hard not to show it. 'Come on, Honey, you wouldn't expect to do a wedding make-up for free, would you?'

'I'm not talking about free. I'm just talking about repairing things.'

'Tonight I'm too pissed to repair a fingernail,' I declared. 'Mind you, mine are rubbish anyway . . .' Anything to get them away from my work and get Honey on to hers. But she was already checking the time with a squeal and hurriedly texting.

Guess who'd promised to pick them up and take them home? Dear old Spencer. He muscled in on all the hugs and air-kisses, of course, though he did apparently draw the line at risking a grope. Anyway, at last I waved them all goodnight, and, locking the door behind them, thought about leaving the kitchen as it was till the morning. I wasn't at all drunk, having made sure I had two glasses of water to every one of wine, so I had no excuse. Before I tackled the mess, however, I did a lot of the other chores, including locking the shutters and checking the security cameras were working. Warm though it was, I even locked the kitchen shutters. There was no point in advertising to any chance snooper that I was on my own.

'My darling, the place smells like a Chinese restaurant!' Griff declared next morning, wafting extravagantly.

'I haven't quite got round to taking the leftovers out to the compost bin,' I admitted.

Very little got past Griff. I felt his questioning eyes on me as I unlocked the kitchen door. And he wouldn't be put off by any questions I might ask about his night out with Aidan. He knew the evening hadn't been a success. But perhaps he'd put it down to the fact that I really just didn't do girlie chats. Perhaps I didn't. But last night really hadn't felt like a girls' night in.

No, I was being paranoid.

Perhaps.

But perhaps I had got away with it. Griff came bustling in from the yard. 'Heavens, my dear one, it's Dockinge village hall today, isn't it?'

In other words, I'd not loaded the van yet – or even started packing for today's antiques fair. For the next fifteen minutes there was simply no time for conversation.

Then something clicked. 'Griff – Dodie's Communion!'

'I'll have to phone Tony while you drive. Just get us there, Lina!'

Dockinge was more of a hamlet than a village until the building of the M26 made it ideal for car-driving commuters. I don't suppose it had ever been pretty, but there was now a flourishing community determined to keep alive – and if necessary resuscitate – village customs, one of which was a bi-monthly antiques fair which seemed to me to specialize in the sort of tat no one else would touch. However, several of Griff's old friends doggedly tried to sell genuinely old artefacts, and as long as they stuck it out, so, I feared, would we.

To our amazement the fair had grown, with a couple of stalls set up in the car park. A cursory glance – I was ferrying boxes of china for Griff to unpack so any glance except at where I put my feet was going to be fleeting – suggested one with a lot of garden statuary. Inside we worked with the silent speed of habit, filling the last gap on the stand and tweaking the final light just as the first punters trickled in.

Not the buying sort of punter. The looking at and shaking the head over sort of punter. I had time to do a quick tour round our fellow dealers' stalls, all of whom, with the exception of the Ty Beanie man, kept checking their mobiles to see if there was somewhere else they ought to be. Or at least to see that more than ten minutes had passed since the previous check. Neither my instinct nor my trained eye found anything worth buying, so, taking charge of our stall, I sent Griff off to meet and greet old mates.

I responded to some emails and texts, then, thinking it would be really bad form to read the book I'd just downloaded, sat back and looked around me. Griff was deep in conversation with a woman who simply had to be another resting thespian: tall, willowy and with rings so large and dramatic I marvelled at how she could move her hands so eloquently.

Eventually I got so bored that I set myself the challenge of making the next punter to drift over buy something. It's not all that hard: once you handle something lovely, it's difficult to put it down and walk away from it. So the idea is to get the potential customer to pick up something – preferably something we'd make some money on. It's easier with jewellery, especially when a man and a woman are involved, but, hey, I never did go for an easy option. As encouragement, I'd even offer a 'best' price, as opposed to the one we'd written down, with very little prompting.

My tally by noon was one failure, one success and one woman wandering off to check with her husband. Since she was still carrying the little Worcester sweet-pea vase in question, I rather thought that was a done deal, too. By twelve-ten it was. Two quick sales. Even so, there must be easier ways of making a profit of twenty-seven pounds.

Fortunately for us, the village WI were on hand with refreshments, and not just the sort of cakes Griff was still forbidden and which I avoided purely to keep him company. Some angel had prepared wholemeal rolls so overflowing with salad you almost got your five a day simply by looking at them. If you ate the lot, it must equate to seven at least. Of course the home-made lemonade was stiff with sugar, but not enough to take away the delicious tartness.

'It was worth coming all this way for the lunch alone,' Griff declared, dabbing his mouth. 'Now, my love, it's time for you to take a constitutional, too. The sun's shining, take your time.'

Should I take him at his word? Why not? There were far more dealers than punters now, some already packing up, although officially doors didn't close until four. The sun took me to the village shop, closed until two, which was no problem since I'd left my bag with Griff, and from there to the church, some 300 metres from the nearest habitation. It was short and squat, clearly very old, its spire absurdly small, as if someone had shoved a witch's hat on to a spare flat space. To my surprise the notice board was up-to-date, promising regular services. There was also information about preventing bat damage: I couldn't be bothered to read whether it was the fabric or the bats that had to be protected. In any case, the main door was locked, surely a good idea in view of what had happened to the equally old Devon churches I'd seen robbed. Presumably the thieves had got away with it; I'd had no information from Devon Police telling me anyone had been apprehended.

Someone had gone to the trouble of strimming the grass between the graves, one or two of which were new. A sudden gust of wind set a wreath bowling away; it was the work of seconds to catch it and return it to fill the gap. You can't just dump a tribute to someone who died only last week, so I stood for a moment in silence. At least I think I must have done, because the next thing I knew I was lying face down amongst the flowers. A thumping headache and a lump on the back of my head too tender to explore thoroughly prevented me from getting up as quickly as I'd have liked, and looking to see who might have socked me – assuming I was thinking so coherently, which, to be honest, I wasn't.

It dawned on me eventually that somehow or other I had to get back to the village and ask for help. Three hundred drunken metres later, I decided I might as well press on to the village hall, where one of the blessed WI ladies could no doubt find some ice to put on the lump. I didn't register much as I staggered towards the car park, except that the garden statue people had finished packing up already and were pulling out on to the road without much regard for the little local bus. Talk about White Van Man. But there was no crash, and to be honest I'd not have made a very reliable witness. It was a huge physical effort that got me as far as Griff before I collapsed again.

THIRTEEN

Despite my arrival by ambulance, it was clear I was going to have a few hours' wait in William Harvey Hospital's A&E, so I sent Griff, who'd followed the flashing blue light far faster, he later assured me, than he'd driven in years, back to Dockinge to pack up and get some of his mates to load the van. Staring at the cubicle ceiling for ever pretty well got me back to my usual state, and I would have been happy simply to discharge myself. But to my surprise a young man turned up with an ID that told me he was DC Conrad Knowles. Asking if I felt well enough, he said he was here to interview me.

Fortunately I'd sorted out a few things in my own mind and began my narrative, though very hesitantly.

'You're lucky to remember anything of the attack,' he said earnestly.

'All I really remember is catching a wreath,' I insisted. 'I'd wanted to look inside the church but it was locked. I was glad it was locked because it was very old – Norman? And I didn't want anyone to take anything from the inside.' Over the paper cup of tea he'd brought along for me, I found myself telling him about the thefts from St Rumon's and St Sidwell's. Not that I could recall their names: I could barely remember the county. But my phone came to my aid and it wasn't long before I'd brought up Henchard's details. This minor triumph – or the tea – encouraged me to ask my first intelligent question: 'You think I might have disturbed another robbery?'

'Sadly, you were too late for that: they'd already hacked out a twelfth-century crucifixion panel from behind the altar. Or maybe it's a good job you missed them. It looks as though they assaulted you as they got away. If you'd interrupted them in the building, they might have used their sledgehammers and chisels on you.'

I patted my mobile again. 'Photos. I've got pics of the

chisels at St Whatsit's. Oh, and the back of the guys' heads. Not much to go on. But Henchard and her spotty sidekick . . . maybe if you called them you wouldn't have to reinvent the wheel?' What about telling him to talk to DS Hunt? No. Different case. But there was one person who ought to know – and whom I'd like to know about my present situation. 'Oh, and do call my mate Carwyn Morgan. He's one of your colleagues, on secondment to Europol.'

'Carwyn? How do you know him?'

'He's a friend.' Sort of. Bother the finer details. 'You could send him my love.'

'You're that Lina!'

There weren't all that many antique-dealing Linas in Kent, surely?

Anyway, suddenly he was my new best friend, and I could trust him to get on with the job. So I relaxed. It was just too much effort to argue when someone in scrubs told me they were keeping me in overnight for observation. I closed my eyes and let them get on with finding me a bed. After all, when I opened them again, Griff would be there.

He was. It was seven o'clock. We sat in companionable silence until I realized he'd have to drive home in the dark if I wasn't careful, and I was going to have a zizz anyway. I awoke to find someone else sitting beside me. Carwyn? 'Carwyn!'

'Bummed a lift,' he said. He probably gave a proper explanation but I was just so happy to lie there holding his hand that I fell asleep again.

Carwyn talked his way into staying the night, convincing them that as a police officer he was there to ensure that my assailants didn't strike again. But he had to leave at six-thirty to get back to France for an afternoon meeting; French time was an hour ahead of ours, of course.

His visit practically had Griff booking the church and having our banns read. Harvey and his pretensions had flown from his mind as completely as if they'd never been there. It wasn't a long drive home from Ashford, so I let all his happy chatter wash over me. I found I was expected to recline on the sofa all day, with TV and audio zappers to hand – not a problem

for once because my head really didn't like the prospect of
bending over broken artefacts. What I didn't expect, however,
was the arrival of my father, clutching some good champagne
and what were obviously garage flowers – it was a good job
I'd organized nice ones for Dodie. The two men bickered with
extreme politeness over two of Griff's best Thai salads, Pa
arguing that I'd be safer in the seclusion of Bossingham Hall,
and Griff pointing out our state-of-the-art security. A text which
arrived during the fruit salad dessert – not that I took it then;
both men would have withered at the awfulness of such a
breach of etiquette – solved the problem to my great satisfaction. Carwyn had booked me a ferry passage and a hotel in
Calais for a bit of joint R&R. This had the effect of making
the old dears unite in condemnation of such a perilous under-
taking. I let them get on with it, actually a little anxious that
I might not feel up to the journey the following morning.

I did.

One reason our relationship worked so well was that neither
Griff nor I ever asked any questions about the other's sex life.
What happened in the bedroom stayed in the bedroom – unless,
of course, it led to a pretty white wedding with bells and
confetti. This was more likely in my case, I suppose, than
Griff's, though I wouldn't put it past him to try if he and Aidan
ever called a permanent truce on their silly tiffs and acknow-
ledged the part each had in the other's life.

So, as he picked me up on my return, apart from checking
that we'd enjoyed ourselves and that my head was better –
though no doubt he wanted to know whether our relationship
was becoming a bit more romantic – Griff let me resume my
life as if nothing much had happened.

Actually, nothing had. Nothing worth reporting on the
evening news, as Pa would say. It was just two friends – no
longer with benefits, actually – enjoying each other's
company. I felt calmer and more refreshed than I had for
weeks, and Carwyn returned to his Europol work braced for
more intensive French classes.

Meanwhile, it was back to routine. Or it would have been,
if I hadn't had a text from DS Hunt who wanted my help. She

wanted it so badly she was even prepared to come over to Bredeham and see me on my own turf.

Despite what I'd said to Honey and Laura, when she asked to see my workroom I agreed, though I did ask her to leave her coat and very bulky bag downstairs.

'Actually, in the bag is something you need to see.' She dug inside and produced a truly hideous vase. She plonked it into my bemused hands.

'Does anyone need to see that?' Griff asked. 'Dear God, is it a booby prize from a fairground stall?'

'Pretty much,' Hunt admitted. 'Actually, someone gave it to my mother-in-law, who loathes it and asked me to drop it into a charity shop.'

'Drop it full-stop would have been better,' Griff observed. 'Are you staying long enough for coffee, DS Hunt?'

'I should say yes, if I were you,' I said. 'It's good – nearly as good as Griff's biscuits. But you didn't bring me that as a present, did you? You want me to do something with it? Apart from smashing it, that is?' I led the way upstairs.

Her eyes widened as she looked round. 'It's like an operating theatre, with all these clean surfaces and bright lights! All these labelled cupboards. But why filing cabinets?'

I explained our system in more detail than the version I'd given to the Pilates women, showing her the paperwork involved. She seemed impressed.

'The only thing you don't seem to have is a drill,' she observed, clearly disappointed.

What the hell? 'Do you want a dental burr or something to dig up roads?'

'Something to put a hole in this vase so we can install a second camera in your friend Dodie's place. In addition to your radio-camera. Have you checked it recently . . .?' she asked, so offhand that I knew instantly what she was carefully not referring to. Goodness, it didn't take long for gossip about a colleague's activities to wing its way round the police force.

'As you know, I've had a head injury and needed to recuperate,' I said, absolutely deadpan. 'The bruise is going down, thank you, but I'm due for a check-up on Friday. Actually, I

thought you might be bringing me flowers as opposed to a
vase.' I stuck my tongue in my cheek so she could see the
bulge. 'Or better still some news of the bastards who robbed
the church.'

'Not my case. But I'll find out for you.' She made a note
on her mobile. 'Now, can you drill the vase?'

'I could. But I wouldn't inflict that on Dodie. Those hideous
knickknacks on her table were a present from a son she doesn't
like, not her choice at all. And in any case, Sergeant, a vase
can't simply appear. Not in a house someone's pretty well
stripped bare. Can it?'

'A present from you? Or from Mr Tripp?'

I didn't dignify that suggestion with anything except a raised
eyebrow.

Her chin fixed in the way it does when people know they're
in the wrong but don't want to give up on what they thought
was a good idea. 'Your father?'

'Credit him with a bit of taste. He's lived most of his life
amid the amazing collection of Meissen and Limoges that's
still on show front of house at Bossingham Hall. Hang on,
I've got an idea coming on.' I clicked my fingers in irritation.
'How about something that might remind her of Bossingham
Hall? So it could be explained away. The trouble is, anything
new is bound to attract attention, so your device would have
to be good enough to pass KGB or CIA muster. If only I'd
not given her a glass vase when I took her Pa's flowers . . .
Let's go and have a coffee and see if we can come up with
something else.'

'What puzzles me,' I said, as we settled in the living room,
'is all that seaside tat on her table. She told me it was to keep
her daughter-in-law, who'd given it to her, on side. Fine. But
what did it replace? That woman's got an eye for good things.
Surely she'd have acquired something apart from netsuke on
her travels? Did she give everything away? Or did it go the
way of the clothes?'

'We're working on that,' Hunt said tersely. 'But her son
insists the old lady's memory is blown, and that she probably
gave away her clothes herself, years ago.'

'My dear sergeant, another biscuit?' Griff asked. 'Except I

find it hard to serve good food to someone who only has a title. Might I ask your name?'

'Fiona. Fi. I used to use the whole name until I married. It didn't sound quite right with Hunt, somehow.'

'Quite,' Griff agreed. 'And I'm Griff to my friends. More coffee? The work of moments, I assure you.'

She raised a pudgy hand: no more. But she succumbed to another biscuit. I knew from experience that the trouble with Griff's biscuits was that it was impossible to stop at one. Or even two.

'She recognized that little rat netsuke by touch as much as anything,' I said sadly. 'And she liked the bright clothes I bought her best. I wonder if she has an eye problem.'

'She's old,' Fi pointed out unnecessarily.

Griff raised a finger. 'Some opticians do home visits,' he said. 'With Moira's permission, I'll arrange one. New glasses could work wonders. Who knows? I'm almost ready for a cataract operation myself,' he confessed, startling the socks off me. 'I went to those nice folk in Canterbury while you were on your little jaunt, my love. Goodness, they're just the people to see dear Dodie!'

Fi looked at him sideways. 'She's become quite a project of yours, Mr Tripp. How long have you known her?'

'Since I became more active in the church after a life-saving operation. When you've had a close look at the Pearly Gates you want to say thank you for not having to go through them immediately, you know. So a few months at most.' His eyes narrowed. 'Like the other volunteers, Fi. I'm DBS checked, you know.'

'Your father,' Fi said, turning to me with a nod at Griff, 'is impoverished, I understand. And – pardon me – might be described as shady. How long has he been involved?'

'They had what I suspect was a liaison years back – I doubt if either could remember the year, to be frank. He'd love to see her again, and as you know sent her flowers – chosen and delivered by me – but Moira said reintroducing him into her life might have a detrimental effect on her mental stability.'

Fi gave a crack of laughter. 'She would, wouldn't she!'

Griff looked troubled. 'Your father came to the village by taxi the other day to see you, my dear one. Could he have taken it into his head to see Dodie while he was over here?'

I got to my feet, arms akimbo. 'If he did, I was spark out and wouldn't know. And – to be blunt – what if he did? He certainly wasn't there to nick anything, shady as you deem him to be.' Any moment now I'd have one of my tantrums, so I made myself sit down again, splaying my fingers to count points off. 'One: we need somewhere to plant a device. I'll see if I can find a souvenir at the Hall gift shop that's suitable. Two – Griff will arrange an eye test. I doubt if we need anyone's permission but Dodie's for that, provided the optician is chaperoned. Three – you, Fi, might like to dig a bit further into the family background and find what happened to Dodie's money. Wherever it's gone, it was well before Griff, Lord Elham or I came on the scene. And four – as Griff's DBS tests may not have made absolutely clear, Tripp and Townend have a reputation second to none for probity.'

To my amazement, she raised her hands in amused surrender. 'Unlike Arthur Habgood? You see, though we've been working flat out on this and other things, I haven't forgotten him. Devon and Cornwall Police have had a word with him about how a probably stolen item came into his possession; he claims that all antique dealers have sources that are well below the radar – says that you do too, incidentally.'

'We did,' Griff said shortly. 'He was murdered.'

'Was he a thief?'

'He'd spot things at boot sales or flea markets. The money I gave him kept him fed, just about. No more, because he'd have drunk himself to death. What about Habgood's supplier? Did you get a name? Because although we're clean, we didn't come down in the last shower, either of us. We know who's straight, who's bent.' He dealt her another of his hard looks. 'Habgood hasn't pointed the finger at my Lina again, has he?'

'He's got form there, has he?'

'Dead right he has,' I said, with a terse explanation.

Fi nodded at intervals, as if my narrative confirmed what she'd already heard. When I'd finished she said, 'Another name he gave us was Titus Oates. I thought he was some sort of historical figure, to be honest, but I find he's been of interest to us in the past.'

'Titus doesn't steal,' Griff declared so firmly I could have hugged him there and then. 'He's a most unusual individual, but theft isn't his line at all. And he'd die rather than bring trouble to Lina's door. Lina's been unofficially sniffing round after some low-life church thieves in Devon—'

'Do I know about them?'

I gave her my Devon contacts' names, more useful to her than just hearing the story from me.

'Titus has told her in no uncertain terms to keep out of it,' Griff said firmly.

'I'm glad to hear it. If you do see Mr Oates,' she said dryly, 'then you could ask if the grapevine's thrown up any ideas about Dodie's thefts. Informants,' she concluded, getting up and shedding biscuit crumbs, 'get paid.'

'I will indeed,' Griff said solemnly, shaking her hand. 'It's been a pleasure to meet you, Fi.'

FOURTEEN

The obvious place to meet Titus was at my father's – but Titus wouldn't dream of doing anything obvious. Phone communication was pretty much a no-no too, now he'd realized that electronic messages could be traced. Semaphore? Smoke signal? A bit of psychic exchange? The best I could do, when I went to Bossingham Hall to buy the souvenir I'd promised Fi, was to nip over to Pa's quarters and leave a message with him asking Titus to get in touch. I wasn't, with our security, expecting him to roll up at our front door, either.

So I returned to my usual existence without holding my breath, but clutching a photo, signed extravagantly by Pa, who relished the whole plan, of the approach to the Hall set in a faux-rococo faux-silver frame.

Griff and I toddled down to Dodie's together, me to check the radio-camera and to tell her that another was on its way, him to mention the next day's NHS optician's visit he'd set in train with Moira's verbose consent.

'National Health? My dear man, I'm in BUPA,' she declared grandly. 'My bank pays every month.'

Did it indeed? For a moment, I wished I was the one entitled to have a few meaningful conversations with her family. As for the camera, it showed nothing of interest, as you'd expect. The junk on the table top appeared undisturbed, and the rat nestled on the teddy bear's lap, Dodie stroking both from time to time.

While I made slow but very good progress on Harvey's vase, Griff contacted both Fi and Moira, who'd agreed to act as chaperone, and also, from the wonderful smells wafting up to my office, cooked another batch of biscuits. My nose also picked up bread and what was probably a chicken casserole.

He'd also found time to organize a salad with some late tomatoes, the dwarf vines still heavy with fruit as they basked on a south-facing wall.

'They're not ripening as fast as I'd like,' he sighed.

'Does that mean you have to make your green tomato chutney? Please?'

'If you'd like some, sweet one. How's your head after its first morning of toil?' He laid a cool hand on my brow, suddenly reminding me of my mother when I was a tiny kid with a headache.

I welled up.

'My love?'

'I'm fine, honestly.'

'And these sudden tears?' He wiped them away.

'Just one of my dratted flashbacks. Nothing to worry about. Now, who are all those biscuits for? You're not planning to corrupt Fi, are you?'

'Poor lady, it's wrong to offer her anything as calorie-laden as that. But she'll expect something when she comes round with the camera for that frame, won't she? And Dodie would like some, I'm sure. I've made enough casserole for her supper, too. I shall have to take it round and heat it myself, of course, since her carer merely provides her with a jam sandwich.'

'You're sure of that? After all, Dodie's memory—'

'Is getting sharper with what Moira would call each interaction. I can't wait to hear the optician's verdict.'

'And, if she needs specs, how will she pay?'

'BUPA, of course.' We shared a grin. 'If only we could find her bank details – maybe Fi will tell us how things are progressing if I offer her biscuits to take home for her children, assuming she has any. Not that I'm bribing her, of course.'

'Her son has power of attorney,' Fi declared, outside her second biscuit. 'So basically he runs her financial life – does everything concerned with money. What I'd really like to do is get a forensic accountant on the case. But,' she continued, in response to my eyebrows, 'there are three unfilled vacancies at the moment, and a big fraud trial coming up. I'd send in an ordinary copper, but we don't want to blow any possible case by muddying the waters.'

'So he can just get away with it!'

'Assuming he's getting away with anything, Lina. He might

be a very caring son. Meanwhile, Dodie's social worker is writing to him to make sure he pays any new bills. I'll text her and ask her about BUPA. You never know when old people may get confused about things like that.'

'Or when they may need urgent treatment,' I added.

Harvey's vase temporarily sidelined, I drilled a minute hole in one of the curlicues of the frame, Fi breathing disconcertingly down my neck. It was the work of moments to insert the little – very little – camera and to replace the photo.

'Well done you. It would have taken ages to find one of our techies with enough time to do it. It's a clever piece of kit – activated by movement. And you'll deliver it?'

'Me or Griff. He's taking up some supper for her this evening. And some bread and biscuits.'

She shot another hard look at me. 'You're sure all this is above board? He's not trying to winkle his way into her affections . . . What have I said?' she demanded, as I gave a shout of laughter.

'He's not the marrying sort, our Griff. And he'd have to fight my father for her. Whatever one has, the other wants it more. Two kids in a playground.'

The antiques fair at the Grand Hotel in Folkestone was one of our regulars. But Griff was torn this time: God or Mammon? Holy Communion or his job? In the end I cut through all his dithering: he would come with me to help set up, dash back to Bredeham for the service, and then come back to me – always assuming he could find somewhere to park, all the roads to the Leas being chockful by then.

In fact I was happy to be on my own, since it was likely that Titus would be there, either with his own stall selling historic books and maps, or simply as a punter, keeping his ears open for gossip, his eyes for bargains. As far as the latter were concerned, he'd be in straight competition with me, of course, something that caused Pa endless amusement.

Griff and I took a funny mix to the fair – some bottom end and some really good stuff, with little in between. We also braced ourselves for a gentle stream of old people forced to eke out their pensions by selling what they thought were priceless heirlooms. The problem was that while most of the pieces were good quality, a lot were simply out of fashion – and fashion dominates the world of antiques as much as it does everything else. It was hard to say no; some of our colleagues would offer desperately low prices, and some actually diddled the sellers. I preferred a straight negative, plus explanation. And sometimes I'd tell them what Tripp and Townend were really looking for, with amazing results at the next fair.

Equally, some people thought we stallholders were all on a tame version of the BBC's *Antiques Roadshow,* eager to do valuations for nothing; they often argued if we suggested less than they expected. One old friend had to summon security when his word was doubted and a whole family surrounded him, yelling obscenities. And then there was the tripper crowd, though they usually only bothered to come on wet days so we could entertain their children – ice creams, buckets and spades and all – for free.

It didn't take us long to set up, and I shooed Griff on his way to church. It was great to see him behind the wheel again.

'Old guy's looking OK,' a voice said in my ear. Titus.

I knew better than to look round and offer a proper greeting. In fact, he continued without a pause, 'That bang on your head. Same guys. Told you not to mess with them.' He was about to move off but I stopped him.

'I didn't mess. Just happened to be there. Innocent bystander.'

'I might believe you. They wouldn't. What's this about blood money?'

'Deal: cash for info.'

'Snout. Snitch. Grass.'

'Call it what you will, it might help when they catch up with you.'

'Told you: going straight. Me *and* your pa.'

He was gone before I could point out that the police might be interested in his past activities, not just his current ones.

Griff turned up rather later than I expected, looking rattled. I assumed it was a parking problem until, over a cup of coffee, he told me about a road rage incident.

'But I've no idea what provoked it, dear one. I know I'm

not the world's greatest driver, but I was buzzing down Stone Street, minding my own business, when this white van came towards me. Next thing I knew it was behind me – at least I'm pretty sure it was the same one – trying to see if it could get up our exhaust pipe. Believe me, it was terrifying. But then I saw salvation in the form of Six Mile Garage. As I signalled, the van came alongside me, and I really thought my number was up. But they suddenly lost interest and drove on. They might have been waiting in ambush later, of course, but I took to the lanes after that, as you can imagine.'

I might have inwardly chuckled at dear Griff being law-abiding enough to signal to his pursuers that he was about to manoeuvre, but I took his anecdote quite seriously. 'I suppose you didn't get a chance to look at the driver? Passenger? No.' What had I expected? But I pressed on. 'What about the van itself? The make – or the number plate, for instance?'

'It was a recent one, of course, that irritating mixture of letters and figures that are impossible to recall. Except two of the numbers were one and three, and I thought how ironic it was to be pursued by unlucky thirteen.'

'So it was a fairly recent model. Anything else – the odd bit of paintwork damage?'

'Is there a white van on the road without one?'

'Point taken.' I was about to fish in my bag and show him the photos on my phone, but we had a sighting of that rare creature, a punter who looked ready to buy. Griff was on his feet in an instant, a friendly and obliging smile replacing his anxious frown.

It might be, of course, that Griff had encountered two different white vans, and had inadvertently committed some offence that annoyed the second. And there were hundreds of vans registered in 2013, not just the one I'd photographed in Devon. What worried me, in a deeply personal way was that the driver had pulled back when he saw the van was being driven by an old man. Perhaps it was old-fashioned courtesy, and if a young man had been at the wheel it would have ended in macho violence. But what if it was a young woman they were after?

This wasn't something I was about to discuss with Griff,

however. Not yet. Not in as many words. What I did float, in a post-lunch lull, was the idea of changing my hair. I'd thought of growing it properly, but it had got to the irritating straggly stage and I was beginning to resemble a sheep. I'd also got into the habit of tucking stray tendrils behind my ears when I was working, not the wisest move when my hands had been dabbling in glue or paint.

Should I have a nice girlie conversation with the Pilates women next time we got together in the Pig and Whistle? Or should I consult my usual style guru?

'Griff,' I said, clutching a handful of the offending locks, 'what shall I do with this? Is it time to go blonde again? Or darker, perhaps?'

'If you were still keen on your retro wardrobe,' he said, head on one side, 'you could go for the Audrey Hepburn look. But now you're addicted to modern fads, it's hard to say. Let me give it some thought.' Had he seen through my ploy? It was impossible to tell.

One thing was certain: I wouldn't show him the photos on my phone until he'd had time to forget this conversation.

FIFTEEN

Monday morning brought the interesting news that Dodie had been referred to a consultant to inspect her eyes: it seemed she had cataracts, with incipient glaucoma. Would BUPA cough up for an immediate consultation, or would she join the NHS queue? My socialist principles told me that it should be the latter, so long as the waiting time wouldn't exceed her life expectancy. My interest in the BUPA option was more to do with what it would suggest about her son's financial care.

Meanwhile, I did something I should have done days ago. I contacted the organizer of the fair in Dockinge village hall to ask for a list of stallholders. It wasn't my job to do so, of course, but I could hardly phone up DC Knowles, although my fuzzy memory of him was of a quietly efficient person – hadn't he summoned Carwyn for me? – and ask if he'd already checked them out. There was one in particular that worried me, with the benefit of hindsight: the garden statuary people, who obviously dealt in stone objects and who had left early.

The fair was privately run, a money-spinner to raise funds for the hall, according to Jane Dockery, the village hall secretary. She'd not organized it – that was the treasurer's doing. She havered for a bit about letting me have details of our fellow stallholders, muttering about the Data Protection Act.

I tried to sound persuasive rather than plain exasperated. 'Jane, if I could lay hands on the little programme we're all given when we go in, stallholders and punters alike, I could just look everyone up. But I was indisposed, you might say, and Griff had other things – like me – on his mind.'

'Oh, you're the young lady who was taken ill. The heat or something?'

'Someone whacked me on the head when the church was being robbed,' I corrected her dryly.

'Of course! You tried to stop the vandals! Oh, is there anything I can do to help?'

'Could you email me the programme? Or send me a hard copy?'

'Oh, Martin will have that, and he's just gone away.'

'Martin . . .'

'Martin Fellows. But if you want, I could dictate it? Here and now?'

Who was I to argue? The task didn't take too long because I knew a good proportion of the stallholders, but I slowed her down as she reached the end of the list. 'What about the outside stalls?'

'The produce? I know it wasn't really appropriate, but we've all got such a glut we thought it might help the hall fund.'

'It was more the statues and pots – the people nearest the hall entrance.'

'Statues? Oh, of course. I've no idea who they were. They said they were someone's friends and that Martin had said it was all right, so long as it was on the usual terms. But they skipped off without paying. Perhaps they hadn't sold anything and were peeved.'

'What a shame,' I said neutrally. 'I suppose you couldn't find out whose friends they were? They had some interesting stuff.' Some of which, by the time they did their flit, may have included the twelfth-century crucifixion panel so rudely torn from the church.

Jane promised to do her best, though she was pretty sure they must have been Martin's friends, since he was the only one who could really give permission, wasn't he? And he was going to be away for at least two weeks. A cruise, she rather thought. Lucky fellows. On the off-chance, I got his contact details – on the off-chance, it happened, of sending them to DC Knowles.

His card was still tucked in the case Griff had bought to protect what he considered a laughably expensive phone – until he'd seen all the things it did besides phoning, of course. Was I phoning as a victim, who was entitled to know how things were progressing in the search for my assailant, or as Josephine Public with news he hadn't asked for and might not want?

In the end I plumped for the former, eliciting the information that police now thought there was a connection between the three church crimes, which were in turn linked to a country-wide pattern of raids on remote churches. Accordingly, the investigation was now being handled by a national task force.

'In other words, kicked into the long grass,' I observed.

'On the contrary,' Conrad said. 'Instead of a few bumpkins dashing round on bikes, a lot of resources will be put into the operation. Do you remember how loads of farm vehicles got nicked at one time? Since the campaign went national, the figures have dropped dramatically. That's what we've got here. A whole team of heritage officers sharing information, finding ways of protecting vulnerable sites, liaising with organizations like English Heritage, and so on. And fewer people like you getting assaulted in graveyards.'

'But no news of who clocked me?'

'Not yet.'

'Look, if you know enough about me to know I'm *that* Lina, you know I'm incorrigibly nosy.'

'Ye-es,' he conceded doubtfully.

'Well, something that neither you nor this here national team may know is that there was an unexpected addition to the Dockinge village hall antiques fair. Not so much a stall, as an outside area devoted to selling garden statues and other stoneware. The owners packed up early and made a rapid exit. They nearly crashed into a bus. I didn't mention it when you interviewed me at the William Harvey because my brain wasn't working. And there's something else you should know.' I repeated Jane Dockery's information, mentioning in passing that Martin Fellows, who had presumably approved their late application, was away for a couple of weeks.

I'll swear I heard him sigh.

'Look, give me Kent's member of this new team and I'll contact him or her direct. Don't tell me: no one's been appointed yet.'

'I'll make sure it's passed on, don't worry.'

But I did.

After our weekly Pilates and drinks session, it was clear that the girls expected to come back to our cottage again.

Anticipating this, I'd already encouraged Griff to host some church meeting there, so I had to spread my hands apologetically. Neither take-out, Indian or Chinese, had a decent eating area, so I looked hopefully at Laura and Honey. Laura's boyfriend was decorating their tiny flat; Honey just said her parents had banned her and Spencer from hosting parties after a Facebook invitation disaster.

'But you're adults, not children!' Laura exploded. 'And what the hell are you both doing, living at home at your age?'

'Loads of people do. Have to. Lina does,' she added with a hint of accusation.

'True. It's not a problem most of the time. Only when we both want friends round at the same time, which isn't often.'

'What about your workroom? We could eat in there.'

I shuddered. 'I know what's in some of those chemicals I use. If you want to risk it, I'll be downstairs!'

'As bad as that?' Laura put in. She'd been looking at the pub's gastro-menu and shaking her head at the prices.

'I wear a mask and goggles when I'm using most things,' I said truthfully.

Even Honey didn't persist after that. And just in case she did, I raised the question of a new look for my hair, which engaged them both in loudly contradictory ideas until we all gave in to hunger and went our separate ways – or I did, at least, since Honey and Laura lived only a couple of hundred yards apart.

The streets of Bredeham were so quiet I almost wished that Spencer had turned up to see us all home safely. But I fingered my torch, heavy enough for a cosh, I suspect, and reflected that I could outrun most would-be assailants. In the event, I didn't have any problems at all. The meeting over, Griff was already in the kitchen, tying on his apron and breaking eggs for his omelette supper. Soon he was making one for me too, and considering the girls' suggestions for my hair. White with a pink or purple streak did not, for some reason, meet with his approval.

Downloading the footage from the camera in the photo frame took even less time than that from the radio, yet neither showed

anything suspicious. As Griff and I were leaving, however, a
Nissan Micra arrived, its unlovely shade of green making Griff
shudder exaggeratedly. A woman not much older than me
drooped out, even her hair dispirited as the door refused to lock.
Her burden of files was out of her arms and into Griff's before
you could say 'case study'. If I'd had the sense I'd been born
with, I'd have been there before him, making sure I dropped
them to give me a chance of seeing the notes on Dodie. But,
as Griff escorted her up the short path with as much grace as
if she were the Queen herself, not one of her overburdened
public servants, I consoled myself with the thought that if anyone
could talk his way back into the house to eavesdrop on the
conversation, it was him. Reluctantly I left him to it: there was
no point in overegging the pudding, as he would say, and in
any case I had some serious work to do on Harvey's vase.

I emerged from my workroom a couple of hours later, stretching
to ease the niggle between my shoulder blades, to hear the sound
of a woman's voice. My first wild thought was that Griff had
persuaded the Nissan-driving social worker to join him for coffee,
but a glance though the window showed me that it was Tony's
totally out of character Juke – twice the size of the Micra, but
an equally off-beat reddy-orange. So the voice must be Moira's.
I stayed upstairs to eavesdrop, more or less shamelessly.

'In short,' she was saying, though I was prepared to doubt
the veracity of that, 'while it was in Dodie's best interests to
have a neutral observer during the case study review, it might
well be argued – and her family may take this view – that with
your background it is not impossible that you may have had
some hand in her present circumstances. We know otherwise,'
she said, raising a hand to silence him, 'but it was a risk.'

'In that case it was most fortunate,' Griff responded, very
dryly, 'that I was able to summon you. I know, Moira, that
you'll be as bound as I would have been by the need for confidentiality, but let's for goodness' sake remember that we're
friends working for the same ends. Let me offer you a restorative sherry – no? A very small one? Perhaps you might like to
try one or two of my cheese biscuits to absorb the alcohol.'

I would, in her situation. In fact I'd prefer the biscuits to the sherry, the very smell of which made me heave: one of my more unsuitable foster mothers had been addicted to it. Meanwhile, though I should by now have put in a sociable appearance, I stayed where I was, hoping the sherry fumes wouldn't drift upwards.

The good news was that Dodie could see an NHS consultant within a month; the bad news was that her BUPA membership had lapsed about a year ago. Emma Foyle, who must be the social worker, said that the case notes showed that Dodie's son had taken the decision when the contributions had risen to what he considered unreasonable levels, and had agreed to fund personally any one-off consultations and treatments required.

'So will he pay for an immediate eye consultation?' Griff demanded.

'He's away at the moment for a couple of weeks, apparently, so Emma considers that in view of the swift availability of free treatment, there's no need to contact him.'

I could hear the smile in Griff's voice. 'Clearly you don't.'

'If a man can afford to go on a cruise, I think he should stump up, don't you?'

Cruise? Wasn't that guy Martin on a cruise, too? But there were lots of ships on the sea, and loads of folk aboard them.

Perhaps the sherry was beginning to go to Moira's head. 'What if he's using her money to pay for the cruise? I'd say rattle his cage now! Spoil the bugger's holiday!' she added recklessly.

It was a good job she lived within easy walking distance; that Juke would have to stay where it was for a bit.

'Besides,' she added soberly – if that wasn't absolutely the wrong word – 'I hear the NHS is operating an unofficial ageist policy, so older people don't get the treatment they deserve. I've heard of so many appointments cancelled, operations delayed times beyond number, that one almost believes it. What if they think she's too gaga to bother with?'

'What indeed? My dear Moira, may I top you up? The merest smidgen? Say *When*! There. Now, how can we ensure that they don't?'

SIXTEEN

Pa's face was a study. I identified pleasure, guilt and apprehension, mixed with something I'd rarely seen before: self-doubt.

'Visit Dodie? You're sure? You're not, are you?'

'It's you that might not be. We've got two cameras set up, remember, to protect her from whoever it is who nicked all her stuff.'

He gave a bark of laughter. 'In other words, don't startle the horses! We always were very discreet, Lina – had to be, with her husband's position, after all.' The impish but tender smile slipped from his face. 'You have – you know – smartened her up a bit?'

'Manicure, pedicure – actually, more like podiatry, removing corns and stuff—'

'Spare me the grim details!'

'Hair-do. Some M and S clothes.'

His eyebrows shot up. 'What did you say?'

'M and S, not S and M.' We shared a sort of laugh. 'New shoes – she's walking much better.'

'All that's good. Main thing, Lina . . .' I'll swear he blushed. 'Main thing, she doesn't smell of pee, does she?'

'Not these days.'

'And she liked the flowers? And the picture of the Hall?' He was sounding embarrassingly like a lovelorn teenager all of a sudden.

'Very much. But her memory's a bit . . . intermittent. You're there to jog it, remember.'

'But not to embarrass the hidden watchers, one of whom will no doubt be you.'

'I can always turn the sound down, can't I? Actually, there will be someone else in the cottage with you. It was the only way we could get . . . It's this woman from the church who has responsibility for what they call vulnerable adults. She's been very useful in dealing with Dodie's social worker, and she's going to make your tea and pass round cakes.'

'Tea! I've got vintage Verve Clicquot in the cellar. And don't tell me she might not like it.' Before I could point out that it might interfere with any mediction she was on, he continued, 'She loves it. Had a bath in it once.'

Talk about too much information.

He got up, suddenly agitated. 'Hair cut. A decent shirt. That suit's a bit too much.'

'How about your good casual trousers and that cashmere jumper I bought you for your birthday?'

He stared. 'A gentleman does not go visiting in a jumper.'

Perhaps not, even when he was a career criminal as well as a serial Lothario.

'There's a sale on in that gentlemen's outfitters you like in Canterbury. I've got time to take you in now if you like. Do we need to sell some more of your treasures to pay for your new outfit?'

'I know I've got Chinese stuff in there somewhere,' he said, gesturing vaguely in the direction of his junk rooms. 'What about Russian? There was this programme on TV the other day . . .'

If Pa was anxious about his appearance, so was Dodie, but the good women of the church rallied round, though Griff insisted that no one should apply her make-up but himself. We provided good champagne flutes and an ice bucket. Griff escorted Moira to the cottage, and I ferried a strangely chic version of Pa, clutching proper flowers (me again) and his champagne. At which point we made a discreet but deeply frustrating exit.

I headed straight to my workroom, to continue work on Harvey's vase. But it's hard to concentrate for long on very detailed work with brushes that are so fine it must be possible to count the hairs. So I did the section I'd promised myself I'd finish, and turned to a job a museum had sent me, a lovely piece of Meissen. As I moved round the room, I thought I could hear raised voices. Were they from the shop? But no one had pressed the alarm button, and Mary was so good at calming down irate customers I thought it best to leave her to it. All the same, I was nosy enough to want to know more. And perhaps I was mistaken – perhaps the noise was coming from the street. A quick look through the bathroom window – I had to perch on the lavatory lid to manage this – showed a very up-market black car parked down the road. I thought it was a high-end Mercedes, though I suppose that's what Griff calls tautology. I froze. That Merc was just the sort of car Harvey would favour. I really did not want him to come charging up into my workroom demanding to see how much work I'd done. Surely Mary would be able to keep him away from me. Nonetheless, knowing that if he upset me, there was part of me capable of violence against the nearest object, I carefully locked both artefacts away and tried to achieve a measure of calm by going through the careful routine of cleaning up after myself. In any case, it was time I collected Pa and returned him to Bossingham, I reasoned, and I didn't want to delay matters by going into the shop.

Gathering my car keys and bag, I ran downstairs and straight out into the street. Even as I started the Fiesta – there was no way I could persuade Pa into the van – I began to beat myself up. I should have seen whether Griff needed help shifting Harvey. But he had Mary and Paul Banner to support him, and I really, truly did not want to see Harvey ever again. Just in case . . .

It wasn't angry voices but laughter that came from the open window of Dodie's cottage. Had I ever heard her laugh like that before? Or Pa for that matter? Or even Moira, who was talking now?

It was she who let me in, shoulders still shaking with ill-suppressed giggles.

I couldn't wait to see the footage on the spy cameras.

On impulse, I asked Pa back to our cottage for a cup of tea. Firstly Griff and I could both hear about his afternoon together. Secondly, and perhaps more importantly, if Griff still had a soft spot for Harvey, Pa most certainly didn't – something to do with Harvey changing his surname, which Pa regarded as infra dig. Neither did Pa approve of his making me unhappy. So if Harvey had managed to sweet-talk Griff, at least I had reinforcements, immaculately turned out and full of jaunty self-confidence.

In fact the black Merc had gone and all was quiet. So I let us into the cottage with a cheery call to Griff. His response was lukewarm at best. My God, what if the stress of all that shouting at Harvey had made him ill? I was in the kitchen in seconds. He and Mary were sitting at the table, the latter white and shaking.

Pa did something amazing: he filled the kettle and switched it on. 'Hot sweet tea,' he declared. 'Builders' is best in a crisis.' It was a good start, even if he wouldn't know where we kept everything else. Griff unobtrusively reached out for china cups and saucers, milk and sugar. Whatever we drank, it would be elegantly served.

'Bloody Harvey Sanditon!' I raged. Anger – at my cowardly sneaking away – burned. It was a good job the cups were Worcester or I'd be smashing them.

'I told you the man was a menace,' Pa declared.

But Griff was totally bemused. 'Why are you talking about Harvey? He's been nowhere near.'

Mary lifted her head. 'This man accosted me when I was on my way to the post. And yes, I thought it was Harvey for a moment – a big, well-spoken man wearing a designer suit and dark glasses. Ray-Bans. No, he didn't touch me. But he snatched one of the packages I was carrying and hurled it to the ground. And said—' she seemed to look at Griff for permission to continue '—that he'd do the same to you, Lina, if you didn't mind your own business. And we weren't to tell the police or anything, or he'd do a lot more damage next time.'

'Did he indeed? Well, maybe, if the CCTV's done its job, we can spoil his fun,' I said, determined not to show how rattled I was.

'That's just it, Lina,' Griff admitted. 'Either he knew the extent of our coverage or he was lucky. His car's parked just within range, but he waylaid poor Mary further down the street. And at this time of the day, there was no one around.'

'And it was one of Paul's golf days,' Mary added, near to tears, 'or he'd have been with me.'

'Have you called him yet?' I asked.

'I don't want to disturb him.'

I nodded. I could understand her wanting to be independent and not spoil his day out.

'He'll be here within the hour anyway,' she added, in a tone somewhere between brave defiance and pleading. 'And I've missed the post,' she added with a wail.

'No problem: the clients will just have to wait another day. Griff'll email them a plausible and heart-rending excuse. What did the guy smash, by the way? Don't worry, Mary, our insurance will cover it,' I added. 'Much better he smash a vase than harm you.'

She started to laugh, drifting into something that sounded close to hysteria. Pa, who'd been sitting silently at the far end of the kitchen table, suddenly got up and pottered off to the living room, returning a few moments later with a cut-glass tumbler half full of Griff's finest brandy. That was Pa for you: couldn't find a mug to save his life, but an unerring nose for the booze cupboard.

'Here,' he said. 'If you don't drink it, I'll have to slap your face, and I don't like violence.'

She gulped some down before she trusted herself to speak. 'The irony is, Lina, that I'd wrapped it with a trip to China in mind – and do you know, it's still in one piece?' She started to laugh again, but a glare from Pa stopped her. She sipped the brandy more slowly.

'What next?' asked Pa, reasonably enough. 'It seems to me to be imperative that you summon the police, Tripp, much as you'd wish to protect my daughter. To apprehend whoever affronted poor Mary, of course. *Noblesse oblige*, remember.'

'It will put her at risk. You didn't hear his threats,' Mary said, slightly lacking in conviction.

Pa peered at her from under his eyebrows. 'We both know that whatever we advise, our girl will do as she pleases. But before you summon them, be a good fellow, Tripp, and ferry me home. It's hardly a secret that there are members of Kent Constabulary whom I'd rather not meet socially. If you want to stay with Lina, you must have a local hostelry. I will adjourn there until one of you is free. Of course it will be open – and if it isn't I am sure that the landlord will discover that he does indeed wish to sell me a bottle of shampoo, possibly his only bottle of shampoo, of course.'

'Don't worry, Pa,' I said. 'Mary and I can deal with the police. Woman power!' I added, hoping she'd still be sober when they arrived. 'Griff will be happy to take you back. Make sure you use the main drive, Griff – our poor Fiesta's suspension isn't as tough as the van's,' I reminded him.

'So it's someone who did his homework pretty well,' I told the worried-looking Conrad Knowles, 'assaulting Mary out of range of our cameras.'

Sitting Conrad down in the living room, I passed him the coffee he'd preferred, and gave an extra-strong mug to Mary. He sipped appreciatively. 'So he hoped to put more effective frighteners on you by bashing your friends. Nice. Are you quite sure you're OK, Mrs Banner? I can organize a call from Victim Support.'

'I shall be fine when my husband returns,' she said firmly. She glanced at me as if to suggest that I'd be happy too with a nice young man like this beside me.

My smile was non-committal. 'The CCTV system got some shots of the car, so you might make out the model number on the back if not the entire number plate.'

'I'll take copies of the footage anyway. But the guy'll be miles away by now. He may even be en route for France.'

'We have close ties with European police forces now, though, don't we, Conrad?'

To my amazement – I'd only made a mild allusion to Carwyn, after all – he flushed. Perhaps he thought I was trying to tell him how to do his job, and resented it. Well, I'd tell him a bit more. 'And even though we've only got a partial registration number, surely your clever computer will be able to work it out. If not, then I reckon Mercedes would be able to tell you who bought a vehicle like that. This year's model, after all.' When he gaped at my apparent knowledge of posh cars, I added dryly, 'You can just see the year on the number plate.'

What was the matter with the guy? He didn't seem to be firing on all cylinders, as it were.

'A man like that wouldn't do his own dirty work, wouldn't use his own car,' he said at last.

'Some men don't like delegating. Some men are so full of themselves they never imagine anyone would disobey their orders – in this case our asking you and your mates for help.'

'So what will you do? Will you make yourself scarce? Another break in France?' he pursued.

'France? Why France, for goodness' sake, when I live and work here?'

He looked strangely relieved. 'You're a sitting duck. And your grandfather. And Mrs Banner, of course,' he added, giving her a worried glance, to which she responded with a gentle shrug.

'If Mary prefers, we'd quite understand if she took a few days off. I could even ferry any items for overseas buyers to her and she could pack them at home – the parcel she'd packed was proof against even deliberate violence, which I doubt mine would be.'

This time she smiled. 'If Paul can bring me I'll be here. Though I'd certainly wait for him to take me to the post office,' she conceded as Conrad raised a warning finger.

'As for Griff and me, we're due a change of car,' I said lightly. 'And this place itself is pretty secure. The main thing, however, Conrad, is that I don't know what I'm doing that this character objects to. Stopping folk stealing from churches? Fingering a fellow dealer called Habgood for handling stolen goods? If you and your colleagues can come up with what I believe you call intelligence, then maybe I can make an informed decision whether to stay or to scarper.' I had an idea I was being too sarcastic, which wouldn't help anyone, even if Conrad didn't seem to have registered it.

He turned back to Mary. 'Now, Mrs Banner, I know you said you couldn't recollect anything about your assailant apart from his sunglasses, but I'll bet you can, you know.' He gave an everyone's-favourite-nephew smile. 'Let's both stand a moment. Taller than me? Shorter than me? The same? OK, about five-nine or ten. Hair?'

'I've just remembered! He was wearing a Panama – the sort my husband wears to the cricket. With a little ribbon round it, red and yellow stripes. A hatband.'

'Well done. He must have looked like an old-fashioned film star.'

'I don't know: those linen suits always look a bit crumpled. And I'd have thought it was a bit too summery for this time of year, wouldn't you? I know I took Paul's to the cleaners a couple of weeks ago.'

'Under that glamorous hat, did you notice his hair? His complexion?'

'The hat was pulled down over his face – just like the baddies in old movies used to wear their fedoras. I just saw myself reflected in those sunglasses.' She demonstrated how they wrapped round his face.

'His hands: they snatched that package. Did you notice anything? Did he bite his fingernails or were they manicured?' He showed his own well-shaped and well-tended hands.

She stared at them fascinated, but shook her head. 'I really can't recall. Really. Ah, that's Paul. I'd like to go home now, please.'

SEVENTEEN

'If that ducky young policeman says we need a new car, a new car we shall have,' Griff said emphatically. 'In fact, we'll go and look for one first thing tomorrow morning, as soon as we've checked Dodie's overnight CCTV footage.'

'You're not going to make me wait till tomorrow to find out how this afternoon's tea party went, are you?' I demanded, arms akimbo. 'Come on, Pa must have spilt a few beans! I didn't have time to ask him when I collected him.'

'Wait till tomorrow? I value your blood pressure too much, my dear one. But I do feel I need, after all the alarums and excursions, a restorative G&T.' He sank into his favourite chair while I did the honours, with white wine for myself.

'Talk,' I said, putting a bowl of olives between us.

He infuriated me further by taking a long, slow appreciative sip. 'I do so miss this. I know the doctors insisted that red wine was best for the heart, but this does soothe the spirit.'

'Griff—'

He gave an impish grin. 'Elham is hardly the most reliable witness, my love, especially outside what I'm sure was the best part of the bottle of champagne he took over. Anyway, he tells me that though he was shocked by the way Dodie had aged—'

'And she him, when she can see properly again!'

'Indeed. Although your ministrations have indeed improved him. Though Dodie had aged, he could still see her former beauty. And after a slow and hesitant beginning, the champagne loosened their tongues and they beguiled each other with reminiscences he suspects brought a blush to Moira's cheeks. Then, because he could see that Dodie was tiring – amazing that the old reprobate could be so perceptive! – he had the bright idea of insisting that Moira join them and giving her a drink too.'

'Which would account for the gales of laughter I heard

when I went to collect him,' I observed. 'So a good time was had by all. Excellent. But I let you down, Griff: when I saw that Merc parked near the shop I assumed it must be Harvey's. That's why, though I heard raised voices, I didn't come and see what was going on.'

'All's well that ends well. Not that it has ended, of course. But a different car you shall have, and we'll get a new van for the business, a strictly anonymous one.' As I opened my mouth, he raised a finger. 'Yes, I deliberately made the distinction. Paul and I have been having numerous quite tedious conversations about tax. I can't just hand over all my assets to you because someone would notice. However, I can give you generous presents. It's your birthday very soon—'

'No, it isn't.'

'Well, you need an early Christmas gift. Whatever. And the first instalment will be a new set of wheels, as Paul puts it. I suspect he's a closet boy-racer. It would be lovely if it could be something really flash, but that would violate our anonymity principle. And Paul is insistent that we buy used vehicles, so that we don't donate twenty per cent of the cost to the government.'

Knowing Paul's views on VAT, I grinned.

'Now, while I prepare supper, my love, I suggest that you go online and start reading car reviews. We don't want to be conned by some oily sales person.'

Dodie seemed no worse for her afternoon tea party the previous day – in fact she was rather bright, holding my hand as she told us how much she was looking forward to the delivery of the anti-dwindling wheelchair that Moira had organized. The Carrs' grandson had been delegated to push her round the village as part of his rugby training. Perhaps if Spencer took it into his head to join us Pilates women again, I could suborn him into doing the same thing just to please me. No. Not a good idea.

'I'm so grateful for all you and your friends have done,' she said. 'So very grateful.' With her other hand she patted the netsuke, then transferred the bear to her lap. 'To have comfortable feet and be able to wear shoes with a modicum of shape – so refreshing. And that lovely lady doing my hair. So very kind . . .'

'I've done nothing,' I said truthfully, 'except to shake things up a bit.'

She squeezed my hand. 'Do you suppose that Elizabeth I ever led her troops into battle? No, she just inspired them! Shakers are worth a very great deal, Lina, and not just for making cocktails.'

Paul insisted on staying with Mary all day, largely because she'd refused to take time off, though Griff pressed her pretty hard to do so. Thanking her, but telling her simply to close the shop when she'd had enough, I was about to leave but popped back to ask, seemingly off-hand, if she'd recalled anything else about Mercedes Man.

At first she shook her head vigorously, but at last, as I held her eye, she whispered, 'His hands were so like that policeman's. Lovely hands. Wasted on a man. But I didn't want to say anything and offend him. Does it matter?'

I hugged her. 'Only if there's an ID parade – and these days,' I added hastily, 'you don't even have to see the suspect face to face. It's all done by video so it's completely safe for the witness.'

Unless you want to ID the police officer beside you, of course.

Dismissing with a sniff all the vehicles he considered aimed at the foolish, spendthrift young – I wasn't entirely flattered that he excluded me so readily from their ranks – Griff pointed at a gorgeous sporty red car swishing past us in the direction of the Audi dealership. Love at first sight for both of us, of course, but failing on two counts: it wasn't exactly unobtrusive and, when we came to test drive it – I know, I know, but blame Griff, not me – we discovered a downside to a two-door sports model, especially when it was low slung with the sort of front seats that hold you in place. I could leap in and out at will, but if Griff had difficulty heaving himself in and out of the front seats, once he was in the back they nearly had to summon a hoist to extract him.

In the end, much as I'd have loved a standard four-door A3

also in vivid red, we settled for a silver one, the same as all the other silver A3s, and none the worse for that. Lots of power, good road-holding (though I didn't observe to Griff that this might be useful if anyone ever gave chase) and much lower road tax and insurance than the original sports model. It was like choosing a sensible marriage over a wild affair. But there were enough bells and whistles even on this to keep Griff amused – or confused – for months.

Now the (cash!) deal was done, it was time to shop for the prosaic van, Griff turning in both the old van and the Fiesta – after an extended bout of haggling from which he emerged the undoubted winner – towards the price of another silver vehicle. Even that was pretty nippy, and again came with more instruments – or distractions – than we'd ever use.

A couple of days later, it was even harder than usual for me to join in the post-Pilates banter at the pub. After all, I'd probably had a more exciting week than most, but there was nothing I particularly wanted to share with the others. The incident outside the shop I could write off, should either of them ask, as a bit of road rage; the new transport wouldn't be on the road till the following morning; and Dodie's business was Dodie's business.

Laura rather shyly invited us back to her flat to eat our Chinese take-out: I had a sense she wanted us to admire her decorating skills. If so, I was happy to oblige, genuinely, as it happens, when I saw what she and her boyfriend had made of an unpromising ground floor flat at the edge of the small social housing estate that stood cheek by jowl with one of the posher parts of the village. Presumably it was in one of the large and elegant houses – many coyly referring to themselves as cottages – that Honey lived.

The meal was as boozy and loud as that at our cottage. Honey gushed over the darling little kitchen – with unnecessary emphasis on *little* – the plain white crockery and the simple wine glasses, almost forcing Laura into confessing she'd bought the lot at Asda. Only then did Honey offer to get Laura's household stuff with her Fenwick's staff discount – though I think both Laura and I suspected that even then she'd still have had to pay a lot more. Just as I'd been on the receiving end of Honey's fire when they were in our kitchen, now it was Laura's turn. What was driving Honey? I didn't know. Perhaps I could help Laura a little by asking Honey why we'd not seen Spencer at the dance classes recently. I braced myself for a barbed reply, but got a reasonable one: he was the only one without a partner, which wasn't much fun. Then came a jibe about me enjoying mixing with a load of geriatrics.

'Dancing's good exercise,' I retorted truthfully. 'As I'm sure Spencer will tell you. Something about kicking people in the teeth, he said.'

At least this time there was no need for me to wait for the others to call it a day: I could leave when I wanted to, which was well before eleven. I had a lot of work to do, after all, not to mention two new (to us) vehicles to get used to.

The only drawback was the walk home afterwards. Laura had probably hoped Honey would leave at the same time, but she declared her intention of helping Laura empty the bottle, which was still three-quarters full. Since I'd already slipped my fleece on I was afraid it would look weak or weird, take your pick, if I sat down again.

Our ways would have diverged after a couple of hundred yards anyway, I reflected, striding out as confidently as anyone who'd incurred a stranger's wrath could – a stranger with a dark car, moreover, on narrow streets only intermittently lit. Stride? I was soon running, and not in a good way.

I got as far as the shops on the village square when I saw the outline of someone tall and broad-shouldered watching me from the front step of the wonderful Indian take-away, in my view streets ahead of the new Chinese the other women insisted on using. Help – even if I didn't actually need it – was at hand in the form of Afzal. He was just turning the sign on the door to CLOSED. He unscrewed the bottle of water he'd been holding and passed it to me. 'Where's the fire, Lina?'

'If I knew, I'd know where to run,' I said.

'You know what they say: if you can't run any more, talk to a mate with a van. It's the last delivery. I'll take it and leave Saeed to clean up. Idle bugger; thinks he's Lewis Hamilton when he's behind the wheel, and far too grand to wield a mop.' He popped back inside, emerging with a cardboard box from which such wonderful smells emanated I wondered why on earth I'd bothered to spend an evening cramming MSG down my throat. The change of plan obviously wasn't to Saaed's liking, but Afzal had long since perfected an almost Gallic shrug. Shaking the van keys in derision might have been less than dignified, but Afzal was a mate and I wasn't about to nit-pick, even when he cruelly observed, as he dropped the box on my lap, that I might be out of condition.

'You try running up from the Glebe Field estate after an hour of Pilates, half a bottle of wine and a really bad Chinese meal,' I said.

'Point taken. But you ought to do aerobic stuff, not just Pilates.'

'You're right.'

'I always am.'

'And so modest, too. The trouble is, Afzal, that like you I seem to work all hours God made – and a few He intended for rest. I do Pilates because it's good for me, just like root canal work, but it never gives me an adrenalin rush or a surge of those hormones that are supposed to make you feel happy—'

'Endorphins,' he supplied helpfully, though it had been on the tip of my tongue. 'Running?'

'It's one thing running just for pleasure, but another running to get home, with someone in a big car known to be after me. Not to mention the guys who gave me a bruise on my head the size of a hen's egg simply for rescuing someone's floral tribute.'

'Heard about that. You're over it now?'

'The bang on the bonce or the fear of a bigger, better bang?'

'OK. So no running, solo at least. Hang on, this must be the place. Parson's Pride. Hell's bells – a bloody entry-phone.' Leaving the driver's door ajar, he stomped off to ask for admission.

I suppose the security was no tighter than ours, but the property was altogether grander, at least judging by the high walls and gates, which, while ornamental, were topped and tailed by serious spikes. The impressive gate posts were home to cameras less discreet than ours – an obvious deterrent. I wasn't keen on the way they were swivelling in my direction, and, pulling my hoodie top over as much of my face as it would cover, I tipped the seat back, so all they'd catch was an anonymous tummy supporting a cardboard box full of their supper.

'What the hell are you up to?' Afzal demanded, dragging open my door. He didn't wait for a reply. 'I hope the snotty buggers know what they're doing. They want me to leave this by the gates for them to collect,' he added, as he relieved me of the box. 'Paranoid or what?' It wasn't clear whether he meant his clients or me.

Back in motion again, with his passenger in a more conventional position, Afzal said, 'I've been thinking. Do you play badminton? Because there's a group of us play every week and we're going to be one down on Thursday. Only you'd have to dress ultra-decent: one's a bit keen on covering arms and legs. Blokes too.'

'Not for anyone would I play in a burqa. And to be honest, I'd be a rubbish partner. I played a couple of times at school. Nothing since. Well, can you imagine it appealing to Griff?' On the other hand, he'd adore watching four sweaty young men leaping around, but Afzal preferred a bit of discretion where Griff's sexuality was concerned. 'He prefers Test cricket,' I added.

'Quite right too. Hey, you ever played cricket yourself? No? Well, my club's recruiting for a women's team and Fozia would love to go along for a trial, but she won't go on her own. Would you do her a favour and go with her? Trackie and trainers are all you'll need.'

'It's autumn, Afzal, football weather.'

'Thinking ahead. You can't just say, "Hey, it's April and we need a team next week." You need to train people, get them bonding. Play some indoor cricket. How about that?'

If it was good enough for Fozia, a woman with a first-class degree in modern languages and no sign of a job other than stacking shelves at Maidstone Sainsbury's, it was good enough for me.

'Ball skills, aerobics and some light weight-training. Meant to be fun.'

'Get Fozia to tell me the time and place and I'll be there,' I promised. 'Here we are, Afzal – thanks ever so much.'

Suddenly he was mimicking a bodyguard, talking to his wristwatch and holding an imaginary gun at the ready. 'OK, sister – coast's clear!'

We might have fallen about laughing, but deep down I knew we were both deadly serious. He made a show of waiting until I had let myself in and given him a cheery thumbs up.

EIGHTEEN

'So you see,' I told Griff as we walked briskly down to Dodie's the following morning, 'the evening wasn't a total disaster. I can't imagine I'll be any better at cricket than I am at dancing, but Afzal's such a good mate it'll be nice to help his sister out. Hang on!' I pulled him bodily into the delicatessen. 'Merc alert!' I hissed. 'Look interested in the charcuterie.'

He needed no second invitation, then browsing the cheese counter and finally the quiche and pie area, accumulating items as he went and putting them in a basket I'd picked up and put into his hand without his even realizing it.

It transpired, when we finally arrived at Dodie's, that from the start he'd intended some of his haul for her. I checked the most recent hidden camera footage, discreetly fast-forwarding the session with Pa: nothing untoward. I was ready to leave when the wheelchair was delivered.

'My transport of delight!' she chortled. 'If only it came with a selection of party balloons!'

The sun was shining. With no rugby player in sight, what could I do but offer to push? And blow up the balloons we found at the post office, tying them haphazardly to the chair and to the teddy's paws? It was probably the most festive mile I've ever travelled. The only problem was that this time, when a black Mercedes hove into view, there was no way we would escape the driver's notice.

At least I could get his number – but just as he whizzed past, a balloon bobbed up and obscured the expensive car.

It was time to tell Harvey his vase was ready for collection and prepare all the paperwork I'd told Honey and Laura about: Griff's job. He'd got me into this mess, and it was only fair he deal with some of the aftermath. He agreed with surprising, possibly suspicious, docility.

What was going on in that head of his? Had he spotted another man he considered might suit me? Who on earth might it be? Then I remembered he'd seen me getting out of Afzal's van, and put two and two together to make not just five but five hundred. Oh, Griff! Afzal might have a nice strong Birmingham accent, and he might so far have resisted an arranged marriage, but at heart he was a good Muslim. In any case there were times when a good mate was better than a boyfriend.

As it happened, Griff had forgotten to tell me that there was a PCC meeting that evening, complete with take and share supper, hence the flans. There was nothing special or urgent on the agenda, he explained, so they were simply going to enjoy each other's company for a change without having to argue about tight budgets. Foolishly I said I'd probably nip down to Afzal's for something wicked. He pulled a face: he might hope for romance in that quarter, but he didn't like leaving me in the house alone, and the thought of my actually venturing out solo appalled him. At night, too! Usually I'd have laughed at his fears; this time I'm ashamed to say that I didn't. However, I was stubborn enough to stick to my guns, so he made me promise that I'd keep my mobile with me all the time. And take the big torch. And wear trainers in case I needed to run for my life. Oh, and if in doubt I should head straight for the rectory, where help would be on hand in the form of a dozen hard-praying pensioners.

Yes, Griff. Three bags full, Griff.

But, guess what, I kept my promise. I actually took myself for a jog, with cricket and general fitness in mind. I'd end up having a curry, no doubt about that, but I'd carry that – it had better be one that didn't come with a runny sauce – in my lightweight rucksack so I could still take to my heels if necessary. And my phone was tucked into my pocket, within easy reach.

Deciding to jog is far better than having to, and I enjoyed padding through the quiet streets, waving to people I knew indulging in an early evening visit to Londis or the chip shop. Mostly I had the place to myself, except for a truck carrying scaffolding; I only registered that because I heard of someone getting killed when a rogue pole slipped from a moving lorry through their windscreen, a form of death that terrifies me. The rest of the circuit was uneventful, and the queue at Afzal's long enough to suggest good business, but quick moving enough to show how efficient the whole team was. Their special jhinga bhindi, some dhal and a couple of chapattis stowed in my rucksack, I set off again, surprised by noises in the otherwise almost silent village: clanks; raised voices; someone being busy.

Nosy? Of course I was. And intrigued. I jogged off in the direction of the noise, fetching up by the church.

I wasn't the only one. Also heading that way was the village pharmacist, Philip Russell, obviously called Phil the Pill, though not necessarily to his face. He was having his nightly tussle with Angus, a dog that knew his own mind, especially when the mind was set on checking each and every one of its canine message boards. Angus was always eager to make new human friends, too, and was yapping excitedly at the prospect of being introduced to, and fussed by, four large men. The lorry I'd seen earlier was parked, and someone had already propped up an official-looking board warning of scaffolding work. Two hard-hatted men sporting heavy industrial glasses unloaded the lorry. Two more, also sporting protective eye and head gear, were already erecting the poles, not needing to use the huge lights still left on the truck because the floodlights the PCC had paid so much to install to show off the fine early Norman building were as good as daylight – though more controversial, given they had a decided orange tinge and some villagers considered them inappropriate. For some reason the two men unloading had taken exception to both Phil and Angus: one was squaring up to Phil, and Angus was now barking, not yapping. Should I intervene? Something told me a young woman turning up would just make matters worse. But I had my phone handy and, still out of their immediate line of vision, snapped away: the truck; each of the workmen; Phil winding in Angus's extendable lead. But now a second thug was approaching Phil. Thug! I never used such middle-aged, middle-class language: what was I turning into? Before I could beat myself up too much, however, I felt a frisson of personal fear. Underneath all his entirely regulation camouflage, I knew that guy from somewhere. No idea where. But I knew he was dangerous, and that I had to do something a bit more positive than simply taking snaps for evidence if Phil was attacked.

'Yoo, hoo!' How middle-aged and middle-class was that? 'Yoo, hoo! Phil! I've been hoping I'd run into you! About that ointment you gave me – oh, I'm so sorry,' I fluttered, 'I didn't realize . . . Hello, Angus. No, this isn't for you. I don't think dogs are supposed to like curry, are they?' I fussed him enthusiastically, quite forgetting I really didn't like dogs.

Phil turned his attention to me and the men retreated. Tucking my arm into Phil's – I'm not sure which of us was the more surprised – I eased him back up the street until we were well clear of the church.

Disentangling myself from him and Angus, I asked quietly, 'Did you know they were going to have the church repaired?'

'It's only five minutes since they had to point the porch, isn't it? So why not do that and this at the same time?'

'Quite.'

'Those guys didn't like me very much. Or perhaps they just didn't like being watched.'

'They didn't look the shy and retiring sort.'

He gave an amused snort. 'They're doing a foreigner, maybe – moonlighting.' He didn't sound at all convinced, however. In fact, he gathered Angus into his arms, slipping some sort of doggy treat into his mouth so he couldn't bark any more.

'Surely the church wouldn't employ dodgy builders . . . There's a PCC meeting tonight. I'll see what they know about it.' I produced my phone again, praying that Griff hadn't switched his off. He had. The call went to voicemail. So did my attempts to reach Moira and Tony. It must be some beano they were having. Under my breath I used all sorts of unclerical language. But a text chirruped its way in. Griff. Was I OK? No, I bloody wasn't! *Is church due for repairs? Scaffolding being erected NOW!* I texted, never using any text-speak abbreviations to Griff, who'd secretly fulminate about the odd missing verb or whatever even as he checked with his fellow PCC members.

His answer was clear enough. *No.* Then he sent another. *We're all on our way to the church.*

Much as I relished the idea of a silver battalion of Bible-wielding pensioners, a confrontation between them and these four hulking men might not end well. Phil agreed.

I texted them back, saying not to be so foolish, and then dialled 999. The call-handler was inclined to be sniffy, wanting to know exactly why we considered the after-dark activities of four men on a church not requiring their presence was suspicious. After a while, however, she conceded that one of their community support officers might call round in due course.

'DCI Freya Webb,' I insisted, name-dropping shamelessly, 'would want action now. Preferably with back-up. These men might well be armed. OK? Call made at 19.54 hours,' I added strategically.

Clearly trying not to laugh, Phil tugged my sleeve, then pointed at the street. I emerged gingerly. A phalanx of Volvos and Honda Jazzes, plus a couple of other reliable makes, was coming down the street at a strict thirty. It was probably silly to expect them to park neatly, given their usual haphazard Sunday morning attempts, but they did their reasonable best, with one man having the foresight to try to box in the truck, despite driving the smallest vehicle of the convoy.

Pensioner power looked really impressive, I had to admit. But they were no match for the four big men, two of whom piled into their truck, reversing hard enough to knock the little Micra clean out of the way. The other two rushed at another car, tearing the occupants out and completing their carjack by taking off the wing of the treasurer's Fiesta.

I fought my way over to Griff, who assured me that he was fine so long as I was. We looked on as Phil, whom everyone knew, of course, managed to get some sort of order – no easy task, given the anger and hysteria the previous two minutes had generated. With considerable aplomb, he herded everyone, including Griff, to his shop, where, he said, there was plenty of paper for people to start writing down their descriptions of the miscreants, and an account of what had happened. If and when the police ever arrived, the victims' preparation should oil the wheels of justice. I caught him eying with concern the couple yanked from their car: they might not need much in the way of first aid – their visible injuries were minor – but who knew better than Phil any underlying health problems requiring prompt medication?

Thinking he'd manage better without me, I gestured that I'd stay where I was, and tapped my mobile: I would get back to the police. He looked reluctant to leave me there, but I waved him away to tend his potential patients.

By chance I got through to the same despatcher. Coolly she assured me that a community support officer had been detailed to come over. Cooler still, I suggested that she send over a team to deal with attempted kidnap (not really, to be honest: they only wanted the car, not the occupants), car theft and criminal damage. And it would help me enormously when I made my official complaint if I could have her name. I didn't get it.

As I ended the call, I started to beat myself up for not doing more to deter either the bloody thieves or to stop the PCC crusade. Not literally beat up: my self-harming ways were under control these days. Weren't they?

Almost. What if the police thought the coincidence of my being around during no fewer than three thefts from church property was suspicious? I was beginning to think it odd myself. My hand was raised to slap my face, was already moving, when it was firmly grabbed from behind.

'None of that, Lina,' Afzal declared. 'I know about self-harm. Fozia cut herself a few times. And I know hitting's not the same as using a blade, but a black eye's not a good look, you know. Not cool.' He dropped my hand. 'The other thing is, you were so busy hating yourself for whatever it was, that anyone could have come up and beaten you up properly. Whatever.' He looked around appreciatively. 'It wasn't you that smashed up that lot, was it?' He slipped off his jacket and slung it over my shoulders. 'Just popped out with a local delivery,' he added, checking his watch: his kindness was costing him business.

I gave a very speedy account of why I was there. 'Talk about lightning striking twice,' I concluded. 'I'd think I was involved if I were the police. Talk of the devil, here they are.'

'Here she is,' Afzal corrected me with a grim laugh. 'I think she might find she's out of her depth, don't you?'

'I think I might be, too,' I said. 'Phil the Pill was here when it all kicked off. I think he'd best be in charge, given the circumstances.' No point in mentioning my aversion to getting too deeply involved this time.

'You handing over to an alpha male? That's a first, Lina!'

I shrugged off his jacket and stuck out my tongue. 'Your fault for treating me like a lady.'

At this point the police car pulled over and parked, in a remarkably leisurely fashion. From it emerged a woman younger and even smaller than me, the woman I'd seen being harangued at Dodie's. Clearly she didn't recall me. Putting on her hat and carefully locking the car behind her, she introduced herself as Police Community Support Officer Ann Draper. We returned the compliment before gesturing at the chaos around us.

'I had a report of minor vandalism,' she said faintly, managing not to gasp, but certainly going as pale as the orange lights permitted.

'Uh, uh. Wrong incident. Or right incident, but wrong information. The guy you need to speak to – who witnessed everything – is in the chemist's shop at the moment, keeping an eye on the victims and the witnesses. I'm just here to make sure the guys who did that' – I gestured at the cars with my mobile – 'don't return. I'm to call for back-up,' I added, when she stared in horror. 'As you might want to. Goodness knows what the woman who took my call thought she was doing.' Perhaps I should boost her ego a bit by pretending to ask for advice. 'Would you like us to make our way to the pharmacy or stay with you here?'

Her terrified eyes answered for her. We stayed.

Once we could all hear the police sirens getting closer and knew that poor PCSO Draper would soon have friends to lean on, Afzal took it on himself to escort me up to the pharmacy, crammed to the gunwales, of course, with Griff's PCC friends. With a horrified shudder at the sight of all the flat heels and elasticated waistbands, he pushed me gently inside and left me to it, telling me he'd be back at work if I needed him.

Everyone was too bound up in their own narrative to notice my late arrival. Not surprisingly, all the talk was of the brazen cheek of the would-be thieves. While the more urban members of the PCC blamed TV for putting ideas into the minds of those with criminal tendencies, a couple with UKIP tendencies were quick to point the finger at anyone from Eastern Europe. A couple of genuinely rural folk were clear that the police should look no further than a travellers' site near Ashford; there was gleeful talk of cars being stolen, stripped and torched right outside the gates, in a nose-thumbing gesture to police, who only ever went there mob-handed. A third man reported that all his corrugated-iron buildings had simply disappeared in the middle of the night. The only thing that all these theories had in common was a clear, loudly expressed belief that the police should be doing a lot more and doing it now.

Without his white pharmacist's top, Phil was much more recognizable as a distinct human being, and one with a smile that ranged from amused to exasperated. He also smelt nice – a good male perfume, not at all pharmaceutical.

'Why not get them to go back to the rectory where they were having their meeting?' I asked. 'It's close enough to walk, since the police would probably want the cars left where they are until they've taken lots of photos and stuff, and there'd be room for everyone there. Where's Angus, by the way?'

'Having the time of his life.' He nodded in the direction of one of the chairs in the window. Angus was occupying a lap, the owner of which was stroking him rhythmically and occasionally feeding him with doggy treats. 'It does the patient good as well – it reduces their blood pressure. But it may well go up again – the sheriff and his posse are coming into town.' He suddenly switched to John Wayne posture, reaching for his six-shooter. No one else saw. I had to turn away to stop laughing.

The street echoed with sirens and pulsated with blue light. Soon the shop door beeped and the community support officer inched her petite way inside, asking thinly and vainly for order.

Phil clapped his hands for silence – and got it. 'Why don't we all go to the rectory to talk?'

There was a lot of rhubarbing. Eventually I caught Griff's

eye. He led the way with a wonderful sashay. Out we tripped in his wake, Angus refusing to be parted from his new best friend, though he danced back to me to check I'd remembered my now decidedly aromatic rucksack. One of the plastic containers must have leaked.

'Venal little bugger,' Phil observed, setting his alarm and locking up. 'Tell you what, when the police have finished talking to us all, we could get some fresh supplies of curry and have them with a beer at mine. It strikes me we could both do with a bit of company our own age after a whole evening of wrinklies.'

Our own age? Not that I'd given it much thought but I'd always imagined him being on the verge of middle age. The white coat, no doubt. In fact, he was probably in his thirties, and while not quite as tall and broad-shouldered as Afzal, quietly attractive in an understated way – blue eyes, fairish hair and skin prone, I would imagine, to sunburn. In fact, I was surprised that Griff, who considered himself a bit of a connoisseur, hadn't remarked on his looks. During working hours, of course, he'd be corralled in his dispensary; customers were dealt with by a team of pleasant motherly women, the sort who'd win prizes for chutney at the WI show.

As one, he and I headed not to the rectory but to the church, where, in true alpha male tradition, Phil headed for the tallest policeman he could find. On the other hand, I could see the familiar face of Freya Webb. Cutting short her conversation with another female officer, also in standard bright-wear, she headed my way.

'You called this in, I gather. And mentioned me by name.' She didn't sound delighted. Why should she? The first look at a crime scene like this was surely taken by someone well below her rank. And she had a husband and child at home.

'Yep. At the time I told the despatcher you'd want more than the poor solitary little community support officer we got. When you've got time, you might want to disembowel her – the despatcher, I mean. We were put at risk and you missed a collar.' I treated her to a succinct account of what she called the incident and I'd have called a crime. 'All the church committee are safe at the rectory,' I concluded. 'I'm on my way there now, but I wanted to put whoever was in charge in the picture. You, then.' I grinned. 'Speaking of which, I've got a load of pics on my mobile. Are you still on your old number? I'll send them through.'

'Thanks. Whatever did we do before clever little things like this?' She peered over my shoulder at my screen as I forwarded them. 'Now, despite all the workmen's gear, that face looks familiar. And that . . . Hell's bells, what the fuck's going on here?' She must be moved: since her marriage to Tim, a rector, she had cut back on her swearing. 'Pensioner power or what? You should have stopped them, though,' she added, looking at me under her brows.

'Stopped the robbers or the silver army? Both impossible, I'd have thought,' Phil said, over my shoulder, making me jump.

I'd forgotten all about him. I'd better remember fast, and introduce them carefully. Freya's expression was hard to read. She knew I was officially with Carwyn, and would disapprove violently if she smelt any suggestion of two-timing. At least, I thought so. She'd referred to Carwyn more than once as a darker horse than most, and never made any girlie jokes about us. But then, Freya didn't do girlie any more than I did.

Mercifully Phil showed no surprise when he learned she was the Detective Chief Inspector in charge, merely saying he'd been walking his dog and encountered the men in question, and that though we were barely acquainted I'd helped him out of a sticky situation. 'Though it did get a great deal stickier when the PCC members turned up,' he conceded.

'OK, we'll get a team up to the rectory to take statements – is Daniel still the priest in charge? Nice man. Almost as overworked as Robin, though it's not as bad here as in Daniel's last parish – he used to call it the Lions' Den.' She'd still not curbed her dangerous tendency to gossip; I was sure Daniel wouldn't like that to get back to his bishop. 'What about you two? Will you be joining the oldies?'

'I've got to go up there to retrieve my dog,' Phil said. Then he added, 'But neither of us has eaten – poor Lina's Indian's been round the block a bit now.' He jerked a thumb at my

now quite pungent rucksack. 'I thought we could get a replace-
ment and eat at mine – Tithebarn Cottage. OK?' Freya's nod
was apparently bored as she wrote it down. She checked her
watch, despite the large and clear church clock only metres
away. 'Should be with you by ten latest, OK? See you then.'

'You'll keep an eye on Griff, won't you, Freya? I don't
want him worrying more than he has to after all this stress.'

'Stress!' Freya crowed. 'That old bugger will think it's a
bit of pleasurable excitement laid on especially for him.'

NINETEEN

Afzal's response to seeing me a second time, and now in Phil's company, was what you might call polite deadpan. His smile and demeanour were totally professional – not so much as a raised eyebrow or a discreet wink in my direction as he handed over our meal. Phil had left Angus outside, of course, hitched to a convenient railing and presumably too stuffed with treats to object to being abandoned. To my mind, the poor thing now walked with a decided roll. Certainly, when we arrived at Tithebarn Cottage, all he wanted was to collapse in his basket.

Phil's place was about the same age as ours, but stripped down and decorated with twenty-first century minimalism. The effect was starkly interesting, and set off quite beautifully a cleverly lit semi-abstract oil painting over the fireplace: a brave splash of reds and purples in the otherwise monochrome surroundings.

Griff would have killed for the kitchen, all good lines and elegance, with cupboards concealing absolutely everything – no friendly clutter of teapot and caddy near the kettle for Phil. He produced modern Danish china and cutlery, which he laid on the sleek kitchen table.

'You don't think it's all a bit much?' he asked. 'I came into a bit of money just before I bought the shop. I was so busy at work I let an interior decorator loose. It was very Fifties – needed bringing up to date, but perhaps not this much . . .'

'I love it,' I said simply, though I hoped the table top was stain-proof. 'It reminds me a bit of my workroom – a place for everything and everything, presumably, in its place.'

While we ate, we chatted about our jobs, and he talked about his education. He had the same sort of background as Spencer, but at least I recognized the university he named because other people I knew and got on with had been there. Politely I asked him why he'd chosen pharmacy – because he liked making people better without having to deal with blood, apparently.

'And you're good at making people better, of course,' he said with a charming smile.

I don't normally like charm, but the observation intrigued me. 'I usually mend pots,' I parried, 'not people.'

'But you got Mr Tripp through that bypass op. And now you're keeping an eye on Lady Boulton,' he said.

'Lady Boulton?' But of course, if she was one of Pa's intimates, as it were, not to mention being an ambassador's wife, she might well have had a title. 'Ah, Dodie. She's a friend of my father's,' I said, rather foolishly, possibly as a result of the lager he'd pressed on me. I really did not want to trade on that connection. 'Do you think,' I asked, glad to have the chance to talk to a health professional about her, 'that giving her a more stimulating life might make her better?'

'It should slow down her inevitable decline,' he said slowly. 'She's no spring chicken, but you and your balloons have given her something to live for, haven't they? They made my day, I can tell you. I could hardly drive for laughing.'

Had he been the Mercedes driver? I could hardly ask him, could I? Come on, Lina, you can't imagine that he was the vicious man in shades who'd parked his Mercedes outside the shop. All the same . . .

Never had a vigorously rung doorbell been more welcome.

I would have put money on Freya joining us at the table and dipping bits of naan bread into any open container, even if it meant risking spicy drips on the table.

'We've found the stolen Jazz,' she said, savouring a piece of chicken Dilshan, named in honour of Afzal's cricketing hero. 'Hmm, interesting texture, that. And it's being checked for DNA. The Barkers – Esme and Harry, right? – are all right, thanks to your ministrations, I suspect, Mr Russell? No, it's Doctor Russell, isn't it?'

'No blood,' he said, in a quick aside to me. 'Actually, I'm not that sort of doctor, DCI Webb: it's a post-grad qualification in the side-effects of analgesics. Any idea what the men were after?'

'I'm sure we can ask them that when we catch them,' she

said, not quite pleasantly. 'Lead, I suppose, though the PCC people I've spoken to assured me it's been treated with smart water and should be hard to sell on.'

'Nothing inside the church itself?' he pressed.

'Why erect scaffolding if all you want to do is break in?' she countered.

'To get through the roof straight into the nave,' I said slowly. 'Or the Lady Chapel? That's the oldest part of the church.' To my shame, I'd never really looked at it in detail, because it was always swarming with worshippers when I was there. 'After all, people would notice if men took a sledgehammer to the door – I should imagine the porch would amplify the sound nicely. But if you look as though you might be doing something official, which is what their warning signs and protective gear suggest, you could spend as long as you wanted inside. You could remove a lot if you covered the scaffolding with tarpaulin and also had a tarpaulin-covered skip.'

Halfway through a mouthful of Muralithan special fish curry, raising her eyebrows and blinking at the heat, Freya said, 'You're starting to think like a criminal, Lina – you must be spending too much time with your father's friends.' She reached for an unopened can of lager.

'Or with the police,' I said cheerfully moving it away from her: after all, hoovering up food was one thing but supping alcohol on duty was another. 'Carwyn, for instance.'

'Not to mention that toad Morris,' she agreed, always ready to goad me about a policeman ex of mine. OK, who interviewed you when you'd had that bang on the head in Dockinge? Young Knowles, wasn't it?'

'Yes. And he talked to Mary when she . . . when she was threatened,' I concluded tamely.

Freya looked at me sharply, as if filling in the dots I'd left hanging in mid-air. 'I'll rope him in to the investigation if it gets that far – see if he's got any ideas.'

Phil spoke before I could. 'Sorry to interrupt, DCI Webb – did you imply that you might not be continuing work on this case? People were hurt. They could have been badly injured. Cars were smashed. Surely that constitutes a crime worth investigating?'

'We deal with each incident on its merits.' She was decidedly irritated. 'We take in a number of variables – the extent of the damage, the ultimate consequences, the possibility of a successful prosecution. And,' she added, dropping the official tone, 'we share the Major Incident Team with Essex these days. This might have to be a small-scale in-house investigation. Or it might move to Essex.'

'You might share some of it with Devon and Cornwall Police,' I pointed out. 'Or, best of all, this new national agency Carwyn was telling me about that's devoted to dealing with thefts from historic sites.' There, I'd jumped on her corns with both feet. Tough.

Phil looked from one of us to the other. 'I don't care who the hell investigates it. So long as someone takes it very seriously indeed. I don't take kindly to being told to eff off when I'm walking in my own village. Or to having my dog threatened. Or to seeing my patients attacked.'

'I thought you were a chemist, not a doctor.'

That's right, Freya, get him on your side. Or not.

'I don't like the thought of the church at the heart of our community being raided for whatever reason. The cheek and arrogance of those men appalls me. They may not have been working in broad daylight, but they might as well have been with those new floodlights. And had it not been for Lina's contacts with church members, they'd have got away with it. It all looked so official. Pharmacists are scientists. We're trained, like doctors, to spot patterns in symptoms. I'd say that such slickness implies practice. And practice might indicate a pattern of past activities.'

Apart from the bit about his scientific background, I'd have said the same myself.

'All I'm saying,' Freya said doggedly, 'is that though we'll do our best, there's no guarantee of success. Especially as not a single one of our witnesses could identify any of the previous offenders we have on our database – yes, we showed them a lot of mugshots, believe me. I don't blame them – none of you could have seen much of their faces under those helmets.' She reached her laptop from her bag and patted it. 'As soon as you've finished your meal, perhaps you'll find time to have a look, too.' In her situation, her fingers red with our curry sauce, I might not have allowed myself that tinge of sarcasm.

'But you yourself said some of the faces I snapped were familiar. Come on, Freya, you're as bad as me: you only recognize bad guys. You'll be able to get your techies to use some classy facial recognition system, surely?' I pushed some of my poor reheated jhinga bhindi at her. And a clean fork. Did the woman never eat except when she was with me? Or did she have a tapeworm? She carried not a single pound of excess weight.

'It's not so much us as the powers that be. The new Crime Commissioner, this ex-traffic warden or whatever he was before he got elected in the lowest ever recorded public turn-out (six per cent, was it?), is obsessed by keeping the M20 open and very little else. I know, I know, commissioners aren't supposed to influence the day-to-day running of the force, but they can skew budgets. Whoever thought they were a good idea? Waste of money – think of their salaries and their expenses!' Some of her diatribe was less audible than the rest: she was grazing as she let off steam.

Eventually Phil passed her a napkin and started to clear the detritus. Should I offer to help? I'd no idea where he'd want to store stuff or throw it away. So probably not.

'Faces?' I prompted her.

Looking wistfully at half a naan bread disappearing into a recycling bucket, she produced her computer. Soon Phil, so close I could feel his breath on my ear, and I were looking at her gallery. Neither of us could positively point at anyone, and, worse, we picked out quite different faces.

'What about your clever computer programs – won't they help? Match your images with the images I sent you?' I tapped my phone. 'While we wait for your technical bods, maybe I should send these pics direct to Sergeant Pat Henchard and see if they prompt a response in her?' It was gross interference and I thought for a moment she'd tell me so. But they were on my phone and I could, of course, do as I liked with them. So I did.

She might have been working out how to bollock me without offending Phil. In fact, when she eventually spoke, she said ultra-casually, 'I've actually got a couple more things to ask Griff. Can I give you a ride?'

Thank you for putting me in a difficult situation. I made a show of looking at my watch. It was, by village standards, quite late. 'Griff's probably imagining those thugs lurking in every doorway to jump on me and beat me up.' In other words, I'd better cut the evening short. I smiled at Phil. 'That food was a brilliant idea. I feel much better now. Next time at our cottage; Griff actually cooks his own from scratch, though he's best with Thai.' In other words, not a date – a family meal.

'I love Thai.'

We exchanged a double cheek-to-cheek air kiss, and I followed Freya out into the dark street: the few streetlights we had went off at eleven prompt, by order of some puritan councillor, so I should have been more grateful than I was for her offer.

She drove in silence, but didn't head to the cottage.

'The scene of crime team should have finished by now, so how about a quick look at what the scrotes might have been after?'

'Wouldn't one of the churchwardens be a better guide than me?'

'They'll tell me what's written in their insurance policy. I want a quick shuftie myself. And you know about such things, after all. Yes, I've borrowed a key.'

Which all sounded a bit premeditated on her part.

'OK. I'll just text Griff and let him know what I'm doing.'

'I told him earlier.'

I expected to have to don some of the gear worn by forensic scientists, but Freya didn't bother; as she pointed out, flicking on all the lights so the church looked ready for midnight Communion, the would-be thieves hadn't actually penetrated the place. Keeping our footsteps quiet, we made a mini-pilgrimage round the church, with me quietly pointing out the obvious highlights: the huge brass lectern; the bishop's throne.

'Is that all? Come on, what else could the thieves have laid their evil claws on if they'd got in?' She grabbed a copy of the visitors' information sheet and thrust one at me.

I blinked. It was written in a style so archaic I'd be surprised if anyone got beyond the first paragraph.

'Bas relief panels?' she asked. 'What and where are they?'

'Those sort of sculptures behind the altar. Got a torch?'

The carved wood panels behind the altar were so dirty and ill-lit it was hard to tell what they depicted. The Seven Deadly Sins, according to the sheet. The beam picked out what I thought must be gluttony and possibly sloth.

'Do you know what the other sins are?' I asked, off-hand. She was a vicar's wife, after all.

'Apart from lust? Not a clue. And the carvings themselves don't exactly enlighten me. But I take it they're worth a bob or two?'

'To a collector, maybe. This sheet says they're Dutch or German. No dates given.'

She reread her copy. 'What a rubbish leaflet. Turgid and uninformative. OK, the Lady Chapel: what's in there?' She led the way, pointing at heavy mustard-coloured velvet curtains behind the altar. 'And what are those hiding?'

I pulled them back to reveal a hideous set of tiles listing the Ten Commandments, in case a previous generation had had a mental lapse like mine with the Sins. 'Any thieves would be welcome to them,' I suggested.

She threw her head back and laughed. 'Straight from a High Victorian public loo! My God, no wonder they keep them under wraps.' Turning round, she pointed. 'What about that picture? The Mother and Child – a bit High Church for this place. Bells and smells next. Not an original, I take it?'

'A Murillo in Bredeham?'

'OK, point taken. No value.' She pointed at the crude wooden and glass frames that had been fixed round some fourteenth-century memorial brasses. 'Oh, Lord, I suppose someone thought they might be strong enough to withstand crowbars. Even I'd get in there in one minute flat. Anything else?'

I led her back to the font: Norman and no doubt valuable, but granite and sturdy.

'Now, you've only got a wooden cross on the altar. Don't you have any church plate? What do you use for Communion?'

'Oh, the chalice? And the silver plates – patens?'

'Right. I'd guess they'd be in the vestry – heavens, another curtain,' she groaned as she pushed it aside. 'Not even a sturdy locked door.' She pointed accusingly at a couple of battered metal cupboards six or seven feet high, one army brown, the other RAF grey. Surplus, no doubt. 'Look, someone's labelled them, just in case the would-be thief's in a hurry: *Altar candlesticks and Crucifix. Second-best Chalice and Paten.* All in cupboards you could jemmy open in a trice, even if someone had remembered to lock them.' She tried the door. It opened. There was no need to comment. 'I assume the best silver's in the safe, such as it is. Combination? Hell's bells, anyone could open that too – well, you could.'

'I'll take that as a compliment.'

She led the way back into the nave. 'There are rich pickings here, all right. Multiply this by other old churches in the area. In the county. Heavens, in the whole country.'

It was as if someone laid a cold hand on me. 'What if the thieves come back?'

'Some of my colleagues have the theory that lightning doesn't strike twice – that the thieves will have been put off and try somewhere else. I don't share it,' she added.

'Hidden cameras are the obvious answer, aren't they? Your colleague DS Hunt had me fix one in the room of someone she suspects is being robbed by her carers. Before you ask, it was because you techies were too busy, and I could sort it in the shake of a lamb's tail.'

She looked around speculatively. 'There are plenty of places to hide one . . . Yes, why not? You want me to get the camera and you'll do the biz?'

'Absolutely . . . Hang on, aren't we about to commit a mortal sin? Aren't you supposed to get someone's permission to put things in churches? The vicar's?'

She sat down hard on a pew. 'Not the vicar's. Absolutely not. He's just a paid serf. I think it's the churchwardens'. And they can't do it on their own if it involves the fabric. The PCC – people like your Griff – have to apply for permission of the diocese, something called a faculty. And damned time-consuming it is. Shit. Sorry, God.' She covered her face with her hands, surfacing as she ran her fingers back through her

hair. 'I'll have to get our crime prevention people to advise
the PCC here and the diocese as a whole in the strongest
possible terms to install CCTV and everything else where it
hasn't been done already.'

'Which will all take time and money,' I said delicately. 'Do
the police actually need all this permission? I've read about
cases where listening devices were planted in suspects' homes
– I bet no one knocked on the door and asked them.'

'That's done on the authority of someone much higher up
in the pecking order than I am – and it's with a specific target.
I don't think generally keeping an eye on a church that hasn't
even asked for it, let alone given permission, would work, do
you?'

'But if you happened to have a little gizmo just lying on
your desk and I just happened to pick it up when I came to
see you about something . . .'

'We'd need a plausible something.'

'Maybe your computer had a glitch. No, Phil knows it
didn't.'

She didn't even try to stifle a yawn.

'Lord, look at the time,' I said. 'Come on, we'll think of
something.'

'I hope so. And I've got an important meeting tomorrow
I've still got to prepare for . . .'

It looked as if she hardly had the energy to lock up and
walk to her car.

'If only we had a spare bed at the cottage I could offer you,'
I said. 'Seat belt, Freya.'

'Shit!' She set the car in motion. 'This camera – I suppose
you wouldn't have time tomorrow?'

'As it happens, I would.' Tomorrow was the day Harvey
was coming in person to collect his vase. Griff assumed he'd
arrive in the middle of the day, having driven up from Devon
in the morning. I suspect that was exactly what Harvey wanted
me to think, and that he'd turn up soon after nine, having
stayed overnight somewhere close. 'I could come over to
Maidstone, if that'd help.'

'Are you sure? Really sure? I know how many hours you
to put in too . . . Thanks. About eleven?'

As she stopped the car in front of our cottage, I asked a question that had been nagging away at the back of my mind. 'Why were you so cagey with Phil?'

'In a case like this it pays to be cagey with everyone. Me *and* you, Lina.'

I couldn't argue with the first half of her sentence. Once she'd sounded off about me and nearly got me killed when the wrong person overheard her complaints. So I nodded. 'Love to Robin and Imogen,' I said, closing the car door quietly to avoid waking the neighbours.

TWENTY

I was meandering along Maidstone High Street, killing time, when who should I run into but Spencer, swinging a carrier bag from an upmarket men's shop. He looked a bit embarrassed, as if I'd caught him in something shameful, but promptly invited me for coffee. I could have said I'd just had one: I was only a couple of paces from the Moonlight, after all. But I made no objection when he fell into step with me, as I still had the small matter of Dodie's outings to float. It wasn't until I mentioned we already had a rugby player onside that he showed any interest. Then, piqued perhaps, he declared that he'd enlist the help of some lads from his club. I'd given him what he saw as the opening he'd been angling for – an invitation to pop round to the cottage to let me know how his recruitment drive was going. I was just going to ask him to text me first when my mobile warbled: Griff, telling me that Harvey had been and gone.

But what if he came back? I was glad I had to see Freya – it was just the excuse I needed not to hurry home to my workroom, to be trapped there if he did. Suddenly – and how paranoid was this? – Spencer, simply because he was a big man, acquired a value as a potential bodyguard.

What was I thinking? The only danger Harvey posed was to my heart. Despite everything, that was why my adrenaline surged, not because I was afraid of violence. And I certainly didn't want, in Griff's phrase, to lead Spencer on. Not fair to anyone.

'Sorry. That was the police – about that little incident at the church last night,' I lied, continuing, 'They want me to go and look at some mugshots.' In for a penny . . .

'Mugshots? Does that mean the men let you see their faces?' he exclaimed, in what almost sounded like irritation at the thieves' inefficiency.

'They were supposed to be workmen – that was the scam,'

I explained. 'And I suppose if a team of scaffolders turned up in balaclavas or ski masks it might have given a few clues about their real intentions.' For some reason I didn't mention all the regulation Health and Safety gear they were wearing.

He shrugged. Griff and his chattering friends would have demanded every last detail, as the meat and drink of village gossip. Spencer didn't even ask how I was involved – though if I'd been keen on someone, it would have been the first thing I'd have wanted to know. Not a man for empathy, our Spencer. And thus not a man for me, not in a thousand years.

Turning in the general direction of the police station, I started my farewells. But it seemed he was going to walk with me. Setting a spanking pace wouldn't shake him off, of course, but it would mean we didn't have much breath for conversation.

We'd just left the pedestrian area when I went flying. I was so close to a lorry that I felt its tyres lift my hair – or it might have been fright. But I didn't end up under its wheels – firm hands on either side grabbed me and yanked me back on to the kerb. Either side? To my right was Spencer. And still holding my left arm hard above the elbow was a complete stranger, a woman in her sixties, I'd suppose. Right now she was staring at my feet.

'It's not as though you were wearing silly shoes,' she declared. 'And there's nothing wrong with the pavement. What on earth were you doing?'

'Can't hold her drink,' Spencer said, with what was meant to be a smile but looked like a smirk. 'Last night's booze too,' he added, obviously enjoying the woman's shocked expression.

'Ignore him,' I said crisply. 'He thinks it's the first of April. Thank you so much for saving me – I hope you didn't hurt yourself in the process?' On the weirdest of impulses I flipped her one of the business cards I always keep in a side pouch of my bag. 'Just to say thank you: if ever you're Bredeham way, I promise you a nice discount on anything you might wish to buy.'

'Antiques? China?' she read, holding the card at arm's length. 'Well, I love my china. I may take you up on that.'

'Please do. Without you I might have been as flat as that card – and a good deal messier.' We shared a laugh I didn't quite feel. How had I ended up in such danger?

We said our farewells. I added one to Spencer, who said he thought he deserved a bit more than a business card for his part in my rescue.

'Not on the edge of a busy road you don't,' I declared. 'I'd best be off – it wouldn't do to keep the police waiting, would it? Cheers!'

As I'd expected, Freya was at her desk, up to her elbows in files when I was escorted to her office. 'Talk about a worka-holic,' I greeted her.

'Takes one to know one,' she retorted. 'Take a pew. OK, what do you know about Philip Russell? Phil the Pill, they call him – right?'

'Right. And I know zilch apart from his drug-dispensing activities. He handled the situation well last night. Afzal considers him an alpha male but doesn't – or should that be *and* doesn't – like him. Male hackles rising. But he served us a wonderful meal, didn't he?'

She ignored my little jibe.

'And Phil spotted a mistake the GP had made in a prescrip-tion when Griff was getting over his bypass, so in theory we both approve of him.'

She nodded without enthusiasm. 'All the same, I didn't come along last night by accident. I blew the date deliberately. I didn't tell you afterwards because I shouldn't be telling you at all. Only Robin thought you ought to know. Russell's got a conviction for assaulting some driver after an accident.'

'Road rage? Bloody hell!' Not being married to a clergyman gave me a certain licence, after all. A woman who self-harmed; a man who'd harmed others. Not a good combination at all. 'Thanks. How long ago, as a matter of interest?'

'Nine years. He pleaded guilty to common assault, escaped prison by the skin of his teeth because he'd got a pristine record and he'd already signed up to an anger management course. He paid a whopping fine. Nothing since, not even a parking ticket, before you ask. Absolutely no record for domestic violence, to be fair, or any other crimes against the person. But . . .' she shrugged.

My voice rose in an embarrassing squeak. 'Domestic violence? Has he had a partner? He didn't mention one. Nor, to be fair,' I added ruefully, 'did I happen to mention my past, of course. It wasn't that sort of confessional evening.'

She nodded sagely. 'Much too early in the relationship. Have you chewed him over with Griff yet?'

'He was already snoring when I got home last night. And I left early this morning to avoid Harvey Sanditon.' To my horror, I burst into tears. I don't do tears, not even wet sniffles. But they poured down my face. 'I'm sorry,' I managed, as she thrust wads of tissues at me. 'I nearly fell under a lorry earlier and it seems to have rattled me a bit.'

'I find this helps.' She put half a four-finger KitKat in my hand. She added, through her half, 'I thought your Harvey was a perfect gent.'

'A perfect *married* gent. But there was a problem . . .' I embarked on a stuttering and hiccupping account of the Torquay evening.

'Yes, I'd call that a problem,' she said, when I finished. 'I'm surprised you agreed to mend it for him after that, verbal contract or no verbal contract. Let him sue, I'd have said. And for all it's a nice vase, surely someone else could have stuck it back together. No? You're *that* good?'

I murmured a couple of museums I did work for.

'Wow. I never realized . . . Well, this Harvey bastard ought to have been on his expensive knees begging you. Mind you,' she continued with a cackle, 'at his age, he might have had difficulty getting up again! Now, these here guys you interrupted last night. For all his history, I think it was a good job you had Phil with you last night. Those photos of yours show blokes remarkably similar to e-fit images we've put together from witness accounts of other incidents, as it happens, even if your old dears weren't much help. And yes, I've asked our techies to virtually remove things like spectacles and goggles and to liaise with Devon and Cornwall techies to see if we share the same villains. With churches in mind, I don't suppose you've got any memories at all of the guy who socked you down in Dockinge? I just want to put everything together for the national team so we don't look too much like country bumpkins. Yes, I absolutely think there's enough to suggest that our friends last night might be part of a much bigger picture. It's a shame: I'd have liked to deal with it in-house, but as I said I simply don't have the resources. I'm asking that Conrad Knowles of yours to liaise between them and our victims. He's due a bit of a career boost, I gather.'

'Have you talked to him yet about the assault on me? And the one on Mary?' Something else she didn't know about, obviously.

When I'd given an abbreviated account, she sighed. 'The trouble is, I'm so immersed in budgets I only see people like Knowles in passing. I'm a bloody pen-pusher, not a cop these days. I deal with the broad picture rather than tiny brush-strokes. Which is why coming out last night was a bit of a treat, in a weird way. But I'll make a point of seeing him. I like to know when people are attacked, even when they're just threatened. Though it really doesn't sound as if the two are connected – posh man in posh car for one, church burglars in truck for the other.'

'Quite. Except that the thugs might have a boss-man . . . Anyway, I did a bit of homework for Conrad on the Dockinge church robbery. There was an extra stall at the antiques fair there the day I was hit. No one knew anything about it, and the owners disappeared without paying for their site. I don't know if he's had time to pursue that lead. Or if he managed to check to see if Dockinge village hall has any CCTV.'

'How do you get on with him – Knowles?'

Some change of tack! I blinked hard. 'Meaning?'

'Straight question. No subtext, honest.'

'Are you asking how well he performs his duties as a detective or how I like him as a human being? There's a world of difference.' When she continued to stare, carefully blank-faced, I continued, 'For all I've not seen many results from him, which may not be his fault at all, he's a nice enough guy. He sent for Carwyn when I was in hospital. And any friend of Carwyn's is a friend of mine, surely.'

'Are you and Carwyn still an item?'

Where was that coming from? 'Until you told me about his record, I thought that was why you were so sniffy with Phil – you thought he was making a play for me, and I was betraying Carwyn's trust.'

'So are you? An item?' She produced another KitKat from her drawer, again giving me half.

A slow meditative chew gave me time to work out, not necessarily the answer I'd give her, but the one I'd give Carwyn if he ever asked. Which he wouldn't, of course. Neither of us had ever even mentioned the change. Perhaps that was why Conrad Knowles had felt awkward about any references to France – because Carwyn had let fall hints that all wasn't well. I looked up from the second KitKat finger. 'Not really. But we've not ended the relationship formally, as it were. And I've said nothing to anyone, not even Carwyn, and certainly not Conrad. So I'd rather you didn't, please.'

'I won't. Except to Robin, who'll want to pray for you.'

'Not a getting-back-together prayer, please. Now, I know you're busy, but there are another couple of names I should float. Another crime here on your patch, another connection with Devon. Again, the groundwork's been done by Devon and Cornwall Police, but a DS of yours, Fi Hunt, is aware of them and may already have more information.'

'Devon? Not your not-grandfather, Arthur Whatsit, again?'

'The same. Now, I've been thinking, Freya, that you shouldn't be putting your career on the line for something I can do myself. Our security team: they'll provide me with a camera, just as they did for that radio – no questions asked.' I didn't mention how much it would cost.

'Could you? Really? Because you know something, I've forgotten to pick one up anyway. I really wonder how long I can do this – no, forget I said anything. Please.' Her eyes filled.

Her phone rang. She took the call. 'Two minutes,' she said, which clearly applied to both the caller and me.

'Arthur Habgood,' she prompted me.

'Handling stolen goods. And it'd be great if you could get someone to run a check on Noel Pargetter—'

'The guy from *The Archers*?'

'Noel, not Nigel. Lives in Devon. Behaving very oddly to Griff. Just a check?'

She was on her feet, grabbing papers. I passed her her bag.

'I'll sign you out as I go.' She set off at a tremendous speed, one long pace to three or four of mine. 'What a crazy life. This and the parish – my God . . .'

Falling into step with her, I gasped, 'Do you ever get quality time for just the two of you? I thought not. Look, why not let me babysit Imogen and you and Robin have an evening with no police and no parish business? You could put her to bed, if you wanted, and go for a meal. Just a drink. Anything. Just be together.'

To my amazement, she stopped and gave me a hug. 'You're a good friend, Lina. We'll take you up on that offer. Thanks for filling me in on the Dockinge business too, and Devon – I'll make sure Knowles has dealt with it and passed it on to the national squad. And I'll also make sure they contact you direct. OK?'

'Nearly. Just one more thing. Your mascara's run a bit.'

I was pretty sure mine had, too.

TWENTY-ONE

Griff was very subdued when I got back, which I took to show some sort of fellow feeling about Harvey's departure from my life. So I tried to take his mind off things with a couple of questions, although they'd flummoxed Freya. 'Have the police got back to Mary about the guy who assaulted her? Not to mention threatening me, of course. That Mercedes driver . . .?'

'Just a text saying they were pursuing their enquiries and that she should report any further incidents via the 101 phoneline. For which she has to pay, of course,' he added dryly. 'No wonder crime figures have dropped if you have to pay to tell someone you've been robbed. Not that you'll ever convince me that there is less crime – all this stuff happening all around us . . .' he chuntered.

I couldn't argue. Despite, or because of, this morning's session with Freya, I was getting sick of the apparent lack of urgency from the police – and the lack of co-ordination, to be honest. But I couldn't fault the officers I'd come across: look how hard, how many hours Freya was working. And Fi had been at my service long after she should have clocked off. Both had to resort to cutting corners to get things done. Finishing my tea and newly baked biscuit, I declared, 'And now to work. I can't wait to get back into my workroom without that vase of Harvey's glaring down at me.'

Griff nodded, and produced something with a flourish. The duplicate of a receipt, signed and dated: Harvey's acceptance of the work I'd done on his vase. And an email from Harvey's insurance company – the payment for the work was already on its way into our bank account.

'Which means,' he declared, 'there's all the more reason to make sure that the repair side of the business becomes yours, nothing to do with me any more. What Paul and I have been talking about is this: I buy you out of the shop. With the capital and a loan, you should be able to buy me out of Townend Restoration. And in time I don't doubt that you'll be able to buy me out of the house, too. This is important, loved one. Very important. Talk to Paul if you don't believe me.'

'I didn't like separating the two parts of the business,' I began, 'so—'

'You might not like the idea now, Evelina, but believe me you'll thank me in years to come.'

I knew he was serious when he called me by my full name. And since Paul had regularly been in my ear, I knew it made financial sense.

'In fact,' he continued, 'Paul and one of his colleagues have already drawn up this contract. I'd like you to read it and talk about it to Paul. And sooner, rather than later, just to put my mind at rest.'

I took it, and toddled up to my workroom with it. One glance was off-putting enough to ensure I put it to one side while I contacted the security team. Apparently they'd had a callout to someone down in Bridge, and the guy dealing with it could come and see me on his return journey. Excellent.

'The less you know the better,' I assured Griff, a couple of hours later, the tiny package from the security team in my hand, as I bearded him in the office where he was dealing with emails. 'So no questions. And no suggestions we discuss it with Tony or Moira or anyone else. Especially Lydia.'

He said nothing for a few moments. 'I suppose this can't wait till Sunday, when we have a reason to be in church?'

'Hythe,' I said, 'The Mayfair. One of us has to be there.'

'Drat. Well, I promised to replenish the supplies of tea and coffee in the fellowship area. We could take them down together and what you do while I'm filling the cupboard I'd never know.'

More or less retracing the route Freya and I had taken, I cased the joint as assiduously as if I planned to rob it, not protect it. Some of the places I'd have chosen to conceal the device because they were such good viewpoints were too high for me. But there was a grimy crucifix hanging over the pulpit, just within reach if I stood on the very tip of my toes. Perching on a kneeler made it slightly easier, if a bit less secure. On the other hand, everyone would see my fingerprints.

Not if I dusted it. The cleaning ladies never locked their cupboard, and why should they? So I did a spot of benign burglary and liberated a J-cloth. Two minutes' awkward perching, and the camera, its feed going straight to our security team's HQ, was in place. I shook the J-cloth over everything the best I could – it wouldn't do for it to look too clean – and descended to the safety of the pulpit. I had a momentary frisson of amusement: what a stage this would be for Griff – a captive audience and every set of eyes upon him.

A couple of days later, Moira bustled in, obviously full of news about Dodie. The NHS had come up trumps with an appointment with an eye consultant only three weeks hence. Oh, and Dodie had loved the huge bouquet that Griff had given her.

For some reason Griff didn't ply her with sherry to celebrate. In fact, rather shamefaced, the moment she'd gone he explained about the flowers. From Harvey to me, of course: 'But I was afraid you might simply have slung them in the compost bin, dear one, and there must have been fifty pounds' worth of lilies and roses there.'

Or I might simply have flung my arms round the wretched man's neck and agreed to resume our relationship. But I needn't tell Griff that. And there was another reason not to succumb to tears: a knock at the door. A peep at our security camera told me it was Spencer with a couple of huge mates, volunteering, he told me as I let them in, for wheelchair pushing duties.

Griff clucked round them, producing strong coffee in mitt-sized mugs and slices of a fruitcake he'd meant for Dodie. 'The only trouble is,' he said apologetically, 'that since this is a church matter, you need – oh, those things that used to be called CRB checks.'

'You'll be referring to DBS checks, Mr Tripp,' said one of the man-mountains politely. 'Ben and I both coach juniors, so we're already accredited for work with youngsters. I know it's supposed to be a different set of checks for oldies, but surely if we're supervised . . .' He and his friend fished out their paperwork simultaneously. Big Ben. Was the other one Big Bill? No, I mustn't even think of them like that.

'Excellent. You're not accredited, Spencer? What a shame. But we could always get the church to do the paperwork for you. No?' Griff toddled off to the office with the papers.

Spencer shrugged. 'Sod it. The whole process is far too damned intrusive.'

Was it now? What did he want to hide? 'Griff feels the same,' I said soothingly. 'He actually threw the forms in the bin first time round. And I point blank refused. So I need an accredited chaperone myself.'

Possibly Spencer looked disappointed. Big Bill, whose name was actually Rob, grinned and offered to escort me. With an identical grin I declined. 'You're the one pushing, not me.'

'But you could hold the old biddy's hand,' he countered.

A little thread of tension slung itself round the room, as if spun by a harvest spider. It stretched but didn't snap when Griff returned, handing the documents back to their owners. 'I've also scanned them and emailed them across to the woman with responsibility for vulnerable adults,' he said, all bustling activity. 'Moira Carr, that is. And she'll be in touch with you as soon as she can. Have you got a match this afternoon?' he asked, as if he was genuinely interested.

The four of them were soon involved in a conversation that left me absolutely cold, all about their team positions with even stranger names (tight head? prop forward?) than the even weirder cricket terminology (short square leg!) I'd come to know and love. Griff interested in such a sweaty, muddy, physical game? Heavens, he seemed to be promising to go along to cheer them on! And the promise seemed to be including me.

Fortunately for me, a text warbled its way on to my mobile. Fozia: would I fancy joining her that afternoon for some ball skills work? Sorry about the short notice but the coach said it seemed silly not to take advantage of the sun.

It did indeed.

'I thought you'd so enjoy it,' Griff declared pettishly as we whizzed round preparing an early lunch so he could get to

Ashford in time to see the start of the game. 'All those pecs,
all those straining quads!'

'You go and lech on your own,' I told him sharply. 'Afzal's
a good friend, and if I can help his kid sister, I will. Just one
thing: don't try to match-make me with any of them. Especially
Spencer. You know I don't like him and I really don't like
Honey all that much. I don't want to complicate things . . .'

I don't think I'd ever had such pure and simple enjoyment
all my life as I did in the couple of hours a dozen or so of
us spent chasing and catching tennis balls on the outskirts
of the village cricket field. Fozia, hot and puffing, said it was
like being back at school again; I said if I'd known school
could be that much fun I'd have spent more time there. She
didn't seem fazed by my quick, understated explanation – one
I'd never have risked with Honey or possibly even Laura –
any more than I'd be disconcerted if she ever wanted to talk
about her self-harm, the scars of which were visible when
she shoved back the cuff on her long-sleeved t-shirt. The
coach, a middle-aged woman called Jan, stern-faced and
whippy as Judy Murray, warned us that a hot bath might be
more beneficial than hitting the pub, after all the bending
and stretching she'd put us through.

'I can hardly wait till next Saturday,' Fozia declared, with
a little-girl skip.

'Nor me. Tell Afzal thank you from me. I'm never going
to be the new Charlotte Edwards, but this is such magic.'

'You might only be playing with a soft ball now,' Griff said
doubtfully, 'but about your hands when you play properly? A
broken finger or two . . .'

He was grumpy because I'd taken Jan's advice and soaked
for a happy and hot-water-consuming half hour. He'd come
back to find the tank almost as chilled as he was. While he
waited, he messed around noisily in the kitchen, wondering
aloud what on earth we could have for supper. Somehow I
didn't think a suggestion that I nip to Afzal's would go down
too well. Heavens, sometimes he and Pa were more like
toddlers than grown men.

It would have been wonderful to see Dodie at her first church service for years the next morning, but as I'd reminded Griff, we were booked for a fair at the Hythe Mayfair. Once again Griff was torn: where did his loyalties lie? I assured him I didn't care one way or the other so long as he didn't spend time hurtling up and down Stone Street on his own again, at the mercy of any passing road hog.

'You could always ask young Spencer to help you?' he suggested, with an ironic smile.

I responded in kind. 'So I could. Don't worry – there'll be someone at the fair we know who'll provide some muscle if I need it.'

There was, in the form of Will Furzeland, whom I'd last seen in Torquay. He greeted me with a smile, and why not? I'd put several hundred pounds his way when I persuaded Griff to buy that lovely miniature for Aidan's birthday – which must be any day now, come to think of it.

As he secured the topmost section of our display unit, we exchanged news of our mutual acquaintances. Finally he dropped the gossipy tone: 'What's this about you actually setting the police on Habgood? Just tit for tat, like? I'd have thought you'd be above something like that.'

'When I see a netsuke on his stall I'd dusted only a week before, what am I to do? Have a quiet word in private? Actually, I would have done – I'd even have had a damned noisy one if he'd been anywhere around. But he'd left that clueless woman in charge.'

'Clueless?'

'Twenty pounds for a brooch I can sell on to a Victorian jewellery expert for nearer a hundred? And the netsuke for about a tenth of its value?'

'You saw her coming, didn't you?'

'If people are straight with me, I'm straight with them. Anyway, tell me about Habgood. Have they locked him up in Dartmoor yet? Solitary confinement for preference?'

He gave me a look I couldn't read. 'You wouldn't shed any tears if they did, would you? Come on, a lot of us sail close to the wind sometimes. Some would say buying good stuff as cheaply as you did wasn't honest.'

We'd had this conversation before, hadn't we? And probably would again. Did he want me to be some sort of angel?

'Isn't it called making a profit?' I asked quietly.

'I suppose it is. But we all need to do that, Lina. Preferably without fleecing each other.'

'And preferably without handling goods stolen from a blind old lady who's already been robbed – literally – of all her clothes and goodness knows what else. She lives in our village. Too sick to get out till I organized a wheelchair.'

To my relief he threw back his head in a generous laugh – perhaps we were going to stay as mates after all. 'Why am I not surprised to hear that you've been busy organizing! But this old dear's really blind? You're not just gilding the lily?'

'She's waiting for an urgent cataract operation. And someone's nicked all that other stuff from her, too. So what I really want is not Habgood's scalp – it's possible he's just earning a crust – but that of the guy who's taken everything from a decent woman.'

'Down to her clothes and shoes? You're joking. No, you're not, are you? No wonder you sound so vengeful. I'll keep my ears open for you. Promise. So long as you spill the beans about you and Harvey Sanditon. He's really lost all his stuffing, if you see what I mean.'

I saw movement. 'You've got a punter heading your way, Will – I'll push off.'

I had a customer too, a woman, who peered at the name over our stall, then at me, and then dug in her bag for something. Suddenly it dawned on me that she was the woman who'd stopped me plunging under that lorry the other day. My smile was huge and genuine.

'Kate Evans,' she declared, shaking my hand. 'And you're the Townend half of the firm, is that right? The one who does all the restoration work? I checked you out online,' she told me, adding with a frown, 'Does that mean that all the stuff I see is damaged?'

At these prices! 'No, items with stickers like this have had work done. Sometimes it's better to sell damaged stock as it is – like that vase.' I picked it up to show her. 'Perfect from one side, but sadly cracked here. A firing crack. I wouldn't dream, by the way, of trying to con anyone, least of all someone who saved my life. And before you decide you can't afford something you like, ask me first.' I gestured expansively: she could browse as long as she liked.

And in the meantime I sold a pretty Shelley cruet and a stunningly ugly piece of Clarice Cliff.

At last Kate alighted on a piece I didn't expect to sell far south, a Midlands treasure by Ruskin, a Smethwick factory started by a father and son called Taylor to emulate the best of Chinese ware, and flambé in particular. Like much of the period, some is so weird in shape and colour that you wonder why anyone bothered to turn on the kiln to fire it. Most, however, is delectable in colour and shape and glaze. This ginger jar certainly was. It was worth a thousand pounds of anyone's money; how much, I wondered, could I reduce it by if she wanted it?

'I can do it at what it cost us,' I told her. As her eyebrows shot up, I added, 'After all, I wouldn't be here today if it hadn't been for you.'

'That young man you were with,' she began. 'Is he a friend of yours?'

I rocked my hand back and forth.

'Do you accept cards?' What had she been going to ask? Something else, surely.

'Of course. Go on, pick it up and check it over.' In other words, fall in love with it, even if I did stand to lose several hundred pounds' profit.

In the end, she didn't buy it. Or anything else. 'You've just got to fall in love, haven't you?' she said with a smile.

'Of course. Although if you were to have a flirtation with an item, I'd be honoured if you'd accept it as a gift.'

'That's too generous for what was simply a reflex action. I'll come to your shop, though. And check out your website again.'

I thought the encounter was over, but she dodged back, looking almost embarrassed. 'How hard is it to look at the CCTV footage of – say – Maidstone? I don't want . . . no, just see if you can.'

'What am I looking for, Kate?'

She shook her head emphatically. 'I really don't want to go

round making accusations. At all.' She waved a hand, ready to move away.

'Hang on! If you let me have your contact details, I'll send details of our stock,' I said. 'And tell you about the footage.' I stowed her card – she was a wedding planner – and waved her goodbye.

It wasn't until we were packing up at the end of the day and my lack of inches needed Will's excess of them that we were able to resume our conversation about Habgood. Apart from an early sale, Will had had a bad day; mine hadn't been much better. The main consolation was that Griff hadn't wasted a day, or spent it hurtling around Kent. The slackness made me realize even more clearly the wisdom of Paul's advice when he had told us to separate the profitable from the dwindling business.

'Habgood's cronies,' I prompted eventually, as Will passed me the last light fitting.

'All I know is that he's got a wide net of people who supply him from car boot sales and the like. No questions asked. But like you said, provenance is all. Or was it Hamlet who said that?' he asked, with a quirky smile. 'My oldest's doing his A-levels, and goodness knows how many versions of his set books we've had to watch on DVD. I don't dislike the man as much as you do, obviously, and to be honest, I still don't think it reflects well on you to bad-mouth him – though I can quite understand why.' Would he ever let this go? It was beginning to feel more like nagging than friendly and constructive criticism. 'But I will ask around,' he conceded.

'No. Don't do that. Please. That's not your job. You've got a business to run and a family to look after. Just keep out of it.' Perhaps I surprised myself by my strength of feeling. 'If by chance you hear anything and can pass it on, that's different.'

He looked at me closely. 'Has something happened today to scare you?'

I shook my head. 'It's just this divvy thing of mine. Sometimes it seems to function with other things besides antiques. People. So please, Will, just keep your head down.' I suspect my smile was watery as I added, 'And maybe we should end this conversation with an almighty row, just in case any of Habgood's mates should be here.'

'Can't do acting,' he said. 'Come on, let's get this lot into your van.'

'Not on your bloody life!'

'What's got into you, you crazy woman?' He looked genuinely shocked.

I dropped my voice. 'See, you can act.'

TWENTY-TWO

Naturally I said nothing to Griff about Kate Evans and her advice. However, having given Freya Sunday evening off, as it were, I texted her first thing on Monday asking for help tracing the CCTV footage – it shouldn't be hard for her given that I'd met her only minutes later and could give the precise location. She texted back almost immediately that she'd been drafted in to help out on a murder enquiry, but she'd asked Conrad Knowles to chase it up as soon as he got in. Did I know what I was looking for?

My attempted dive under a lorry. The one that had upset me and helped reduce me to tears.

She texted back: *Illget him to priotise. X*

I got the gist, anyway.

For some reason, though I had to sit firmly on my anxiety, I didn't hold my breath. But I did make a note to call him the following morning just to remind him of my existence. Then, after my now less regular check on Dodie's cameras – nil returns – I settled down to a delightful day of really pleasurable work . . . apart from the smells drifting up insidiously from the kitchen; Griff had decided to make chutney. Eventually I gave up and took myself down to the shop to get some kids' tennis balls – soft, not much bounce – that happened to be on offer at this time of the year. As I told Dodie when I nipped in to see her for a few of what she called her anti-dwindle moments, I was going to hurl these at the back wall of the yard to improve my throwing and catching. It turned out she'd played cricket when she was a girl – she almost pronounced it *gell* – in the days of long socks and divided skirts. We parted with our usual hug and soft kiss.

The smell of vinegar and spices still clung to Griff's skin, despite his shower and change of clothing, as with the rest of the dance class we practised – endlessly – a quickstep figure called the fishtail. His feet flashed through the steps, apparently instinctively. I didn't help my cause by trying to look down at mine to see why they weren't working. Any day now I might chuck the whole course in – but that would upset Griff and deprive him of a session of nice aerobic exercise. There was a large notice on the board too – that learning to dance helped prevent Alzheimer's. I marked, learned and inwardly digested, and resolved to button my lip a while longer.

Spencer was making one of his rare appearances, completely monopolizing poor Dee and her long-suffering feet. The only bonus was that they weren't mine. At the end of the hour, back in street shoes (we all wore special soft-soled dance gear), we inevitably fell into step; I made sure the conversation followed strict rugby lines. My thanks to him and his friends were lavish, and sincere. At this point Griff virtually pleaded with him to submit the appropriate vetting form. Sensing that this time Spencer might actually get angry, I changed the subject abruptly, reminding Griff that there was some TV programme that he wanted to see and had forgotten to record. It might have been beyond rude actually, but I had an idea that Spencer was relieved. So what was he hiding? Late though it was, I thought about texting Knowles. Or did he deserve an evening off too?

The blinking eye of our answerphone announced what turned out to be a message from Phil. Landline? Of course – we'd never exchanged mobile details, had we, probably thanks to Freya's intervention. He reminded us that we'd spoken of Thai food, and that what was supposed to be a better than average place had just opened in Canterbury. Would I care to join him – Griff too if he was so inclined? Tomorrow?

'No. It'd mean missing Pilates,' I told Griff, who was rubbing his hands with glee at the thought of my having a decent respectable man to wine and dine me. He waved aside the socially and physically inept Spencer; Phil, with his flourishing business and bijou cottage, might be the answer to Griff's prayers – not for himself, of course, but for me. 'And I wouldn't want,' I added with a smile that Griff would interpret as coy, 'to sound too keen. He mentioned you too, remember, and you're joining Aidan for that am-dram production in Tenterden.

I know you're only going so that you can both have a good
sneer, but you can't really stand Aidan up, can you?'

'He wouldn't think twice,' he said flatly. 'But Phil only
asked me as an afterthought – you can tell from his voice.'

'Whoever he invited, he's going to have to find another
evening,' I insisted. 'Am-dram for you, and for me Pilates
with the girls it must be. Will you call him? I've got a really
important text to deal with.' I ran upstairs to prove the point.
But I got no reply from Conrad Knowles. The next day I even
tried phoning, to no avail. Any moment now I'd get so pissed
off I'd dob him in to Freya.

Compared with the ball skills work, Pilates epitomized dullness,
but I knew it was doing me and my back good – I was almost
beginning to think of it, with all its individual bones and muscles,
as a separate entity. I certainly didn't enjoy Laura and Honey's
company nearly as much as I enjoyed Fozia's, but I went along
with them to the pub as usual, and then nearly fell off my stool
in surprise when Honey invited us back to her place – her
parents', of course – to eat our latest Chinese feast.

It turned out to be Parson's Pride, the very house to which
Afzal had delivered an order when he'd been taking me home
– high gates and entry-phone, which I now saw protected a
big garden, lights giving some indication of its range, and a
floodlit four-square Georgian house to die for. We entered by
what would once have been the servants' entrance, a kitchen
so large that pretty much the whole of our cottage would have
fitted inside it. For chicness it rivalled Phil's. The table was
already laid for us. At one point Laura asked for the loo, and
tried to open the door she probably assumed – I would have
done – led to the hall and a cloakroom. It was locked. Honey,
rather giggly even for her, shooed her to another door, which
opened, Laura announced when she emerged, into the biggest
loo in the Western World. I was filling the water jug at the
sink (I knew my place) when a car crunched the gravel outside,
heading to the rear of the house – stables now converted to a
garage, at a guess. Then there were footsteps past the kitchen;
the walker was heading to the front door, no doubt. Motion-
sensitive lights switched on and off to mark their progress,

the only remotely environmentally friendly part of the lighting system I'd observed.

Honey was full of Spencer's good deed in recruiting people to help what she infuriated me by referring to as 'Lina's old bat'. I joined in, though I did mention the other young men involved too. As for Dodie, I said firmly, she might be old but she was bright and canny, and everyone who met her liked her.

'But fancy you refusing to go along to support Spencer's team!' she said, provoked. 'That wasn't very nice, Lina, after all he's done for you.'

All what? Getting others to do his dirty work? 'I'd got a prior commitment, Honey. Just as I had with you two tonight when someone asked me to do something else,' I concluded lamely, not wanting to feed Phil into her conversational mincer. 'Aren't I a dreadful Goody Two-Shoes! The way I was brought up, I suppose.' They weren't to know I was being deeply ironic.

'Someone was saying Griff isn't your real grandfather,' Honey said, as if that might provoke me.

'Oh, he's not. He adopted me.' This wasn't legally true, because I'd been too old when we had the idea.

'Why?'

'Because my mother died when I was young, and my father wasn't exactly . . . I'd not rate him very high in the father stakes.'

Laura abandoned her chopsticks and picked up a spoon. 'Someone said your dad's a lord.'

'Yep. Not a famous one, though. Doesn't live anywhere as grand as this. He only has the servants' quarters, which are almost as basic as in the days when there were servants. Before they could ask the perennial question – if I was a lady, with a capital L – I spread my hands, opening my eyes wide. 'This is some pad, Honey. No wonder you don't want to move out.'

'Oh, I'd go if I could afford it. Don't you worry, I'd rather live in a place like yours, Laura.' Were we seeing the real Honey for once? 'No one keeps an eye on when you come and go, after all. I mean, it's nice having a rich dad, but not if he's a bit of a control freak. He says he's just looking after me, but it doesn't feel like that. I mean, I'm nearly thirty, for God's sake!'

'What about your mum?' Laura asked.

'Jumped ship years ago. I still see her, obviously, but I don't like her new man, not one scrap. The way he looks at you . . . I don't like the bitch who's likely to become my stepmother either, ingratiating cow. I said to Dad, just give me some money and I'll get myself a place in Canterbury and a little car, something like your new one, Lina, and leave you to it. I mean, he's rolling. He says this is cheap plonk—' she pointed to the bottle of excellent Marlborough Sauvignon Blanc she'd just emptied, and reached for another from the giant American fridge. 'Twelve quid a bottle, and he calls it plonk!'

Laura giggled. 'I could take a couple of these home if you wanted to get rid of them.'

'He's just got himself a new car – OK, second-hand, but new to us. I don't suppose he got much change out of fifty K. And he won't fork out for a little runabout for me.' Her lower lip wobbled.

So my handsome new Audi was a little runabout, was it? Motoring luxury, in my book.

Laura caught my eye, jerking her head minutely. I nodded. It was time to leave Honey to what would probably be a monumental hangover the following day. 'I've got to be up before seven, Hon,' she said. 'Working day. Shall I pop that back in the fridge for you?' She screwed the top back on the Sauvignon and got up. I followed her lead. At least we could walk part of the way together. And this time I'd got proper trainers in my rucksack.

'Oh, Dad'll take you home. He'd like to show off his Merc . . . But he said!' she added, whining like toddler, as we both shook our heads.

Laura patted her stomach. 'After all this food it'll do us good to walk, won't it, Lina?' She watched as I changed my shoes and slung my rucksack on. I also added a little gadget I'd found online: a torch you wore round your head. I might look weird, but it would be good to see where I was putting my feet. The trusty truncheon torch lurked in the rucksack. 'You're not expecting me to run, Lina? I only do walking.'

'Of course not. It's just that I'm really into this cricket thing and want to get fit so I shall jog from yours to mine.'

Honey roused herself from her sulk to say, 'OK, if you insist . . . No coffee? All right, I'd better buzz you out, then. He'll be really pissed off, though.'

'Mercs, a place like this, security gates – what's your dad do to get this much money then, Honey?' Laura, who'd drunk rather more than me, had the brass neck to ask. Good for her.

'Recycling or something,' Honey said, off-hand.

It felt like a lie. At best a partial truth.

As Laura observed as we set off down the drive together: 'I don't know if I want to do this again,' she said quietly, watching the gates swing open. Giggling, we dived through as if dawdling would get us sliced sideways. She continued, 'I just get so sick of her sense of entitlement. I worked my way through Uni and we saved up for ages to get the deposit for our flat, and you should see our poor old car. But she thinks she should get everything on a plate. She sneers at my things, too. Like my poor plates.' That sounded suspiciously like a sob.

'She shouldn't. Sure you couldn't spend a fortune on them but you chose wisely – nice simple designs, nothing fussy.'

'You mean that? And you're a china expert? Thanks!' She gave me a tiny hug. 'Another thing· I wish she didn't drink so much – it's not good for her.'

'It's not. Perhaps she drinks because she's so unhappy. Remember the fancy dress I told you about? At Torquay? And how I sang, "Only a Bird in a Gilded Cage"? Do you think Honey might be like that bird?'

'Locked in the servants' quarters! Did you see? We might have been guests, but we weren't getting into the house proper, were we?'

'You're sure it was locked? Literally?'

She nodded, fit to shake her head off.

Curiouser and curiouser. I'd have to hope we did get another invitation there after all and I'd try the door for myself. 'You see, all I meant was that she was trapped by her father's money.'

'There are worse things to be trapped by. Being poor, for instance. My parents were actually driven to using a food bank till I found out – but I wouldn't want Honey to know that. Redundancy. Illness. Two professionals and they have to choose whether to keep their own roof over their head or to eat.'

It was my turn to hug her as she sobbed to a halt. 'What a good job they've got you. And of course I won't tell anyone, anyone at all. Tell you what, it's time the church had a new project. I doubt if it'll help your parents specifically, but we could organize donations to whichever is our nearest food bank. Actually,' I added, to lighten the moment, 'when my pa heard about bottle banks he had the notion that if you put empties in, you'd get full ones out . . .'

TWENTY-THREE

My jog from Laura's was almost uneventful – but not quite.

I told myself that it was because I saw danger in every black car – pretty stupid statistically, if you think about it. In any case, I really could not believe that Honey's father would be so outraged that someone should reject his wheels that he would get the new black Merc – another one to worry about! – out again and prowl the streets of a sleepy village looking for the ungrateful ones. But I did see the same car a couple of times, so I took to one or two car-unfriendly lanes. These added a few minutes and removed a few more calories – always welcome. Of course, they came with hazards of their own: evidence of lazy dog-walkers. They'd gathered up the mess but then left the poo bags on the ground. Some kind soul had actually festooned a couple on someone's hedge.

I was no longer alone. Other footsteps were following me. Just another jogger . . .? I didn't spend too long on speculation. I might just get away with turning round and confronting whoever it was, but this wasn't a great place to do it. On the other hand, it was a great spot for anyone with enough speed to attack me from behind. So stopping and fishing the mega-torch from the rucksack didn't seem the best option. If only I hadn't had quite so much wine: my head would be clearer and my legs stronger.

Whoever was behind me was definitely gaining, and I had to do something simply to reassure myself that this was an innocent health freak and not someone with evil intent. I tried accelerating. No good. The footsteps kept pace. Should I slow down and wave him past?

Not without seeing him first.

Turning at right angles to the path, I bent, as if to tie a lace. I could look up to face him, illuminating his face with my mini-headlight, of course. We might exchange a friendly smile and a comment about the weather. I'd also be in a position to do an explosive start. Unless, of course, my would-be assailant – I hoped I was getting ahead of myself here but couldn't be sure – took advantage of his height to wallop me over the head. Heavens, I was getting paranoid, wasn't I? Or at the very least obsessed with potential head injuries.

All the same . . .

All the same, when a man wearing a balaclava for running on a mild night slows down and raises his right arm as if to strike, you might be entitled to feel mild suspicion. I dodged to my left, ready to sprint, but the hand I was using to boost lift-off landed on something squidgy and vile. OK, it was still in a polythene bag, but there was no doubting what it was. Or that it would constitute the only weapon I had available. Even our grim-faced cricket coach might have cracked a smile as I grabbed it, threw and scrambled to my feet.

I've always been able to run fast, and this time I ran very fast. I needed somewhere, someone, safe. Now.

And found it in the form of Phil and Angus, out for a gentle stroll. Angus carried his lead in his mouth, which gave the impression he was grinning with pleasure. At arm's length, Phil carried a full poo bag.

'Are you all right? That didn't look like a quiet jog to me – it looked as if you were pursued by the hounds of hell.' He didn't sound very happy, but why should he if he thought I'd preferred a run to his company?

'Pilates night,' I gasped, breath coming harder than I liked. I supported my hands on my thighs. 'We always have a girlie get-together afterwards. This time it was at the edge of the Glebe Field estate. And I was quietly padding home when another jogger tried—' What had he tried? What could I tell the police? 'Let's just say I didn't want to wait to see what he wanted to try.'

'Have you got your phone? Well, dial nine-nine-nine. Please.'

I shook my head. 'Actually, I don't want the police to know I retaliated in a way I shouldn't.'

'You kicked him in the balls? Well, why not?'

'Uh, uh. I was on the ground at the time. I put my hand in

something when I slipped. Oh, it was in a bag like Angus's. But I don't know that you're supposed to use dog mess as a weapon.'

Without a word – was one necessary? – he peeled a wad of sanitized wipes from a sachet he produced from his pocket, going up at least sixteen points in my estimation. The tissues went into a convenient poo bin, along with Angus's donation.

'Did you see enough of your pursuer to identify him?' he asked, as he wiped his own hands.

I shook my head. And then stopped. Was there something? But it wasn't a strong enough suspicion to mention to anyone else. And not to a man with a record for losing his temper, who might be tempted to deal with the offender himself, assuming he could find him, of course.

By now Phil was speaking urgently. 'But you will report this to the police, won't you? This man might try to hurt other women. And he might succeed with someone who couldn't find a suitable weapon—' despite himself his face cracked '—or run impressively fast.' Then he started to laugh. We both did. It was very hard to stop. He succeeded first. 'Do you think Griff's back from his theatre trip yet? I wouldn't want you to be on your own after that sort of incident. Come on, Angus and I will walk you back to your cottage.'

And they did, Angus circling me and looking up from time to time with a bit of a whine and an encouraging wag of his tail.

'I'll be all right now. Thanks for coming with me.' I hoped my voice had a note of finality. Apparently it didn't.

'Look, you're still trembling.'

I was. I couldn't fit the key in the lock. 'Too much exercise after too much MSG, maybe,' I said with a grin, passing the key to him. But I felt awkward. Would I feel safer or less safe if I asked him in? Angus solved the problem for me: the moment Phil succeeded in opening the door, he dashed in. I had to get in quickly too so I could deal with the alarm, capable of rousing the entire South East if provoked. Which left Phil standing on the step, yelling to Angus, who had taken an immediate liking to Griff's favourite chair and was already falling asleep on it. Or so he pretended. He was certainly genuinely snoring by the time I'd equipped Phil and me with a glass of wine that was decent enough but not in the same league as Honey's so-called plonk.

'You really should call the police, you know,' Phil said firmly. 'Now. In case the guy tries to strike again tonight. Just omit one salient detail.' Any moment now we'd be hysterical again. 'Go on.' He got up and passed me the handset, at which point Griff appeared, so I withdrew to the kitchen, passing my untouched glass to Griff with a resigned sigh.

It took me seven minutes to get through on 101, and the despatcher was actually yawning as she repeated the details. 'OK. I'll ask our patrols to be extra vigilant. I suppose you could ask the council for any CCTV footage of the area. That sometimes helps.'

'CCTV in a village the size of Bredeham?'

'And I'll get one of our officers to call you,' she added, in what sounded remarkably like an afterthought.

'Would you rather I dial nine-nine-nine?' I asked tartly.

'If it had been a genuine emergency I'd imagine you'd have dialled that in the first place.'

Which, if not exactly good PR, was hard to argue with.

Griff insisted that he'd told me about a forthcoming trip to London to catch up with some old theatre pals over lunch: 'Before the next funeral, dear heart. I know I told you; your brain must have been clogged up with other things, and why not?'

Since that was the excuse I always made for Griff when things slipped his mind, it was unanswerable. He didn't even tell me how worried he was about leaving me on my own, setting off in what he considered his Town clothes (somehow you sensed the capital letter) at a jaunty pace. He'd got an open day return, on the grounds that his boozy lunch might extend into the evening.

It wasn't until he strode off that I became suspicious. Of course I'd had a lot on my mind, but it wasn't as if he'd just jogged my memory. I was certain I knew nothing of his plans. Which suggested to me he'd not told me, and when he was secretive it was usually for a reason. Sometimes it was because he wanted to give me a nice surprise; sometimes he knew I'd deeply disapprove. The pit of my stomach told me it was the latter.

He was going to see Noel Pargetter, wasn't he?

And even if I grabbed the van and hurtled to the station, I'd not get on the London train. I simply couldn't stop him.

Unless he'd left his phone on?

Of course he hadn't.

'Noel Pargetter?' Pa repeated stupidly, his voice tinny and distant. 'What do I know about Noel Pargetter?'

'That's just what you're going to tell me,' I said through gritted teeth. It was a good job I was phoning him, or I'd probably have had my fingers round his throat choking the information out of him. 'If you don't know anything, Titus does, and I bet he's just across the room from you waving his hands around and putting his finger to his lips to shut you up. Right? OK, put me on to him.' There was a pause while the handset was dropped – by Pa – and picked up – probably by Titus.

'Griff's gone off to see Pargetter,' I said. 'Should I be afraid?'

'Dartmoor or London?'

'London.' Except he'd have to go to Paddington to get a train west. And he had warned me that he could be late home. All the same, London to Devon and back in one day, with all the changes involved if he wanted to get to Shepdip Farm, was pushing one's travelling luck. 'I think,' I added, less certainly.

'What does he want to sell?'

'Who?'

'Griff, of course.'

Not those Russian objets d'art! 'Nothing, as far as I know. Why?'

'Because that's how Pargetter makes his money. As a high-class fence. Not stolen objects, oh no, wouldn't soil his lily-whites for them. Just iffy things that he'll sell to a mate who doesn't ask too many questions. And he'll take a big cut.'

'By iffy you mean . . .?'

'Second World War stuff that's never found its way back to the original owners' families. Odds and ends that may just have dropped off the back of a lorry in Afghanistan. Good things, no provenance.'

Or maybe even the odd netsuke stolen from a widow in Bredeham? No, small beer, surely.

'Can you give me back to Pa? Thanks. Pa, has Griff been in touch with you about anything recently?'

'What sort of anything?'

'Any sort of anything? Russian, for instance?'

'Only to talk about you. He's got some hare-brained scheme to stop you paying inheritance tax when he pops his clogs. Told him I didn't like it; told him you wouldn't wear it.'

'I want you to swear on anything you might believe in that it was nothing to do with Fabergé. Or icons.'

'Why should it be?' He sounded genuinely puzzled.

'Titus, please.'

A growl. 'What now, doll? Really busy.'

'Pargetter. Is he dangerous?'

'You mean physical? Himself?'

'Too ill for that, surely. What about heavies?'

'Nah. Murders reputations, not bodies. Him and that posh mate of yours have had a bit of a falling out, I hear tell. The one your Pa here loathes. Don't know why.' He cut the call.

And with that I had to be content, even though I'd have given a tooth to know what had caused a rift between two men I didn't even know knew each other: Harvey and Pargetter? I'd probably never solve that problem but at least I could put my mind at rest over the icons. Telling Mary and Paul I was slipping out, I confess I nipped up to the self-store. To find everything was exactly where it should be. So should I worry less – or a great deal more?

I'd hardly got back and locked the car away, promising myself I'd try, no matter how hard it was, to concentrate on painting a cherub's hair, when the doorbell announced an inconvenient caller. It was none other than the tiny police community support officer who'd been sent to tackle the gang raiding the church: Ann Draper – that was it. Taking her through to the office and offering her the most uncomfortable chair – there were all those curls to give individual attention to – I gave a succinct account of what had happened, omitting the missile I'd had to hand, as it were. Truthfully I told her I couldn't identify the face lurking in the balaclava, but had been afraid for a moment that it was one of the church gang.

Rolling her eyes, she agreed that scarpering had been the best move, but lamented the absence of any hard evidence, of course.

'You're not talking about the sort of DNA you'd get from a physical attack, are you?'

'Skin under the fingernails is always useful. But without evidence, all I can say is that you should avoid ill-lit streets at night, even though I'll try to get a couple of colleagues to drive round and establish a presence. Stick to the main roads.'

Which would have meant never emerging from the cottage after dark. 'The trouble is – if you check police information on that natty little tablet of yours – that a guy with a big black car has already made me feel unsafe on streets big enough for cars: the Mercedes driver who assaulted one of my employees in order to threaten me.'

She checked. Her eyebrows, already higher on her forehead than you'd expect, because she'd tied her hair back tightly in an Essex facelift, struggled even further north. 'I think I need to report this to my superiors, don't you?'

'I'd be really glad if you would,' I said, with no irony at all. 'By the way, do you know a guy called Conrad Knowles? CID?'

'Oh, he's gorgeous, isn't he? I always imagine him in sequins on *Strictly Come Dancing*.'

I had a horrible feeling a penny might be about to drop in the deepest recesses of my brain. 'I've been trying to get in touch with him,' I said. 'About the assault on me in Dockinge, for a start.'

'Oh, do you need Victim Support? I can put you in touch with them.'

'Actually I don't. But I do need to contact Conrad. And he's not responding to my texts or voicemail messages.'

'You wouldn't expect him to. He was overdue his annual

leave and Human Resources said use it or lose it. He's in France, I think, staying with a mate.'

And I would bet that balding cherub I knew which mate. 'Can you do that? In the middle of a case?'

'Oh, someone else will take over his urgent caseload. We do have lives, Lina.'

'I nearly didn't have mine,' I said. 'How would I know who's taken over?' I'd ask Freya, of course. But Ann didn't need to know that.

She shrugged. 'His DI, probably.'

'Who is . . .?'

She checked her notepad, tapping a couple of times and sucking her teeth. 'Well, Springer's on maternity leave and Black's long-term sick. The new acting DI's in court all week. And there's a big push on desk-solvable crimes. They sit in rows glued to computers. The most effective use of resources,' she said glibly, and quite without irony herself.

'And leave people like you to do the dirty work.'

She blinked. 'There's no need to put it like that. Except,' she said slowly, 'I suppose you're right.'

TWENTY-FOUR

When I picked Griff up at the station I found him in the company of Spencer; apparently they'd travelled back together. Griff seemed quite happy to wave him goodbye without trying to drag me into any conversation, and sank into the car with a sigh.

'Plays his cards close to his chest, doesn't he?' he observed, nodding at Spencer's retreating back. I'd offered him a lift but he'd rather curtly declined. Sauce for the goose time, no doubt. 'All those questions. And he never wants to give any answers.'

'Sounds familiar,' I said. 'Honey's the same. If only we knew what they wanted to hide.'

'Yes, indeed,' he agreed without interest.

He was clearly in need of a restorative something or other by the time we got home. He might have been a bit disappointed when he found a cup of jasmine tea on the table beside him.

'And how were your fellow thespians? Or should that be in the singular? Oh, Griff, what have you been up to?'

He put his head in his hands. 'Yes, I did talk to Noel Pargetter. He and I go back years, as you know. And he's dying, though he didn't admit it in so many words. He got completely the wrong end of the stick about our relationship, dear one, and thought I'd in some way betrayed him by returning to the closet, as it were.'

'Didn't you ever mention Aidan while you were having lunch with him?'

'Indeed I did. But Noel deduced that it was your presence in my life that stopped me doing what I always meant to do – dancing off into the sunset with Aidan. And in a way it did. The way that Aidan reacted to you – continues to react to you – worries me deeply. He's become such a snob, hasn't he, the poor old dear? I can't think what he'll make of that miniature of your unknown ancestor, by the way. One day I must research her and find who she is. He'll be torn in two – desire to have an excellent addition to his collection and irritation at having to see your features. I shall have to give him something else as well – one isn't seventy-five every day.'

'Surely he'll be having a huge party?'

'To be honest, although he has loads of concert and theatre and opera-going acquaintances, he doesn't have very many close friends. The Grim Reaper, my love, took a lot of our contemporaries way before their time.'

'And is that all you talked about – you and your relationships?' I removed the empty cup and poured him a G&T which he sank with alarming speed. 'Or did his fencing activities come into the conversation? I was so worried I pumped Titus and Pa for information,' I added, almost but not quite too embarrassed to confess.

'As a matter of fact they didn't. I'd meant to explain my fear that the Inland Revenue would get hold of all the money needed to keep things going when I die; I meant to ask him to help.'

'The Russian stuff? Griff, no! You mustn't. All your principles—'

'It's all right, my love. I didn't. I thought of the look on your face if I did. And actually, the look on his face. So I still have to find a way round this, dear one.'

'Not an illegal one. Not after all the morality you've drummed into me. Please.' I'd have loved to ask about the suggestion he'd put to Pa, but decided against it. I managed a smile that felt weak and pale. 'One way is to live a long time.'

'I've already done that. And I hope and trust I have more years to come. But one never knows, dear one. I want us to expedite this sale. Lina, you've not even read Paul's proposal, have you? Shame on you. Child, we have to do something or you'll have nothing left. You have to own the shop; you have to buy me out of the restoration business. Even this cottage, if possible. When the local authority sells this place to pay care home fees, where will you live? Business premises too – capital gains tax! I rarely do this, but I'm setting you a deadline: I want that contract drawn up properly and signed by this time next week. Do you understand?'

My brain did. But some part of me certainly didn't. And was very worried.

'Good. Meanwhile, I also spoke to Noel about your *bête noir*, Habgood. There's no doubt they know each other. Professionally, if that isn't too high-flown a term. Who supplies whom I wouldn't know. He certainly didn't like you going public with your accusations against Habgood.'

'I'm not surprised. They make a lovely pair, don't they? Handling stolen goods . . . Titus thinks Afghan artefacts have passed through his hands. Iraqi, too, and Syrian, I should imagine. And Egyptian, after all the chaos there. A lot of thefts from underprotected Greek museums . . . How about antiquities from closer to home? From historic churches, for instance?'

Griff shook his head slowly. 'He was outraged by the damage inflicted on those churches – I've already forgotten their names, dear one, to my shame. And I think it was genuine anger at the thought of places he knew being horribly violated. It's almost as if his head is in some sort of cultural, perhaps empire-building, time warp: somehow it's all right to steal from Johnny Foreigner? And he clearly believes some items are safer over here than at the mercy of religious extremists who want to destroy what they believe are idols. Who can argue with that?'

Perhaps this was a night when I should ease his alcohol ration: bringing a plateful of olives, I also topped up his glass.

'I don't know that I ought,' he said, drinking deeply anyway. 'I had the best part of a bottle at lunchtime. There again, why not?' He looked into a distance I couldn't see – a last meal with an old friend, however corrupt, perhaps reminding him of everyone's mortality.

As for his account of their conversation, I believed him implicitly. Or not.

I discovered, when I came back the following morning from my regular brief trip to Dodie's to check her still innocent footage, that I had a whole lot of new friends, including our diminutive PCSO, Ann Draper. Overnight, it seemed, someone had removed all the manhole covers and drain grids from

Bredeham, not as some giant practical joke, Draper assured me as I ushered her into our living room, but almost certainly to sell as scrap.

'Hang on. I thought there's a national initiative to curb that sort of thing – rules for scrap metal dealers about not making cash payments and so on. Everything to be properly receipted and recorded.'

'In theory,' she said carefully.

'But in fact it's a law more honoured in the breach than the observance,' I said, with a rueful smile. Her blank expression suggested she hadn't registered the allusion. 'OK, how can I help?'

'It's your CCTV cameras. Did they pick up anything?'

'Let's look, shall we?' I led the way to the display console. 'Didn't anyone spot the thieves? After all, you can't just pick up a manhole cover, tuck it under your arm and stroll off with it.'

'Apparently people thought they must be from the council. Though one lady did get a bit worried and went down to have a look. When the men simply melted into the darkness and didn't reappear, she felt suspicious and phoned us. 101, though – or we might have caught them red-handed.'

I knew the feeling. 'Any reason why people thought they were official council workers?' I asked, automatically shielding the keypad and tapping in our code. I supplied the answer to my question. 'Lots of official-looking signs?'

'They *were* actually official signs. The council lost a lot during some recent roadworks. A prank, they thought, at the time.'

And of course it was much easier for all concerned to continue with that assumption.

'One good thing,' Draper continued sunnily, 'is that it should be the end of problems in Bredeham. Lightning never strikes twice, does it?'

'It has already. The attack on the church and now this. How about the adage of bad things happening in threes?' And I knew just the place they'd be after. But I shut up. She was out of her depth, and Freya and I were now back at the point where at least I could pick up the phone and talk to her.

We watched through all the footage together. I'd an idea she'd expected me to fade discreetly into the background, but I rarely did discreet when it was my equipment involved and I was in my own home.

Draper was right. They really did look like genuine workmen. As before, they'd erected their signs, this particular set warning about raised ironwork. Someone had a sense of humour, obviously. But the downside for them was the same as for the church raiders – they couldn't totally hide their faces. I was as sure as I could be that some of the faces were the same, though no doubt a court of law would prefer the evidence of police facial recognition systems. I downloaded the footage for Draper, who toddled off happy in the knowledge she'd done her job well. She didn't need to know that the moment I'd closed the door on her I was texting Freya with the information and telling her I'd really welcome another talk. The old Freya would have refused point-blank. The new one texted me that as soon as her meeting in Canterbury with church representatives was over she'd pop over to Bredeham to see me. How about the church as a venue, so she could see how good my camera was?

I sat quietly at the back of the church, waiting for Freya to deal with a flurry of texts and watching the sun play on the stained-glass windows. It seemed ages before she got to her feet and, saying nothing, wandered round looking at the carvings we'd last seen by artificial light. The Seven Deadly Sins still didn't show up clearly – in fact daylight dimmed them even further – but the gleaming brass lectern might have had 'Steal Me!' signs all over it. Inside the vestry, where I followed her, the metal cupboards looked even flimsier.

'At least the churchwardens here have agreed to move the best plate to the vaults in Canterbury Cathedral for temporary safe-keeping,' she said, following my gaze. 'They don't need a faculty for that. In fact this morning's meeting accepted most of what the Crime Prevention team and I had to say, which was in essence that for the time being at least they had to take extra precautions. The problem was implementing any major changes. Most churches don't have the funds, for a start, and in any case, as Robin says, you can't turn the House of God into a fortress. There's always a debate about keeping churches open all day every day. Robin and Daniel take the view that it's the only way, but they have churches in the middle of villages at the very least. I'm truly worried about isolated ones like the one where you were assaulted. We've passed on our concerns to the rural deans. But you're worried about something more specific, I'd say.'

'Yes. I'm convinced that they'll have another go at this church. I know it's in the heart of the village but those were serious efforts they were making when Phil interrupted them.'

'Is that founded on fact or just your weird divvy intuition?'

It would have been easy to take offence at the word 'just'. 'There's a feeling in the village that now they've got all our drain-gratings and manhole covers they'll move on to the next victim. OK, my intuition, mainly: the people whom I interrupted in Devon wanted carved panels; the people who socked me in Dockinge wanted church sculpture.'

'I'm not surprised you're anxious. But with luck, thanks to your camera, we might be able to pick them up before they lay their filthy mitts on anything else.'

We moved back into the nave.

'Have you spotted my camera yet?' I asked cheekily. 'I bet it's spotted us. There is just one thing, Freya,' I said, apparently innocently, as we both turned towards the altar, nodding in a sort of bow of acknowledgement, 'how come you're involved in this? I thought it was supposed to be Conrad liaising with the Heritage Squad or whatever they call themselves.'

'It was. But it seems he was due annual leave and when I heard how few senior staff were available I volunteered my good self. Better than a murder for getting home at a decent hour. Although you've not been there to nag me every minute of the day, I've already been in touch with Devon and Cornwall Police, and have been trying to get up to speed on the observation you made about your Dockinge village hall incident. You're not the only one to be suspicious of a stall set up at the last minute, with the holders disappearing before everyone else. I am. Very.'

'And not even paying,' I added pseudo-self-righteously.

'Quite. If they'd paid their ten quid or whatever I wouldn't have cared enough to chase up on the bus driver, who I located in about ten minutes and who gave a nice clear description of the van driver. He also said the van was probably overladen and he hoped someone would spot him and escort him to a weighbridge. So well done you.'

'I never thought I'd ever hear you say that.'

'Funnily enough, I didn't either.'

'Tell you what, here's a challenge: if you're a clever detective and can locate our camera, I'll get on to the security firm and ask them to release footage to your email address.'

She handed over her tablet with a sideways glance and went on an exaggerated search, like a child hunting a prize in a party treasure hunt. By the time she'd located it, the file had arrived, and was showing an ecclesiastical version of the no-shows on Dodie's cameras: no one was doing anything they shouldn't.

Again like a child, a guilty one this time, she put her hand to her mouth. 'I forgot. Some PCSO contacted me about a problem you'd had with someone knocking you to the ground. No?'

'Not quite. But someone seemed to chase me through Watery Lane and the Washes. I was convinced he was going to thump me. But I managed to give him the slip. I almost cannoned into Phil taking Angus for his evening constitutional a minute or so later, and they escorted me back home.' I paused to acknowledge her sky-high eyebrows. 'Maybe I should have dialled nine-nine-nine, which was what Phil suggested, but – to be honest – not many of your mates would have approved of my method of slowing Chummie down,' I explained.

Silent reverence or not, she threw her head back and yelled with laughter. More soberly, she asked, 'Have any other women runners reported being stalked?'

'There aren't a lot of runners of either gender in Bredeham. But I'll email the women I'm doing cricket practice with and ask if they've had any problems. Warn them too, of course.'

'Good. And we'll put something on our Facebook page. And Twitter. Where did you say you were running from?' She got to her feet and led the way out.

'If you've got time for some of Griff's coffee and biscuits, we could go back via the house I graced with my presence and you can see. Be prepared for serious security – at least as good as Griff's and mine, I'd say.'

'You've got some posh friends,' she said, as she drew the car over so she could take in the place's glories. I'd not have described her as enthusiastic. 'Parson's Pride. Wow. Appropriate name or what? What's it like inside?'

'I've only ever been the wrong side of the green baize door. Someone I know from Pilates lives there. She invited me and another friend for a Chinese the other night. We ate in the kitchen.'

'But you're nobility! Sort of,' she conceded, with an ironic grin.

'Best mates with the Indian take-away driver,' I said, and explained how I'd waited for him to complete his delivery slumped down out of sight.

'Why? Your sixth sense functioning again?' She set the car in motion and headed towards our cottage.

'Maybe. Or maybe an extension of my common sense. I thought some guy in a big black Merc was tailing me, and since it was someone in a big black Merc that had scared poor Mary rigid by warning me to stop doing something unspecified, I was a bit rattled. And now it turns out that Honey's dad drives—'

'Don't tell me – a big black Merc?'

'Exactly. And though we were guests in his house, he locked us in the kitchen. OK, the biggest kitchen you've ever seen outside Downton Abbey, and palatial with it. It's even got its own magnificent cloakroom, but all the same.'

'Name? Anything else you know?' There was no doubt her ears were twitching.

'It's awful. I don't know his name. His daughter's just Honey, his son Spencer. The other girl, Laura – to my shame I don't even know her surname. It's all first name stuff.'

'Youth culture,' she said tersely.

Given the middle-aged milieu I frequented, I took that as a compliment.

'Honey said her parents were separated, both in other relationships, and that her dad made his money in recycling. But

I thought she was being economical with the truth. Funnily enough,' I added, as she pulled up outside our gates, 'her brother Spencer is dead secretive about his father, too. I always think it's nice to know a bit of background about a person. Just a bit. Well, he really doesn't want us to know what he does. Or what his dad does. He told me about his schools – fairly posh, I think – and his rugby playing. But how he spends his days I've no idea. Now, Griff likes him, so before we go in let me tell you I really don't care one scrap for Spencer. Like me, he won't go for DBS accreditation. You know I'd rather not court humiliation because my past's a little murky. So what does that make his? Of course, like me,' I added, with an ironic preen, 'he may have been a model citizen of late. Helping you lot rather than helping you with your enquiries.'

'So he might. Why don't you like him?'

'I used to have the feeling he was trying too hard to find out all about me; he was overfriendly. But then when I was telling him about the guys trying to break into the church, he didn't get excited at all – no sense that I was putting myself at risk, no jealousy I was with Phil. No empathy. Almost an irritation that the guys weren't properly masked. Weird. And then – something else you mustn't tell Griff or he'll die of terror – while I was with him I nearly fell under a lorry.'

She snapped her fingers. 'Your text! The CCTV footage. I completely forgot about it. Too busy with someone having placed a pot of geraniums where someone's stomach should have been, I imagine. Shit! Forget I said that. Please. Me and my big mouth.' She looked and sounded as contrite as she ought to be.

'You obviously need that coffee,' I said mildly. 'And – please – not a word to Griff. About anything that might alarm him. At all.'

TWENTY-FIVE

I n the event, a text made about an unexpected meeting caused Freya to sink her coffee, so quickly that I thought her throat must be asbestos-lined, and hurtle back to Maidstone. 'Sodding budgets again,' she declared, grabbing a biscuit. Waving her thanks to Griff, she dived out of the door, pursued more slowly by me. 'And I've not forgotten the CCTV stuff,' she mouthed. 'OK?'

When I asked Griff idly if he could recall Spencer's surname, his face was a perfect blank. 'I don't think I've ever known. Why do you ask?'

'You know me – always nosy. The funny thing is that I've never known either – nor Honey's, of course. They certainly know mine. They've Googled me, just like you checked on Pargetter.'

It struck me that one way to save the undoubtedly over-stretched Freya a little work would be to find the name of the owner of Parson's Pride; of course she could do it in minutes, but I suspected she didn't have a nano-second to spare – even delegation took a breath she didn't have. On impulse I phoned Afzal: straight to voicemail. Next I tried the Pilates studio and got Greg, the owner, first ring.

'Lina, you know I can't tell you people's names. Data protection and all that.'

'It's just that she had me for supper the other night – lovely place, Parson's Pride – and I wanted to send her thank-you flowers. I don't think *Miss Honey, Parson's Pride* would be quite enough for Interflora, do you?'

'Sounds too *Gone with the Wind* for words! Well, if you know her address . . . and you've eaten there, you say? What's it like inside?'

'Amazing. Wow, Greg, you'd fit the studio into their cloak-room. So it's Honey . . .?'

'Blakemore. There. Oh dear, Lina, I really shouldn't have done.'

'If the library had been open I could have got it from the Electoral Roll, couldn't I? So don't worry. See you, Greg! Thanks!' I was already texting Freya. And embarking on a spot of Googling on my own account. I needed a first name for Blakemore senior, didn't I? Easy peasy. Mortimer. And Mortimore Blakemore in connection with recycling? Google had no suggestions at all. More information for Freya.

I was just settling, rather belatedly, to my morning's work, when Mary phoned across from the shop. Someone was asking specifically for me. And she had one of my business cards.

Kate Evans? Wiping my hands, I headed downstairs.

It seemed that this time she *had* fallen in love with items on our website, things I was more than happy to give her a huge discount on – especially as I knew how much Griff had marked them up in the first place. I'm never sure how much I like the most richly gilded modern Crown Derby; in the right setting it looks superb, of course, but in the wrong place it can appear to be simply vulgar. However, I am always amazed by the skills of the original craftsmen, and certainly wasn't going to do anything to deter Kate from buying a pair of 1930s plates.

We talked about some of our other stock – all very relaxed and pleasant, had I not already missed so much work time. Mary wrapped the plates to perfection, and Kate prepared to leave the shop. But just as Mary was pressing the button to unlock the door, she turned back. 'Did you ever check those CCTV pictures, Lina?'

'The police are on to it,' I declared confidently, my fingers crossed behind my back.

'Excellent. You need to look after yourself. Or I won't be able to plan your wedding, will I?'

Mary might appear to be a vague and slightly ditzy woman, but she'd been a teacher for many years and knew when someone had said something of importance. As soon as she'd relocked the door, she turned to me, suddenly gaining a couple of inches and a bucketful of authority. 'Well? What was all that about? CCTV, Lina? And the police?' she prompted. 'And you can plead that you've got paint drying till you're blue in the face, but I can tell when something's up, even when Griff can't.' And then she blew my defences completely by pushing a tin of her home-made scones in my direction.

Coming completely clean was the best option. 'The day Harvey came, I made myself scarce by going into Maidstone. While I was there, I was walking along a street and found myself almost under the wheels of a juggernaut. Kate Evans and Spencer grabbed me by the arms and pulled me back, just in time.'

'Spencer: he's the young man that goes dancing. So you were seeing him to avoid Harvey?' She screwed up her face as if it helped her understand better.

'Not quite. We ran into each other. By that time I was heading off to see Freya but he insisted on accompanying me. You know Griff rather encourages him, Mary . . .'

'He just wants to see you settled happily. So the CCTV . . .?'

'When I met her again in Hythe, she told me I ought to check it. No idea why. Freya said it would be easier if she did it. So it's in her hands. All safe and sound.'

'Go on, convince me. Freya's got too much on her plate, according to Griff, to know what day it is, let alone what she should be doing. When did you ask her? Shrug all you like, Lina, you can't tell me you didn't ask her some days back and she's still promising immediate action.' She picked up the phone. 'Go on. Call her. Or I'll tell Griff.'

'I'll text her the moment I get back to my phone.'

'Good. I want your word on that. And didn't you promise Griff to read through Paul's suggestions for the future of this shop? Have you got round to it?'

'I couldn't understand a word,' I confessed.

'Bring it down here and we'll go through it together. Believe me, Lina, this is more important than the application of one more coat of paint. And then we'll go through the contract together. But not until you've been in touch with Freya.'

Somehow Paul and Griff had valued our stock and premises at way below what I'd have imagined, and in normal circumstances any bank would have been happy to give me a loan, with the restoration business as collateral, whatever that was.

'But we're not living in normal financial times, are we, Paul? Banks aren't friendly things with handfuls of cash to throw at potentially good businesses. We both know some are actively closing down firms that are actually in profit so they can realize their assets.'

Paul oozed exasperation. I was supposed to be the artistic half of Tripp and Townend, not the one who knew a bit about current affairs. He insisted he still had plenty of contacts from his accounting days, and had no doubt he'd find one to support me. Would I give him the go-ahead?

With Griff breathing down my neck, how could I refuse? But the proof of the pudding, as the cliché goes, would be in the eating.

There was still no response from Freya, but that was typical of her. So I did the obvious thing. I got out Kate's business card and phoned her.

First I established that she'd got the plates home and liked them enough to keep them: it was Tripp and Townend policy to exchange items if they didn't work in their new home. Then, PR done, I said, 'I know you don't want to accuse anyone of anything, but the police are being remarkably slow in dealing with my request about the CCTV footage. Something clearly worried you when I slipped. Off the record, could you tell me what?'

She clearly did not want to be pinned down.

'If the footpath is uneven, I should report the near-miss in the hope that the council will repair it before someone takes a real purler.'

Silence.

'Kate, there's that old punchline – *did he fall or was he pushed?* Are you worried that my fall might not have been accidental?'

Pause. 'I didn't like your friend's joke about you being drunk.'

'The man's an idiot. Absolutely not a friend of mine. Though perversely he fancied me. Might still do. But I don't care the click of my fingers for him.'

Another pause. 'Perhaps he thought you might find him more attractive if he rescued you from a dangerous situation?'

'Kate, you really do think he pushed me, don't you?'

A pause so long it was nearly another silence. 'Yes. I do.

But you must see for yourself,' she said with a rush. 'And
don't say anything, anything at all, to anyone, till you've looked
at the footage yourself. And, Lina, I'd much rather not have
to say all this in court, you know.'

'Of course.' Though I couldn't see – if it was a case of
attempted murder – that she'd not be invited into the witness
box. 'Kate, you've been more than helpful. And I'm so glad
the plates are happy in their new home.'

It was time for another phone call. To Jane Dockery. Did
she know if Martin Fellows was back yet? I really needed
details of that phantom stallholder. 'And I can't just phone a
man I've never met and ask him, out of the blue, to give me
information, can I?' I concluded sunnily. If I'd thought I'd get
anything out of him, I wouldn't hesitate, of course. But there
were times when a subtle approach might work better.

'Actually, you might know him,' she countered. 'He's got
family your way. No? Very well, I'll put it down on my To
Do list.'

'Jane, it really is quite important. I know I'm being a pain,
but . . .'

'Data protection phooey,' Freya declared. 'Have you noticed
when people are too idle to do something they blame the
Data Protection Act or "Elf and Safety"? Of course this
Dockery woman can tell you Martin's address. But my
computer can do it more quickly.' Tossing me an apple, she
sank her teeth into hers as she tapped away. 'Yes, here we
are. Martin Fellows. The Big House – that's an original name
for you – Middle Bredeham. Must be some pad to have such
a perfunctory address.' She clicked again. 'Hey, come and
look at this.'

I went round to her side of the desk to peer at the screen.
'It's a gem, isn't it? Perfect Tudor – all those tiny bricks in
herringbone patterns. And look at those curly chimneys.
Amazing. So how is a man who owns a place like that associated with a one-horse village antiques fair? Why bother?'

'That's what I intend to find out. Actually, no, not me in
person, because I've got something else to do. But I got talking
to this bright young woman DS in the loo the other day –

seems she knows you. Something to do with an old lady you've been keeping an eye on. Had loads of clothes stolen? Well, she was at a loose end and I sort of co-opted her.'

'Fi Hunt? She's been in the thick of liaising with Devon and Cornwall about the theft of Dodie Boulton's netsuke.'

'Quite. In fact she should be knocking on the big front door of the Big House about now. I really want to pull all this together, Lina. Sometimes I disappear under all I have to do, but sometimes, like you, I get a niggle that won't go away and I have to act on my gut instinct and prioritize that. And I've got a niggle now. To do with all this business. But first, let me take you down a couple of corridors. I've got something to show you.'

'I take it it's not pictures of Imogen . . .'

Nor was it. Banks of screens surrounded an Amazon of a woman, who looked as if she'd rather be out on the streets sorting out brawls herself rather than merely directing her colleagues to trouble spots. Acknowledging Freya and me, she slid her chair to one particular monitor, its frozen frame showing a young woman in mid-flight towards a lorry.

'And this must be the star of our video,' the Amazon declared. Her badge insisted she was Finuola Byrne; perhaps she was an indirect descendant of Finn McCool. 'Trouble is, we can see you here, Miss, and here.' There I was, beside Spencer, with another figure, presumably Kate Evans, hurrying up. The next frame showed Spencer apparently putting his arm round my shoulders to hug me. Then there were two hands on my back, but they must have been pulling me back, as on the following one I was between the two of them, dusting myself off. 'Nothing worth having of the alleged incident itself. Not from that camera. However,' she added, with the air of one about to pull at least a hare out of a top hat, 'there is another one here.' She clicked her mouse efficiently. 'There. I'd say the guy was looking round before that arm went out. And it was only when that woman's arm shot out to grab you that he opened his fist and grabbed you too. But that's only my interpretation. Who knows what madam here thinks?' She winked at me, looking across at Freya.

'Or what defence counsel would make of it,' Freya said

cautiously. 'Thanks, Fin. Did you have time to check any other sightings of Chummie? Aka Spencer Blakemore, of course.'

'Sorry, Guvnor. There's a lot going on, this time of day. RTAs; tailacks; road rage. But I'll hang on ten minutes at the end of my shift to go through it all, just in case.'

I was about to protest that she oughtn't to give up her spare time, but found I could only add my thanks to Freya's.

As we walked back to her office, I said, my lips strangely rubbery, 'Why should a bloke who's appeared to fancy me pull a trick like that?'

'Perhaps,' she said slowly, her voice disconcertingly kind for a woman whose usual mode was bracing, 'it was just a trick. Perhaps he would have pulled you back in the nick of time, hoping to look like a hero in your eyes.'

Just what Kate had wondered. This time I had enough time to think.

'That's a bit subtle for Spencer. We'd been talking about the business of the fake scaffolders. And I just thought that a man interested in me as a person might have been more interested in how the whole business had affected me.' I recounted our conversation. 'But all he was interested in was that the guys weren't wearing balaclavas. Weird or what.'

'Weird indeed,' she said. But then she was paged and had to dash off.

Feeling as if someone had punched me all over again, I headed – carefully – back to the station.

TWENTY-SIX

My usual brisk walk from Bredeham station felt more like a trudge, as if I was carrying a lot more cares on my shoulders than I ought. One of my immediate concerns was Griff's safety. If Spencer had been cross-questioning him, did that mean he was next in line for a push? The funeral of his dearest friend wouldn't make a good birthday present at all for poor Aidan, would it? But on the other hand, having Griff under his roof to celebrate just might improve what promised to be a pretty dull event. I'd certainly be a lot happier if he was tucked away in genteel Tenterden.

I was so busy working out how I could organize this subtly – or even not very subtly – that I nearly walked into my father. To be fair, he was the last person I expected to see strolling round the village.

'Slouching, Lina. Come on, shoulders back, chin up – I'll stand you a drink.' Taking my arm he propelled me into the Pig and Whistle, sitting us down at a table for two and raising a lordly finger to the bartender. Instead of responding, as I expected, with two of his own, the young man trotted over obediently. 'Your usual, sir?'

'Of course. And one for yourself, too, don't forget.'

The lad tugged his forelock – really! – and scuttled off.

'Your usual?' I prompted.

'Often drop by when I've been to see Dodie,' he said. 'And I've brought her in that contraption of hers a couple of times. Didn't your mother ever tell you it was rude to stare, young lady? Of course I bring her here. Why not? Both consenting adults. Those church folk of yours do their best, but they can't make her laugh like I can. And I've got a bit of time on my hands now.'

The bartender reappeared with champagne, an ice bucket and two chilled glasses. He dived off, reappearing with some nibbles. I was so disconcerted I didn't pick up on Pa's last sentence until too late.

He was already talking again. 'I hear you go round pretty regularly. But she says you never stay as long as either of you would like. Something about a debarring certificate. Couldn't make head or tail of it.'

'If I go as a church representative, I need to be signed off as a good citizen. If I go as me, as an antiques dealer, I might arouse her family's suspicions – they might think I'm after her stuff.'

'They might if they ever showed their noses.'

'Noses in the plural, Pa?' Heavens, the champagne was good.

'Two lousy sons. From two lousy husbands. A bit naive, my Dodie – got in with some bad lots,' he declared, entirely straight-faced. 'That ambassador chappie, Boulton, he was her third. Decent, that one, but dull as ditchwater. First one gave her Tiny: premature, you see. Second husband was a prize shit: he begat – that's the sort of word Tripp would use, eh? – Tim. Tiny, Tim – get it? I promise you that was what they were always known as.'

'But Dodie's social worker, Emma Something or other, always refers to the son. Just the one.'

He topped up my glass. 'Of course. No one ever refers to Tim. The black sheep. Well, Tiny's pretty grey too, come to think of it, as sheep go.' Without missing a beat he asked, 'Did you know they're planning to use them to mow the front lawn at the Hall? Wanted to know what I thought of the idea. Fine, so long as you don't expect me to walk on it, I said. And think of all that crap being trodden into the carpets.'

'Dodie's sheep,' I prompted. 'Start with the black one.'

'Drugs, booze, gambling . . . Big gambler. Lost his pa's car once, they say. Not your average Mini, either. Should have told you, the father got custody. Son wouldn't have anything to do with poor Dodie. Families, eh?' He reached and stroked my cheek with the back of a finger. 'It seemed Tim blamed her for everything he did. Walked out of his pa's place one day. No word of goodbye. But they knew he'd gone for good because he'd taken the best silver. They covered it up – blamed some chance burglar long since in France. And that was that. Never saw him again.'

'And Tiny?' My heart felt sore at the thought of all the family strife. How could such a nice woman as Dodie inspire such loathing in her own son?

'Tiny was a mummy's boy. He's still in touch with her, after all. But he takes after his dad, and if he isn't the one who's stolen all her clothes and other bits and pieces I'll eat that bucket. Actually, I could eat anything.'

'In that case, you can eat it at ours. I've got a plan, Pa, and all you need do when I put it to Griff is nod sagely. OK?' I jammed my thumb into the neck of the bottle – I needed to be sober – and led the way to the cottage.

Griff would probably have been delighted to go off to luxuriate in the best of Tenterden's wining and dining, all within reach of Aidan's fabulous house, but he didn't want to leave me in Pa's company. Or worse still, on my own.

To hell with being subtle. 'Griff, you've been talking quite a bit to Spencer – the arch-interrogator. I might be paranoid on your behalf, but there's something I should tell you.'

By the time I'd finished my story, both men were red in the face with anger. 'And the police have done nothing?'

'They've hardly had time, Pa. They've got fewer resources, less money, more targets. Freya's taken on someone else's case load as well as working on a nasty murder—'

'Not that man with a pot of geraniums where his stomach should be?'

'How do you know about that, Pa? They've imposed a media blackout.'

'Grapevine. But he's dead. What about you? You might have been.'

'True. But the CCTV footage also suggests he might have grabbed me at the last minute to stop me falling. So it's by no means a clear-cut case. He might even have staged it to make himself look heroic.' I was less convinced by the theory each time.

Pa wasn't impressed either: 'I'd have thought that a rather passé notion.'

'Anyway I had this Kate woman on the other side, and I'm here talking to you both now. So your taking a couple of days out of the way somewhere would be ideal, Griff.'

He was almost sold on the idea. But not quite. 'I'm not leaving you all alone in this cottage!'

'No. You're not. Tonight Pa and I will pick up some of Afzal's finest and adjourn to Bossingham Hall. I hope you keep that bedroom aired, Pa. And we'll share our feast with Titus. Because if anyone has the low-down on Dodie's low-life sons, he will. OK?' Griff was wavering. 'And tomorrow I can take some work down to do in the shop. Oh, anything,' I said as his eyebrows shot up – he knew I preferred the lab-like conditions of my workroom. But something started to ring in my head. I patted the kitchen table. 'Honey,' I said, surprising them both. 'When she and Laura ate here, Honey went on and on about what I could mend and what I couldn't.'

'Honey is Spencer's brother,' Griff told Pa, *sotto voce*. 'I thought it wonderful that our girl had friends of her own age. Now I begin to wonder.'

I looked at my watch. 'Phone Aidan now. You'll just have time for a late supper. I'll get a taxi and pack your overnight bag.' With enough clothes for at least three days, though I didn't need to say that.

The moment we'd waved him off, I phoned an order through to Afzal. The last person I expected in the queue when I stopped to pick it up was Phil, who greeted me with a smile and cheek-kiss that raised both Afzal's and Pa's eyebrows. Pa seemed more impressed than Afzal, maybe taking Griff's view that a man I could introduce as Dr Russell must be a good thing. For a moment I was afraid he was about to summon him to dine with us at the Hall, but in the end he just thanked him for all he did for Dodie and hoped they'd meet again.

Phil waved at our still empty bag and at his: 'We still haven't had that Thai meal, Lina.'

'I know. I'm sorry. Things have been a bit complicated. But as soon as Griff gets back – he's helping a friend celebrate a big birthday – we'll phone and fix something.'

'It doesn't have to include Griff, you know.' He coughed.

'Actually, we could all adjourn to my place again, if Lord Elham wouldn't mind.'

Interesting use of the third person; perhaps he couldn't get his head round calling him My Lord. And why should he?

Pa rose to the occasion admirably, despite all that shampoo. 'My daughter and I are entertaining another friend at my home, Dr Russell, or we'd certainly have accepted. You'd have been welcome to join us, but my friend is an acquired taste.'

I nodded. 'Very much so. But as soon as I know when Griff is coming home, I promise I'll call you.' It was time to collect our goodies; what I hadn't quite bargained for was Afzal coming from behind the counter and enveloping me in a bear hug. I was more than happy to hug him back – mate, not date, remember.

I gave Angus a good pat as we left; he whined hopefully, wagging his tail until it really did seem to wag him.

'Didn't like to say anything in front of Griff,' Pa confided, as I picked my way gingerly up his rutted drive, 'but there's a bit of a problem with your room. The truth is – well, it's a bit full just now. This job I'm doing, you see. But don't worry, I can fix the security system and you can slip through into the Hall and pick your own bedroom.'

'This job, Pa – you promise it's legal?'

'It's pretty well for the Crown itself,' he declared. 'But no more questions, Evelina; I shall reveal all in my own good time.'

Titus was already in the kitchen, and to my amazement had laid the table – clearly there were hidden domestic depths to the man. He and I removed the little plastic boxes from the insulated bag and microwaved them, laying them on the peninsula of old-fashioned cork mats he'd had the forethought to find, probably somewhere in Pa's hoard.

'Between these four walls,' he declared, as he helped himself to rice.

Pa pointed to the ceiling. 'In other words, this whole conversation is *sub rosa*,' he confirmed. 'Here, what are you doing?'

'Leaving now,' I said. 'You know I need information that will stop people assaulting me and robbing church artefacts, in whichever order. You also know I can't stop it on my own. Or even with your two standing shoulder to shoulder with me. Pensioner power may have worked in Bredeham, but it might have come at a hell of a cost. You'll have to trust me to work out what material I can pass to the police. Or say nothing. Or decide for yourselves what to tell me. OK?'

Titus looked at the feast as if I might take it all away. 'You could freeze it for another day,' he told Pa.

Pa hovered in a state somewhere between sitting and standing. 'Not having my girl killed for the want of a few words.'

I pressed him back on to his chair, sitting beside him and taking some naan. 'Shoot, then. Shoot and eat. Dodie's sons, Tiny and Tim.' I deeply resented the fact that one of them shared a name with my bear – who, in my haste to depart, I'd forgotten. That decided it. There was no way I'd sleep on my own in the Hall without him. 'Well?'

'Does the name Mortimer Blakemore mean anything to you?' Pa pulled a nice furry rabbit out of his hat. What a shame he could tell from my face that I recognized it. 'Oh.'

'Only as the father of Spencer, the guy who might or might not have shoved me under a lorry, and Honey, who wanted to know all about my repair business. And as the owner of a house to die for.'

'Never did like that expression.' Titus sniffed approvingly at the chicken Dilshan.

'And,' I declared, 'he and his kids keep their cards as close to their chests as you do, Titus. Come on, give, the pair of you.'

They exchanged a glance. 'What about Martin Fellows?'

'Ah – he's Mr Elusive. He organizes antiques fairs in a village called Dockinge. As far as I know, he doesn't live there. And he may or may not have rented out a site to a group who were ostensibly selling garden statuary, but I think robbed the church there and gave me a shocking headache. But he's been off on some cruise . . .'

'You've nothing to connect the two?'

'Only the fact that one is into recycling, the other antique fairs – not a close connection.'

Titus shook his head. 'You want to sell something dodgy, it's a car boot sale or local antiques fair, doll. Got word all sorts of one-off stalls have popped up at his fairs. How does retro designer clothing grab you?'

'Designer as in Dior? As in Dodie's Dior?' Even as he nodded, I was asking, 'But how did he get hold of it?' I raised a hand. 'Mortimer – he's Tim, isn't he? Just the middle of his name? And Martin must be Tiny. They're brothers. They're her own sons. One – the one who's still in touch – gets power of attorney, stops her BUPA membership and, oh, he steals her stuff and finds a way of getting rid of some of it; the other presumably takes on what he can't and "recycles" it!'

Titus continued flatly, 'Word is he recycles other stuff too. Big stuff. Impressive stuff.'

'Stolen stuff,' Pa put in. 'Stolen to order, so not strictly recycled.'

'Church stuff?' Heavens, this was catching.

'That's what they say. Goodness, my girl – what are you doing with that phone of yours? This is the dinner table, for goodness' sake!'

Shamefaced, I was about to put it away. But a text warbled its way in, and I knew I had to take it. Raising an apologetic hand, I got up from the table. 'It's from our security firm,' I said. 'There's activity near our cottage. They wanted to warn me. I'll have to go.' I dotted a kiss on Pa's head. On impulse, I slapped Freya's business card on the table between them. 'Call this woman now, and tell them what you've told me!' I left the Hall at a run.

I'd never put the Audi to the test before but had to now, treating the poor thing like a rally car as it bucked and bounced its way down the track and into the lane. Even then I didn't dare floor the accelerator: it was country roads I was driving through, with a couple of elbow bends between Bossingham and the main road that had been known to defeat even trained police drivers, two of whom had once arrived unheralded in the graveyard of the parish church by dint of driving straight through a fence.

I knew, of course, that the security team would be there long before me, summoning the police if necessary – preferably via their hotline, not the 101 service. And if this wayward farm vehicle didn't pull off soon – it was far too wide for me to contemplate overtaking – everything would probably be done and dusted before I reached the outskirts of Bredeham.

It was. The street outside the shop and cottage was deserted. Via our Bluetooth connection, the duty security officer – Imran – phoned me to say it had all been a false alarm. 'You're sure?' It still seemed strange not to hold the mobile while I talked.

'Absolutely.'

'Before you go, tell me how long it took your mates to get here.'

'Sixteen minutes, door to door.'

I didn't so much think as know. 'Get them back to the village – to the church,' I said, flooring the accelerator. 'Now.' He may even have heard the squeal of the tyres.

The people we were dealing with weren't stupid, were they? They'd know – they'd have timed them – that once the security team and the police had left the village, they'd have a little time to strip the best stuff from the church. With luck they wouldn't know about the camera, wouldn't know that any movement would trigger it. And once the alarm sounded, the team could turn on their heels and race back. U-turn. Silly Lina. But by then they might have torn out the brasses or broken up the wooden carving. Not on my watch they wouldn't. At least I hadn't come unarmed this time. I had a spray that managed to be legal. Not pepper, but probably almost as effective, since the person on the receiving end finished up with a red face – and if he or she tried to wipe it away they ended up red-handed. Literally.

This time the vehicle parked outside the church was a plumber's van. Did churches need plumbers? I'd never given it much thought. Someone had lifted the stopcock cover and a convincing-looking cast-iron rod poked out. Was I mistaken? Or were these guys just good at window dressing? Holding my phone – set to camera – in one hand, my spray in the other, I was ready to move in.

'I thought you were at your father's,' a voice said quietly.

Phil. Angus was checking out a lamp-post.

'I was. Our security company said there was a threat to the

cottage and to come home. I was just going back to Pa's when I saw this.' I curled my thumb at the van. 'What do you think?'

'I think you're right to be anxious. Last time you called someone: can't you do that this time?'

I went one better. I texted Freya and security, telling them: *Look at church camera feed now!*

'You're not going in, surely?' He gripped my forearm quite tightly.

'Genuine plumbers won't mind. Fake ones might be hacking bits off the church even as we speak. So yes, I'm going in. Be prepared to trip anyone making a quick exit, right? Oh, use Angus's lead!'

It didn't take long for my eyes to get used to the comparative gloom in the body of the church. Or for my camera to snap four people in jumpsuits; each carried a jemmy and black polythene sacks. But then – who was that behind me?

TWENTY-SEVEN

I smelt something before I even heard or sensed a movement. Something – no, someone, wearing perfume or cologne. And a Tony Blair face mask. An ex-Prime Minster was going to crack me on the head. But this time I wasn't going to be socked. The spray was out and fired before I was even on my feet to run. Poor fake Tony Blair: the person behind the mask was howling shrilly, mostly with rage. The noise made the four other identical Tony Blairs wheel round to face me. All had chisels in their hands; two of them brandished hammers. The camera must be working overtime by now – but it would be useless, of course, in recognizing the men behind the masks. As one they headed towards me.

Once they got within range of my spray, I'd be within reach of their chisels. But I might still buy myself a couple of minutes.

I was right by a shelf full of hymn books – hardbacks, solid. I thought about Fozia and cricket practice, and all those balls thrown against the wall. I can't claim to have hit with each book, but the barrage certainly took the Blairs aback.

Four of them in front. There was still the one behind me, too, who'd be as angry as a wasp by now. On impulse I dropped the book I was holding and ran forwards, grabbing an implement I'd found so useful in Devon: a warden's staff. This time I didn't dare poke at the men. The odds were too poor. So I headed for the pulpit. There was only room for one person at a time to climb those steps, and once installed I could jab down at anyone coming up. There was still some dye left in the spray too, with luck.

Custer's last stand – in Bredeham.

Part of my mind wondered why Phil, who must have heard all the noise, hadn't dashed in like the cavalry to my rescue. God knew I couldn't hold out much longer – in fact, since I was in His house, I really could have done with some of His assistance.

But I didn't expect Him to send in an armed response unit, and I especially didn't expect them to have their weapons pointing at me.

I couldn't obey their orders to lie flat on the ground either, could I? So, watching the Blairs prostrate themselves, I stood with arms spread as wide and weaponless as I could make them, the staff, my phone and spray clattering from my splayed fingers on to the tiles. The longer my arms stayed airborne, the greater was the impulse to drop them, but you don't argue with the barrels of what looked like very serious weapons. What little I could see of each face was certainly very grim indeed.

'How did I guess?' Freya's voice rang out from the church door. 'OK, Lina, come on down. But keep your hands where we can all see them. The rest of you can gather up our erstwhile Middle Eastern Peace envoy – or at least his representatives in Kent. Been on the Red Eye flight, have you, gentlemen? One at a time, mind. And keep them separate.' She raised one hand, stopping her colleagues short. 'Tell you what, let's see the rest of their faces. Stay where you are, Lina. I said— Oh, shit!'

I could no more have stayed where I was than flown to the moon. I was down the steps and heading towards the masks. Who did I know who wore cologne? Phil the Pill. Honey – no, hers was always upmarket and feminine – and Spencer Blakemore. It had to be Spencer, didn't it?

It was. They had to tear me off him.

The police removed the masks from the other three not much more gently. I didn't recognize any faces and waved them an ironic goodbye.

As they took Spencer and the other ex-Blairs away, I rested my hands on a pew. That was that, then.

Had I messed up everything? Had I ruined the police case?

Then it dawned on me that someone was missing: the person who'd crept up behind me. I could have sworn that he'd rushed at me as I ran to the pulpit. So where was he now?

I put my hand on Freya's arm, touching my finger to my lips. 'One got away,' I mouthed.

'Couldn't have. You're sure?'

At this point a figure emerged from the rear of the church, for some reason wearing dark glasses. She waved. Honey?

'I came in to see what was going on,' she said blithely. 'And there were all these policemen looking fierce. So I thought I'd better stay where I was.'

'Quite right,' I said, heading towards her with a smile. I could sense Freya's alert tension as she followed. As if it was a social occasion we exchanged air kisses before I introduced them. I made sure that Freya was close enough to grab her if necessary. But I wasn't in any great hurry. 'I'm sure I dropped something earlier,' I lied cheerfully. 'Just hang on, then we can walk home together.' As if. But I left her no time for argument, slipping off with a wink to Freya.

Got it! Tucked behind the very back pew was a jumpsuit, just like the men's. And a dirty tissue showing that someone had scrubbed at their red eyelids. Evidence. I knew better than to touch it.

Time to stroll back to Freya. 'I must have been mistaken. But someone else had left something behind. Heavens, Honey, I know Pilates has given you wonderful core muscles, but are you sure you should have put them to that sort of use?' I pointed at the damaged wood.

She started swearing and clawing at me, until Freya pinioned her. She completed the performance by spitting at me. It would have done me so much good to get into a catfight and crack her skull on the church floor. So much good. Or I could have outsworn her. Easily.

But not here. Not in church. Though I could hardly breathe, though I was shaking with the effort not to be violent, I managed to say, without so much as a quaver in my voice, 'Judas!' And I turned on my heel and walked back to the altar.

I'm not quite sure how long I was on my knees, long enough for them to cart Honey off, however, because when I opened my eyes I found Freya on her knees beside me. After a while, she asked quite matter-of-factly, 'OK, what damage have the buggers done?'

'I've not had time to look,' I said, realizing that just behind us some people were rapidly shimmying into protective suits. Someone handed one to Freya. I pushed my luck. 'Got a spare?'

It seemed they had. Freya snorted as she tossed it to me. '"Elf and Safety" – hitch the trouser legs up and don't dare fall over. That's better. Fits you like a drink of water, doesn't it?' If she meant it was so large it almost dripped from me, I suppose it did. 'Let's have some lights over here!'

And there was light.

She twitched the gloves she'd pulled on; we all did. And like her I ran my fingers over the chisel marks, surprisingly limited in scope and fairly superficial. 'Could you fix it?' she asked.

'A woodwork version of me could. But not me. By the way,' I added, turning, 'have you noticed the lectern's not where it should be?'

'Check their van,' she shouted over her shoulder. 'The plumber's, of course!'

For some reason Freya insisted on my accompanying her to Maidstone, where she installed me in a soft interview room, with tissues and teddy bears for company.

'We're a bit busy tonight,' she said, flipping over a couple of KitKats. 'If you want to curl up and have a kip, that sofa looks comfortable. I'll get someone to bring you a blanket.'

'I could always sleep at home,' I said mildly, breaking the KitKat and handing her half.

'Not till we've thoroughly checked the cottage; something was going down there earlier, and we want to make sure everything's OK. So I could do with your keys and your burglar alarm code, please.'

'The place has got one or two hidden surprises,' I said. 'I'd get Sam from security to go with you. Or I could show your mates myself.' I really didn't want to hand over anything to anyone. Paranoid or what?

'You're staying here till we know it's safe. I promised your pa. Oh, yes, he was on the blower the moment you left

Bossingham Hall. Didn't make much sense at first. Had he
been drinking?'

'When has he not been drinking?' I said cautiously. She
was still after Titus, after all, and he'd probably been standing
next to Pa when he made his call.

'Your mate Oates sounded sober enough. Sober enough to
give me names. Didn't even bargain for immunity from prosecution.' She paused expectantly.

'I think he deserves it.'

'You would, wouldn't you? Look, I've got to mop things
up here and liaise with Devon. I'll get whatshername to debrief
you and also fill you in. Fi Hunt. Only don't give her so much
as a crumb of that.' She pointed to the KitKat. 'She's not up
to speed on her fitness tests.'

I might have been braced for a night identifying vile people,
but Fi brought me the frustrating yet suddenly welcome
news that the police computer system had crashed. 'I'll give
you a ride home,' she said. 'Your security people and our
SOCOs have been through the cottage and found nothing.
But if you happen to wake in the night, don't be surprised
to find a couple of our lads parked outside. Just to be on
the safe side.'

To keep my mind off the appalling situation Titus might
have put himself in, just to save my skin, during the drive I
talked nothings with Fi, who was happy enough to give me
the run-down on the problems of being a mother and full-time
sergeant. Our route took us past Dodie's cottage.

I pointed. 'What's she doing up at this hour?'

She slammed on the brakes and put the car into screaming
reverse. 'Let's find out. No, you stay here.'

As if.

The front door was unlocked. Calling out, we pushed it
open to find a scene of chaos. The radio and picture of
Bossingham Hall were in pieces. The tatty ornaments were
shards scattered over the carpet.

'Dodie?'

She'd got as far as her bedroom, and was lying still
dressed on her bed, clutching the bear now called Mop. As

I ran to her, to take her hand, I could hear Fi yelling for an ambulance.

'Bossy,' Dodie murmured. 'I knew you'd be here.'

I touched my lips as Fi came in. She nodded, quietly stroking Dodie's tears away.

'I won't leave you,' I whispered. 'But you mustn't leave me – understand? Try and tell me who smashed your stuff.'

'My boy.'

Her son! If he'd been in the room just then it would have taken more than four police officers to tear me off.

But she was reaching for my hand again. I had to bend close to hear what she was saying. 'That lovely girl of yours, Bossy – those clever cameras of hers . . . He didn't like them. Always did have nasty tantrums. Couldn't control himself then. Not now. And his brother.' She gripped my hand tightly. 'My will, Bossy! That solicitor of yours. He's got my will. And I want to be buried with Mop. No one else will ever love him as much as I do. Do you understand?'

'Let's not talk about dying now,' Fi said briskly. 'Can you hear that? That's an ambulance on its way.'

'Life'll be so much better when you can see properly again,' I said. Anything to keep her with us.

'I'd love to see your face,' she said, reaching for my cheek. 'Yours and your dear girl's. Look after her, Bossy. And you look after him, Evelina.'

'Of course I will.' I had to try to speak normally; my sobbing wouldn't do her any good. As the paramedics filled the doorway, I added, 'Now, these nice people will make you better. I'll come in the ambulance with you.' I pressed her hand, kissed her cheek.

'Not going to dwindle.' I think that was what she said. 'Balloons!'

I held her hand to my chest so she'd feel my heart beating, and just talked. Nonsense, I suppose. But they say hearing's the last sense to go.

Suddenly, her eyes opened and she said, with amazing clarity, 'Do not resuscitate. I absolutely forbid it.' Her head turned slightly towards me. 'Good night, my darling. Remember, balloons. And Mop.'

TWENTY-EIGHT

However much I wanted to hide my head under the duvet, clutching Tim and howling, I had to get up. Freya had texted me to say she wanted to see me in Maidstone at eleven to disentangle all the threads. Which of us was to pull which thread I'd no idea. In any case, I had that statement to make.

All I told Mary and Paul was that Griff was away for a few days and that Dodie had died. If they assumed it was a matter of ripe old age, that was fine. They would hold the fort as they always did, entirely competent, and I hoped a good deal safer now Maidstone police station was crammed to the gunwales with the criminals that had once threatened Mary – and me, of course.

What had happened to Phil? And how could I have forgotten to ask about him? Fear gripping my stomach, I made myself look in on the pharmacy en route. The kindly and competent ladies behind the counter, renowned for never flapping, were in headless chicken mode. There was no sign of Phil, one whispered to me, or of Angus, or even a locum. No, Phil wasn't taking any calls, and – her voice dropped lower – there was no sign of anyone at his cottage. When she asked what I thought, it seemed better not to voice my fears. The trouble was, which did I fear most, that he was a victim or a perpetrator?

There were other fears to deal with when I saw Pa and Titus getting into a mini-cab outside the police station. Neither saw my frantic gestures, but theirs were the first names I shot at Freya as she came down in person to sign me in.

'The name Pargetter mean anything to you? Yes? Well, Titus has just given us enough information to see him die in jail.' Thank God Griff didn't get him to handle our icons. 'OK, that may not be long away, because he's clearly a sick man, but they've also given us some of his contacts' names

– and guess who figures amongst them? One of your old friends.'

Mouth dry, I think I swayed.

'That's right. Arthur Habgood. You weren't thinking it was that louse Sanditon, were you? Actually, are you all right?'

'A friend died last night. In my arms.' I found I was shaking. Before I knew it I was in that soft interview room again.

'Does Griff know?' she asked, the moment I'd explained.

'Not yet. I need to tell him myself. I even left a large notice in her house forbidding the church visitors to tell him. Pa needs to know too. So let's get the news of the living out of the way so I can go and do what I have to do. What are you doing?' Tapping at her phone didn't seem particularly helpful.

'Texting Daniel. He's a good parson. He'll help you. OK, where do we start?'

'All the Tony Blairs. Spencer and Honey apart, of course. Freya, cut to the chase. I need to deal with Dodie's death, not play games. Spencer, Honey – what about Blakemore senior?'

'He didn't soil his hands doing the dirty work. So his face isn't indelibly red. He was pulling Spencer and Honey's strings, of course, and involving them in the family business. Which I really do not like. You probably don't either, since their brief was to first try to suborn you, and when that failed to keep an eye on you.'

'Like Spencer shoving me under a lorry?'

'He chickened out.' She reached for my hand and held it – a most un-Freya like gesture. 'I'm glad he did. And I'm quite glad you declined to work for his dad. He's a bad lot: not only did he have a team of heavies in Bredeham, he actually had another team working on St Dunstan in the Dunes, chiselling out a reredos at exactly the same time – quite an empire he's built. But we got a tip-off – some career criminals still respect churches, it seems – and nabbed them too. He was miles away, of course, busy having a row with his mother, him and his brother. Yes, Fi checked – still working six hours after she should have clocked off, bless her.'

'Tim and Tiny . . . Can they be charged with hastening Dodie's death?'

'It'd be the icing on the cake if they could, wouldn't it? We and the Crown Prosecution Service will be looking at every possible charge. Robbing the old lady apart, they've done inestimable damage to our heritage, and to other people's. The trade in stolen church and other historical artefacts runs right across Europe. It looks as if I shall be seconded to the national team to help sort it out. Robin and I will have to take you up on that babysitting offer of yours, if that's still OK?'

'You know it is. Can I ask you a few more questions? Phil the Pill – why didn't he try to help me?' It came out as more of a wail than I liked. Anger would have been altogether better.

'That's our fault. Ours and your security service's. We thought he might be acting as obbo. Well, not me, someone whose common sense had gone AWOL. And then, when they realized he was kosher, they took him back to one of the response vehicles for his own safety. His and Angus's. They didn't want him yapping at men with guns. So it seems as if Phil's on the side of the angels. Even so . . .' She looked at me meaningfully.

I gestured – that was irrelevant at the moment. 'But he's in the clear? Excellent – the village needs him. But why's he not at work this morning?'

'Some idiot put some of those instant plastic handcuffs round Angus's mouth. It took a while to get them off. I think Phil and Angus were probably at the vet's earlier – should be back at work by now though, surely to goodness.' She looked at her watch and nodded disapprovingly at the notion that Phil might be skiving.

'Hmm. More to the point, Pa and Titus: they went off looking perky enough. Do I take it they'll be able to finish this big project of theirs?'

She grinned. 'It's so amazing, isn't it? It'd almost be *lèse majesté* to arrest them.' Her phone chirruped while I breathed a huge sigh. But why did Freya know about whatever it was and not me? Alone in the playground again, it was hard not to let my lip tremble. 'Excellent. Thanks.' She cut the call. 'Daniel's picking up Griff from Tenterden; he'll know how to tell him, and all the other members of his congregation involved. Robin's dropping Imogen off with one of his parishioners and coming over to take you to your pa's – he knows him of old, after all.' She coughed with what might have been embarrassment and looked at me under her brows. 'Do you want me to suggest Carwyn gets compassionate leave?'

'Him *and* Conrad? No, there's no point in poking sleeping dogs, with or without plastic binding round their muzzles. I'm just glad it's easier for people to come out these days. But Robin's a really good idea. Thanks for contacting him. Freya, why do I feel so flat? I should feel something about Honey and Spencer's involvement . . . What an idiot I was to think she wanted me just as a friend.'

'But you stood firm when they asked for your services, Lina, remember that. And Daniel says to tell you something else.' She patted her mobile. 'That whenever he spoke to Dodie, which was quite a lot recently, she told him she wanted a quick end.'

I nodded, trying not to sob. 'She didn't want to dwindle.'

Which is what I told Pa, in his strangely clean living room. He and Titus had already broken out the bubbly to celebrate getting on the right side of the law for once. And it didn't seem at all wrong to toast Dodie's memory in another bottle. It was the way Pa would always deal with tricky things, and I was his daughter, after all. Robin was more cautious in his consumption: he'd be the one driving down the still-unrepaired track, after all.

'We'll have her wake here,' Pa declared. 'No, not here in my rooms. Far too ordinary. I'll tell the trustees we'll have the yellow saloon for the day.'

He did too, and got his way. Dodie had hers, too. To go with her statement ring and amber beads, I found Dior stilettos and a fabulous Chanel suit for her last journey. Mop, decked in a new bow, was going with her to meet her Maker, who, Daniel declared in his sermon, must surely have a soft spot for teddy bears. I said in my brief, tough-to-articulate eulogy, I hoped He might have a similar weakness for balloons: if in life Dodie had had them tied to her wheel-chair, now the whole hearse bubbled with them. Her sons weren't amused, but it might be hard to smile when you were handcuffed together. As they shuffled out of the church between two burly security guards – it seemed that keeping an eye on villains wasn't in the police remit any more – I caught up with them.

Looking from one smug face to the other – they weren't yet prison-pale and had been allowed to wear classy suits from their old lives – I told them what I thought of them: 'You don't belong to the human race. Imagine those long-term raids on your mother's property, when you have more than enough of your own. And what about corrupting your own children, to the extent they ignored their lovely grandmother entirely – they even made jokes about old people as though they no longer deserved respect. You turned them into criminals – you made them befriend me so that I'd work for you. When that didn't work, you wanted them to kill me. Even a rat had more soul. Even a louse.' Add in a few expletives and you get the message. Add in blows to their faces. And a head butt or two.

But I didn't say or do any of those things. It was as if someone had laid a calming hand on my shoulder, pinioned me when I surged forward.

Did they drop their eyes in the face of my silent scorn? Not a bit. They oozed the most loathsome sense of entitlement – only resentful, it seemed to me, that they'd been caught out. And they'd just left a church they'd employed other vile, venal men to desecrate. Holding the gaze of first one then the other, I said the only words appropriate to such a time and place: 'May God forgive you.'

One day I might forgive them myself. But not yet. Sorry, God, I'll work on it.

While they went back to custody, everyone who'd made Dodie's life better, from the care-worker who'd given her the red scarf to the retired podiatrist who'd helped find non-dwindling shoes, came back to the Hall in a convoy of minibuses so they could all get tiddly. Pa had sold a fine jade carving to pay for the booze; the village deli catered, charging only the cost of the ingredients; Afzal chipped in with tiny savouries and some remarkably vivid Indian sweets.

Phil, closing his pharmacy early out of respect, was there of course, with a partly shaven and strangely subdued Angus. Freya had come to the funeral to represent the police and then stayed behind for reasons best known to herself, despite all the pressures on her time. She gave me a reproving look every time she saw Phil and me exchange a word.

No one wanted to leave early, which turned out to be a good thing. With no explanation, an hour or more into the wake, Pa despatched me to the hall to find the dinner gong: 'Bash it as if you're announcing the credits to a movie.'

I did. And very therapeutic it was too. When I returned, he took my hand, said, 'Ever since my daughter and I came back into each other's lives, she's been determined I should turn over a new leaf – not one to forge a document on, incidentally. And now I have, and, apart from Lina, the leaf is my proudest creation. Ladies and gentlemen, please accompany me to the library.' With remarkable grace, he indicated that Griff was to take my other hand. Perhaps he was afraid I'd faint. And I might have done. There, in a beautifully lit glass case, was Magna Carta.

'Commissioned by English Heritage and the British Library,' he said. 'To celebrate the anniversary of Runnymede. The originals can't tour the length and breadth of the land. This, and the other five I've worked on, can. And I'd like to dedicate them all to Dodie's memory.'

Who could argue with that? No one here. Everyone's glass mysteriously filled again and another toast was drunk.

But then a nondescript man sidled up to me. I'd taken him for a security guard, since he'd seemed glued to Magna Carta. But it seemed he wasn't. 'There is one more thing you have to do for Lady Boulton,' he said quietly, passing me a business card: *Derek Waters, LL B* and a lot of other letters. A solicitor? What had I done? 'I'd like to speak to you in private. I had hoped to do so here today, but I can see that it would be inappropriate. Might I ask you to come to my office tomorrow morning?' He fished out his iPhone. 'Would eleven be convenient?'

Looking at his unsmiling face, I rather thought it would have to be.

TWENTY-NINE

Though Pa and Griff both insisted – separately – that one of them, but not the other, should accompany me to Mr Waters' office, I told them that this was something I had to do alone.

I was just about to pop into the shop to say goodbye to Griff when I heard raised voices. *Déjà vu!* No, it was Griff and Paul talking. Paul still hadn't found a financial backer for my take-over bid, by the sound of it, and Griff was quite frantic. So I walked across the yard, and then walked back again, calling cheerily. One glance at Griff's face was enough to show me how desperate he was. Had those tests shown something really nasty? None of my previous attempts to probe had worked, and clearly this wasn't the time for another. But I set off for Canterbury and Mr Waters' office with a heavy heart.

It was housed in one of Canterbury's lovely old buildings, though I sensed that Waters might really be a glass and stainless steel man. But his coffee came in a silver pot, and the cups were china. Three cups. He looked impatiently at his watch – several times – and made a few remarks about the previous day's activities: the service went well, the rector spoke well, the wake went well, and Pa's bombshell – no, it didn't just go well, it was impressive. He might have been a dentist making conversation while he waited for a local anaesthetic to work before he dug into a tooth. I responded as enthusiastically as if he was.

At last voices in the outer office heralded a knock at the door and the grand entrance of a TV expert in Oriental art. Without lights and (possibly?) make-up, Wesley Jago's face was rather more interesting, and his smile as charming (and alarming) as Harvey Sanditon's. I put his age as somewhere in the early sixties, and silently admired a very fine signet ring, as good as Noel Pargetter's magnificent specimen. He took one sip of his coffee and set the cup and saucer aside on the mega-desk. Mine joined it, the very smell putting me off. At this point Waters dug behind his desk and produced a cardboard box, which he laid midway between me and Jago.

'Before I open this, Lady Boulton required me in her will to read the accompanying letter to you, Ms Townend. Are you ready?'

Though I was terrified of hearing her voice from beyond the grave, I nodded. There was no one, not even Tim the Bear, to hold my hand.

'*My darling child,*

You have given me more than pleasure in the few weeks of our friendship, reminding me of the good things of life. You bought me clothes and a reincarnated Mop. You brought back into my life my dear lover, Bossy. Both he and Griff, whose company gave me hours of gentle pleasure, love you dearly, and want a future for you, though neither feels confident of providing it for you.

I want to thank you for what you brought to my cottage, and thank Bossy and Griff too. The only way I can think of doing this is to leave you what little my marauding family have left me. It should be enough to make you independent of them – though I can't imagine for an instant your ever abandoning them to the sort of life my family left me. But if ever you need your own roof over your head, you now have mine. I have no doubt you will make it beautiful. But you need a beautiful life of your own too, and accordingly I leave you my dear rat netsuke (I hope you'll keep him for ever), the little box of treasures locked behind that fake socket and the contents of the loft strongbox, which I advise you to sell. Mr Waters can assure you that I was entirely in my right mind when I made my will and if some of the words in that are his not mine it is because I wanted to make everything watertight.

I leave you with all my love and I hope a few happy memories too.

Your devoted friend,

Dodie Boulton

Perhaps Jago understood I simply could not speak. While Waters produced the rat netsuke, which found its way straight into my hands, he busied himself opening the cardboard box and laying out its contents – the netsuke from the loft strongbox, of course. He picked up a couple at random, and then more and more, deliberately arranging them in some sort of order neither I nor, to judge from his expression, Waters could fathom.

At last he turned to me, his face inscrutable. 'As you know from your own work, Ms Townend, there are good and bad examples of all types of artefacts. It has taken me half my lifetime both here and in Japan to study netsuke, and I will be more than happy to pass on some of the information I have gleaned to you. I should imagine from your reputation in the world of antiques you'd prove a worthy student.' He dug in his sleek briefcase and produced a book which he signed and passed to me with a smile. 'With my compliments. You might want to read it before you take my advice about the sale of these masterpieces.'

My mouth said, 'Masterpieces? I don't imagine you use a word like that lightly.'

'Oh, I don't. Believe me. Now, you see this semi-circle. What do you make of it?'

The last thing I wanted to do was perform my divvy's party trick. But I almost felt Dodie's hand on my shoulder. 'They're truly mine? I can handle them?' Yes, the trick I used to persuade customers to buy worked just as well on me. They were mine. And then I knew the answer to his question. 'This end is the bottom end of the collection, and this the top.' Perhaps I should have made that a question, out of politeness, but it came out as a statement.

He didn't seem offended. 'Excellent! Your little rat, the one

your friend wanted you to keep, comes very much at the
bottom end – something to love and cherish for your friend's
sake, I'd imagine.'

I nodded.

'On the other hand, as you've realized, at this end, the values
go up. And up. You'd expect this – it's signed by a master – to
fetch at least twenty thousand pounds, perhaps more at an
international auction. This one is unique.' He picked up another.
'At least I've never seen one like it. So I can't put a value on
it except to hazard fifty thousand.'

At last my mouth said, 'I could do so much with that much
money . . .'

'You could do a very great deal,' Waters said repressively,
'but only within the terms of the will. You can't just give it
away. My client meant it for you. Her cottage – your cottage
now – is in need of extensive repair and modernization to
make it truly habitable. That will take a proportion of what
Mr Jago raises for you. Even when it's completed, you don't
have to move in unless you want to – you may wish to stay
with your Mr Tripp. But if he ever needs care you can't manage
and has to go into a home, the law says that he must sell his
assets to support himself. And that's where Lady Boulton's
bequest will come into its own. It's either that or, Ms Townend,
you simply have to marry Mr Tripp.'

'What the hell . . .? I can't believe you said that! It'd be
incest!' Mouth open to scream more abuse, I was on my feet,
ready to overturn his massive desk.

'Exactly. Morally if not literally. I believe Mr Tripp and
Lord Elham discussed this with my client. So please sit down
again and understand exactly how much you need a home that
is absolutely your own.'

Just in time, I managed to control myself. I needed to sit
on my hands, but still I sat down.

He continued seamlessly, 'You also need to buy Mr Tripp
out of your joint business, as much for his peace of mind as
for your future.'

Jago coughed gently. 'It seems to me that Ms Townend is
somewhat overwhelmed.' I liked his understatement. He turned
to me. 'I sense you need company and reassurance. I'm about

to have lunch with my wife, daughter and new grandson. You'd
be very welcome if you cared to join us.'

'You're very kind.' To my surprise my voice sounded almost
normal. 'But I need to talk to Pa and Griff first.'

It was Waters' turn to cough. 'I too have booked a luncheon
table: Lord Elham and Mr Tripp should be arriving there
within the next ten minutes. I would like to join you at some
time to clarify a few matters and for you to sign some documents. I'll arrive for coffee, perhaps. But in the meantime,
Ms Townend, permit me to offer you my congratulations and
also my thanks.'

'Thanks? What on earth for?'

'In my profession, we see many lonely, embittered old
people. Your own father, my client too, of course, was decidedly odd at one time, yet now he functions extremely well.
As we saw yesterday. Poor Lady Boulton might have spent
the last weeks of her life in lonely despair: thanks in no small
part to you, she didn't. The rector spoke of her serenity in her
last few days. Of course, her sons did their best to destroy
that, but you were there at the end.'

'By sheer chance.' I swallowed hard.

'Sometimes I think coincidences are meant,' Jago said
kindly. 'Is that another box, Waters?'

'Yes. It contains the items from her little safe, Ms Townend.
I know she'd like you to wear some of them.'

Jago leant across. 'That Georg Jensen necklace might have
been designed for you. It's got such chutzpah!'

My hands shook so much I could barely hold it. Waters had
to fasten it.

As I raised my head I found enough breath to say, 'Dodie
didn't dwindle, did she?'

The next few days were very busy. I had to make sure Pa was
packed and ready for his UK tour – preening, he insisted it
made him sound like the pop star he'd always wanted to be
in his youth. Griff had to be nudged and chivvied to the next
of his tests, the precise nature of which he still refused to
discuss with me. A museum wanted its star ceramic repaired
yesterday. The police needed a lot of my time going over

statements and so on, and I was asked to be an expert witness in an entirely different trial, this one in France. Carwyn brought over what he called the 'invitation' in person. We let each other know where we stood, and because we'd always liked each other as friends, our hug was entirely natural and loving. I promised to dance with both him and Conrad at their wedding.

Next week, while Griff went on a cruise (the sea-faring sort) with Aidan, who'd booked it as a birthday present for himself, I'd spend a few days at Wesley Jago's home so he could tell me which of the netsuke he thought I should sell now and which to hold on to. The question of Griff's icons and enamels still lurked, of course, but that was a problem to deal with another day.

One Saturday morning, I ran into Freya at the hairdresser's – at long last I'd made a decision about my new style.

'Going on a date, are you?' she asked without a smile.

'I'm going for a meal with Phil. But one shared bowl of rice doesn't mean I see him as a lifetime partner, Freya. He and I have been through a few bad things together, and might as well enjoy a few pleasant times. But the only thing I'm worrying about now is if the weather will clear up for our cricket practice this afternoon.' I smiled. 'Bathing Imogen the other night made me realize there might be other things to life than dealing with two cantankerous old men, no matter how much I love them both. There's a world out there for me, isn't there?'

I might not know exactly what it held yet, but throwing a few tennis balls round in the warm autumn sun had to be a pretty good start.